SUNSET

Sunset © 2002 Hugh Hazelton

Acknowledgements:
Published in the original Spanish under the title *Puesta de sol* (Ottawa: Girol, 1997). ISBN 0-919659-35-7). Translated by permission of the author, Pablo Urbanyi.

Cover art: "Garden of Earthly Delights" (detail), Hieronymous Bosch.
Design and in-house editing by the publisher, Joe Blades.
Printed and bound in Canada by Sentinel Printing, Yarmouth NS.

Also published as BJP eBook 48, ISBN 1-55391-015-X (PDF), with distribution via http://www.PublishingOnline.com.

The publisher acknowledges the support of the Canada Council for the Arts and the New Brunswick Culture and Sport Secretariat-Arts Development Branch.

Broken Jaw Press
Box 596 Stn A   **www.brokenjaw.com**
Fredericton NB E3B 5A6   jblades@nbnet.nb.ca
Canada   tel / fax 506 454-5127

National Library of Canada Cataloguing in Publication Data
Urbanyi, Pablo, 1939-
[Puesta de sol. English]
        Sunset / by Pablo Urbanyi ; translated by Hugh Hazelton.

Translation of: Puesta de sol.
Also available in a PDF format.
ISBN 1-55391-014-1

        I. Hazelton, Hugh, 1946- II. Title. III. Title: Puesta de sol. English.

PS8591.R34P8313 2003   C863   C2003-902005-3
PR9199.4.U73P8313 2003

SUNSET

by
Pablo Urbanyi

translated by
Hugh Hazelton

Fredericton • Canada

Once again, to
my wife Catalina
and my children, Pablo and Mafalda

Acknowledgements:
To my friends Alberto, Pepe, El Negro, and all the others who've helped me put up with the difficulties of life, and to the Kalpakian family, for teaching me to face them. To Eduardo Andújar and Patricia Campos, for their advice and literary corrections. And finally, to Dr. Jorge Blanco, attorney and ex-diplomat at the Argentine embassy in Ottawa, for his legal advice.

"I would like you gentlemen to tell me," said the Fairy, turning to the three doctors gathered around Pinocchio's bed, "whether this unfortunate puppet is alive or dead."

When he heard this, the raven stepped forward and felt Pinocchio's pulse; then he touched his nose and the little toe of his left foot; and when he had finished his examination, he solemnly pronounced the following words:

"In my opinion this puppet is completely dead; but if he's lucky enough not to be dead, then he must unquestionably be alive."

"Are you sure of what you're saying?" asked the Fairy.

"Absolutely," replied the raven.

"I'm sorry to say that I am not of the same opinion as my illustrious friend and colleague, the raven," said the owl. "It is my belief that the puppet is still very much alive; but if he unfortunately is not alive, then he must undeniably be dead."

"Are you sure about that?" asked the Fairy.

"Positively," replied the owl.

"And how about you? What's your opinion?" the Fairy asked the talking cricket.

"I think that the best thing any prudent doctor can do, if he doesn't know what to say, is to keep quiet."

— from *The Adventures of Pinocchio*, by Carlo Collodi

Dear Doctor Brahe,

If it weren't for the date so indelibly printed on our son's birth certificate, which I found while going through my papers, I would never have realized how many years have gone by since I promised you the enclosed report. Back in those days (perhaps you remember him, despite all the patients you've had), everything seemed to be in your hands, from our son's miraculous cure and ensuing life, or half-life, to his subsequent death after being admitted to Argerich hospital. In a moment of need, as we waited for his destiny to be decided, I offered to put my wife's and my own feelings into writing, to express the thoughts, desires, hates and fears about the child that, tenderly — or perhaps cruelly — we had christened "Meningito." Possibly I was more attentive at the time or else was trying to justify what I was afraid might appear to be (and possibly was) a crime. You told me that writing was an excellent way to soothe the soul, and that my manuscript would be a most original testimony — and of great use to science.

I have written down almost everything, I think, on a series of numbered file cards.

I have often asked myself — and still do today — why I never got around to revising them and sending them to you before, or why I didn't give them to you in their original form before I left. None of my reasons seem particularly valid. It could have been from spite. After all the ambiguities, doubts, and fears you created in us, my wife and I judged your conduct severely — I more so than she. Perhaps I was mistaken.

Later, due to things as absurd and banal as the passage of time and the fact that life inevitably moves on, I never got round to sending them to you. Work, revolutions (so typically Argentine), our other children, and a slow, painful forgetting all kept me from doing so. Neither the imperious necessity to write about our experience nor the wish for complete oblivion, spurred on by the hope of forgetfulness, ever came. I didn't want to remember where I had put the file cards; but, as if by magic, they suddenly reappeared, demanding to be exorcised. And finally, if my memory serves me right, you were no longer young even back then; as a neurologist and psychiatrist who knew the human soul, the goodness and wisdom that apparently or actually did emanate from your words is only achieved with age. As the years passed, the question that we used to ask ourselves may indeed have become more meaningful every day: "Don't you think Brahe must be dead by now?"

No, you haven't died: a long life was bestowed upon Doctor Brahe. The file index, which accompanied me like a small urn over thousands of kilometres, is next to me now, on the left side of my desk, waiting for me to open it and keep my promise. Propped up against it is an Argentine magazine, open to the page on which your photo appears. The title of the article is "ARGENTINE SCIENCE: TO YOUR HEALTH!" It's about the international award you received for the discovery of a new disease; the journalist's verbal gymnastics make it sound more important than the Nobel Prize. I smiled at this touch of nationalistic banality, but I smiled even more — with a touch of tender bitterness, as if time had never passed — at the way you explained to the journalist how to pronounce your last name, just as you once explained to me in your office.

About the file cards: I vaguely remember how (it must have been some twenty-five years ago now), when I offered to write them up, you asked me, in order for things to be done "seriously," to include all possible details, including the age, sex, financial circumstances, and background of everyone, including grandparents and relatives, who had in any way been involved in our son's fate. The more details, the better, and, perhaps in order to get me excited about the idea and to make things easier for me, you told me not to worry about including an excessive amount of information or about being too chaotic in the way I wrote, because either you or your assistants would prepare a final version.

In searching for the right format — something that would be more than a mere notebook or the kind of diary I'd be likely to forget in some café, though really more out of practicality than anything else — I found my inspiration in the method I'd used as a carpet salesman: a box of file cards on which I would jot down information about my customers.

I eventually bought one, a card index with some five hundred separate files, out of which — with the feeling of doing something highly professional, numbering them on each side — I think I've filled out some three hundred or so. At first I used a ballpoint with a hard, fine tip that helped me vent my anger; later I switched to a fountain pen that glided along smoothly and gently, freeing me from my bitterness.

Whether sandwiched among the pages of my agenda or, preferably, in the inside pocket of my jacket, a file card was always with me. I would write on the train, in cafés, or in the shop where I worked; I was especially prolific on weekends, when the silence, the fear, the feeling that "there's nothing left to say or do," and the waiting all made me ever more anxious, while hope seemed increasingly futile.

My present task isn't going to be that difficult: I just have to open the box that's been closed for the last ten or fifteen years, put the cards in order if need be, and type them out neatly. I remember that some of them are dirty and stained — I'd like to say with the tears I've shed, but in reality it was with *mate* or coffee.

In fact, the mere thought of opening the box brings back my old trembling: the hope of forgetting has become a drug, and the remedy, homeopathic. The illusion that I might finally exorcise the dream that has haunted me for decades, in which Meningito pays me a ghostly visit every night, is gradually becoming weaker. Must I confess that, despite everything, I now actually hope for it to recur?

Where am I writing from now? I don't think it's very important. This is a country with long winters and short summers, but with green, well-kept lawns with lots of flowers and numbered trees. It's a utopia in which El Dorado — order and cleanliness all year long — has become reality. I've started writing this in winter, in a house, next to a window; outside lies a snow-covered field with scattered pine trees, through which there is no path. The sunlight reflects violently off the windowpanes but gives little warmth.

Finally, I make no apologies for the quality of my writing in this report. There was a time when I wanted to be a writer, as attested by a large cardboard box labelled "research material" that my wife used to bring me — and still does — as background for my "great novel," as she would say. My inspiration, however, never turned out to be anything more than a springtime itch, like that of an eighteen-year-old who has fallen in love and wants to become a poet in order to better express his passion.

That journey took a year, Doctor. And, since we travelled much of it together, it's best to leave the farewell for the last.

Entry 1
Ancestors and Origins; My Parents

Argentina is a nation of immigrants that came in search of the same El Dorado that the Spanish had sought and never found centuries before. The majority of new arrivals, waving the banner of civilization in their relentless advance, brought along the stuffing of one culture or another to make up for the emptiness left by the slaughter of the Indians.

My parents were also immigrants, with their own stuffing and breastplate of European culture from Hungary. Besides their culture, they also brought along my sister and me.

My father never really succeeded in the New World. His little workshop for making wooden toys never grew into a factory with smokestacks reaching into the sky for the greater glory of God. All he was able to buy was a modest house on the edge of the pampas, with a large kitchen and a front door and windows that were open all summer long. In the winter, as the wood stove stoked with scraps from the shop purred along, he would tell us about the glories and refinement of that fabulous European culture which he used to justify his failure. "I'm imbued with the standards of the European industrialist, with a sense of integrity and fair price. But here I find myself living among bandits, against whom my armour and moral and ethical straitjacket don't give me much protection. There's no doubt about it, son" (or "children" if my sister were there) — "I made a serious mistake. Instead of conquering and pillaging, I worked." He would sigh. "I wasn't brave enough to loot. In other words, I didn't make history, and no one will ever write a biography of me as an example of all the poor people who have come to this country in steerage and ended up finding their fortune."

He lived protected by the breastplate of culture until the rust of time and history finally punctured it. He was somewhat of a leftist, a great reader who was proud of his independence and carried around a full load of Enlightenment ideals; sometimes he tired us out or bored us with his utopian vision of the future, of the paradise that science and progress would eventually provide.

His name, like mine, was Pedro, and as the years passed, the neighbours began to call him "Don Pedro" out of respect. When my son was born, he became a grandfather.

Note: I realize now that I when I wrote these files, I never put in anything about the background of my mother — our son's grandmother. There wasn't really any need to. Suffice it to say that, despite her sometimes unbearable penchant for exaggeration and theatricality, she lived with her feet planted firmly on the ground, without ever mentioning European culture. She's outlived a good many people and, at eighty-two years old, continues to ignore her doctor's advice by dining on grilled meat, smoking a pack of cigarettes a day, and indulging in a glass or two of red wine. Her name is María, and she's now known as "Doña María." I also haven't spoken of my sister, Veronica. She's seven years younger than I, and luckily these events never affected her much.

An observation: My trembling stopped when I opened the box of file cards. All that's changed is that they've yellowed a little with time.

ENTRY 2
My Wife's Parents

Among the waves of immigrants that washed ashore in Argentina were a number of repentant thieves and bandits who promised God that, if He helped them get ahead, they would go straight for the rest of their lives and even give donations to the Church and the poor. I'm not sure this was exactly the case with my father-in-law. He was a Dutchman (or a Dane), who went to Scotland when he was young. There he got involved with the daughter of the chieftain of some clan, and, though the details were never made clear, she evidently slipped up and the chieftain, in order to preserve the family's honour, made them get married. Seeing that there weren't many new lands left to conquer in Scotland, they immigrated to Argentina, bringing along their daughter, who was to be my future sister-in-law. Legend has it that he worked from sunrise to sunset like a tireless and exemplary Puritan, buoyed up by hope and faith as he struggled along, and slowly amassed a small though well-earned fortune. Reality has it that he never donned an ethical straitjacket and outdid every bandit he ever met, buying and selling and plundering his way the length and breadth of the country. Whatever the case, perhaps someone should have written his biography as a model story of success.

As was only natural, he also had a breastplate of European culture, one which he padded with Scotch whisky and Dutch and Havana cigars. The fact that he spoke English was definitive proof of both his own superiority and that of his family. At age nineteen, I was, for him, the poorest of ragged gypsies: a long-haired Hungarian who was obviously unworthy of his second daughter, Ana, and yet had the nerve to keep courting her. I only saw him once in my life, on a summer night when, impelled by love, the warm weather, and desire, I went to Ana's house to look for her. I found him seated on the porch of their beautiful home, smoking a cigar and drinking a glass of whisky. When I had introduced myself and asked for Ana, he honoured me by getting to his feet. Wobbling a little, he staggered forward to welcome me in the traditional Scottish way. In a strong voice accustomed to giving orders and in an even stronger accent, he waved his cigar and shouted, "I don't know you. You scram. Get outta here." I remember he was bald.

As far as Ana's very British family went, I always existed as though I didn't really exist at all. Even if I'd made love to her right there against the pillar next to the front door of their house, it still wouldn't have changed things. Their culture was fully armoured. I don't want to speak badly of my father-in-law. Even though he never wanted to see me, deep down he wasn't a bad person — maybe he was even human. Although he often threatened to disinherit his daughter if she married a gypsy like me, Argentine law wouldn't allow it. Ana's inheritance was the pillar upon which we would eventually build our own nest of eternal happiness.

Note: I notice that I've also forgotten to mention my mother- and sister-in-law. Seeing as they have a substantial role in this story, I'll say a few words about them. Both were alcoholics, a fact they concealed beneath their armour-plating with elegance and aplomb. My sister-in-law had failed medical school. Later on I'll describe how they cheated Ana out of part of her inheritance and how my sister-in-law's machinations twisted and sealed our son's fate.

Entry 3
Ladies First: My Wife

In spite of being born in Argentina, I don't think Ana arrived in the country until four or five years after I did. Up till the age of eleven or twelve, she lived in what might be termed the armour-plated cage of Anglo-Argentina, consisting of her family, the English-speaking neighbourhood, the Protestant church and its British minister, the tennis club, and her private English school. She hardly spoke any Spanish, other than a few laboriously pronounced words, until she entered high school, where she finally learned it. That was where I met her, in Secondary V, when, thanks to the progress of modern society, the barriers that separated the sexes were finally lifted in what was technically known as a "mixed school." As always happens in such cases, despite the romantic conversations we had later on about being destined for one another, we in fact met by pure chance. Due to her last name and thick blond hair, which almost covered one of her large blue eyes, the kids called her "Blondie" or "The Brit." She hardly spoke at all in class. She was a good student — quiet, attentive, and rather tall — and she walked with a slightly lilting, languid gait; she seemed to leave part of her body behind at every step and then have to wait as it slowly caught up to her. Her beauty was intimidating.

Entry 4
Myself

As my father aged and continued to bounce from one failure to another, I grew up to be just like him. When the kids in the fields and vacant lots where we used to play soccer would ask me my name, I'd tell them it was Pedro, and they'd immediately reply, "Pedro, eh? Then you must be Polish," because of all the Poles, Ukrainians, and Russians who had that name. "No," I would answer, "I'm Hungarian." "Oh, so you play the violin," they would say, associating Hungarians with Gypsies. They called me "Little Polack." Due to my lack of European armour, or simply because a kid doesn't yet have any, I turned out to be a child of the pampas and the star-filled skies of Argentina. I spent my early years, those of primary school, out in the country, walking to class every day across the fields. Sometimes I'd hear a voice call from a milk wagon, "Hey, Little Polack, you want a ride?," and I'd climb up on the cart driven by Mr. Sartori or Mr. Mansilla. Longchamps, the small town where I spent my childhood, had a simple topography: the main road had a bar called La Bocha, the Spaniard Manuel's general store, Tío's pharmacy, and a blacksmith's shop; a street that ran off it had a church and a hardware store; there was also a train station with a café and lottery kiosk, and out beyond it the school, a second store, another bar, and a bakery or two. This was my world, in a village where at that time gauchos still raised dairy cattle. I think I could truthfully say that between horse-breakings, cook-outs, rodeos, cockfights, and clandestine horse races, roaming through small farms, some of which had been abandoned, and stopping by country stores where the kid who helped out would be having a glass of gin, I grew up among gauchos and knew more about them than a lot of academics who specialized in their lore. But the march of progress, science, and French culture — particularly that of Monsieur Pasteur — caused the gauchos to disappear overnight. In the name of national health, and to avoid the gauchos diluting or adulterating the milk in any way (which in fact they did) and, oh yes, in order to get rid of germs and bacteria, the government passed a law decreeing that all milk had to be pasteurized. The gauchos became tied in to large milk-producing companies such as La Armonía and La Martona, as well as to the law of supply and demand — all of it easy enough to explain, I suppose, but in the end, they simply had to give up. Many of them disappeared when the companies brought in uniforms for their employees — evidently the traditional *bombachas* or baggy pants gauchos wore weren't considered hygienic — while the older ones retired to country taverns to play cards and drink coarse red wine. From then on you had to buy milk at the store. The milk that Argentines drank was still adulterated, of course, but now it was pasteurized and had a trademark. That's the way the country worked.

I finished primary school and went on to high school. Now that I had to walk down to the station every day with a group of friends and take a train to school, my world began to broaden. It was also at this time that I started to read endlessly and omnivorously and to take an interest in the ideas that governed or could change the world. After school, I started stopping by cafés in Adrogué, Lomas de Zamora, and Temperley for small talk and intellectual discussions; later on I would do the same in Buenos Aires. I suppose it was around the same time that, stimulated by all my reading, my personality took on its present form: irritable, rebellious, and generally rotten, according to some. My father's attempts to buckle me into a suit of European armour by enrolling me in language and history classes at the Hungarian Centre, or by sending me off to various boy scout camps, all fell flat. Yet although it was true that I never donned a European breastplate or acquired much of a taste for one, I nevertheless inherited that bitter, ironic, skeptical way my father had of speaking — one that was both very Hungarian and very Argentine.

At fourteen or fifteen years old, I lost my virginity — or gained my manhood — in a way quite different from the usual one of the time, which consisted of waiting in line in some construction site. I'd made the acquaintance of a railway worker named Pepe, who spent his days off earning a few extra pesos by selling the favours of The Turk, an Arab woman who earned a living for herself and her children that way after her husband abandoned her. One Sunday afternoon, on my way to play soccer, I came across Pepe drinking *mate* in front of the shack he lived in next to the playing field, and he asked me if I had ever known "the face of God." He went on to offer me a "first-rate service," with "imported meat" for the feast, complete with condom and "payment on easy monthly terms," since I was short of cash.

I entered a room with a radio playing tango music, lit by a halo of light that came through a window covered over with newspapers. Trembling, I groped forward in the darkness. A few words from The Turk — "C'mere, I'm not gonna bite you" — led me to where she was. Her sure hands moved over my body; my nervous ones were stopped before they could make it as far as the face of God: "Oh no: don't touch the hardware." I looked into her dark eyes in the dim light, beautiful eyes that entertained themselves by gazing up at the ceiling, but that were also opaque, dry, and indifferent. And in hopes that her eyes would prove to me that I existed and was really there, I dutifully carried out my part of the initiation ceremony. Once it was over, without having once seen the face of God, though with something indefinable now known, I found myself missing warmth and love. The bitter taste of an unfinished experience stayed with me.

At any rate, what I had discovered was useful for bragging about to my friends at school.

Note: I've just finished typing up this file and have read it again. I can't help asking myself whether I'm not needlessly drawing out the story. I think I must be, because it sounds like I'm describing Paradise Lost. After what happened later became part of the public domain, this village, which was like a second cradle to me, turned into a bed of thorns, as stories spread of a Pole and his blond wife who drowned children in the bathtub — legends that continue on even to this day. I also forgot to note down something important. Perhaps due to my father's influence or because it was always in the air when I talked with my friends, it was at this time in my life that I began to have vague, tenuous ideas about a better world and, even more tenuously, about a world which I would actively help to build.

Entry 5
The Foundation of a Family or a New Generation: The Romance

The new stage in human development represented by the "mixed school," with the two sexes studying in the same classroom, turned out to be difficult to digest. We boys looked on the girls, just as they probably regarded us, as creatures from another planet. It was no longer a question of blathering on about "chicks" and how to handle them, but rather of what to do with the ones that were right there in front of us. The barriers that had been removed didn't help anyone overcome their shyness, and despite having earned my diploma in manhood from The Turk, I was still as bashful as the others. Since I didn't have the faintest idea of how to initiate a conversation, I resorted to another of God's — or life's — countless gifts: writing. With a great deal of effort and thought, crossing out and correcting and then making a final draft, I managed to write Ana a letter. After consulting a few friends, who told me not to make problems for myself, I had it delivered to her by a small, chubby schoolmate with glasses who was overjoyed to be on the first mission of what later turned out to be his profession: an errand boy.

It's a summer weekend. I'm writing with the Parker pen that my employers gave me when I left my job selling carpets, trying to round out the beginning of the file a little. I put the fountain pen down on the desk and smile, either out of good nature or pain. Before continuing, I try to remember what was going through my mind as I wrote Ana that letter. It went something like, "Dear friend Ana ... I ... or rather, you ... we, yes: I do not believe that it was simply by chance that we ..." Did I use a formal style, trying to be romantic, or an everyday one? I'm sure she must have kept it, along with other letters and notes from those days.

I raise my head and, as if returning to the other side, I find myself in a country house with a beautiful overgrown garden. I see our two small children playing in the sandbox. Ana, my wife, is putting clothes out to dry on a line in the backyard. I'm tired; I've wanted to stop writing for a long time, to finish up, complete the files, and perhaps send them to Dr. Brahe or else put them away forever. I stand up, push open the screen door, and step outside.

I go over to her and catch the fresh smell of wet clothes. She smiles at me in that same reserved way as always. I tell her, "Listen, that letter I sent you that brought us together, or got us interested in one another, do you still have it?"

She hesitates. Her smile fades.

"Why?"

"I'd like to read it."

She thinks for a moment.

"It must still be around somewhere."

"Could you look for it?"

"Yes, all right, when I finish here ..." Her blue eyes stare into mine. "I think, though, it would be better if you didn't read it."

"Why? Because of the stupid things I said?" Now I'm the one smiling.

"No, it's just that ... you know ... so many things have changed."

"Because of the lies I wrote?" I ask her.

Before I even say it, I know she won't answer. Her response, all the same, is to keep her eyes locked on mine: I'm free to interpret or think whatever I want.

"I don't think that I ... so many years have gone by ... I don't know why ..." and, not knowing what else to splutter, I walk off. Or do I escape?

I pick up the Parker again and continue to write. It was a long letter, I remember that. It must have contained a lot of unintentional lies, the product of my youthful enthusiasm. At that age you believe your own inventions. It was only years later ... Yes, sometimes, even now, I still tell her I love her.

I remember the answer that the happy messenger brought back to me on his return mission. It was a page torn out of an exercise book, without any greeting or prologue whatsoever: just two short sentences and her signature. "Yes, you can meet me when school gets out. I don't mind, but I'm not sure I'll like it either."

Note: Ana was not my "first true love" after The Turk; there was another I had some doubts about, even though she swore it had been "the first time" for her. Had I ever made the blunder of telling Ana that I had left that girl for her? It was more than likely. Like anyone else, I was capable of telling any sort of lie in order to gain some "proof of love." I believe — I want to believe — that Ana's look that day didn't speak of that sort of lie, but of something much deeper. I gaze out the window; I see a snow-covered winter landscape in a strange country. Our children don't live with us any longer. At night we're alone, but the hour of confession never comes, if there is indeed anything to confess and if confessions actually serve any purpose other than making things worse. I know that we have always supported each other. The silences between us are growing deeper. A few glasses of wine now and then help us endure them and survive. Maybe it's just the years passing by. All the same, I think I'm still alive, with a profound desire to smell the fragrance of grass, to look up into the starry summer night, to catch the fresh, wet scent of the clothes as Ana hangs them out on the line, mixed with that of her own body. Now we have a washing machine and a clothes dryer. We've succeeded in seeming to be civilized. The clothes we wash have a soft, delicate, impersonal odour.

Entry 6
The Romance Continues

That very day, or perhaps the day after, I ran out of school when the final bell rang and waited for her. We said hello to each other formally, as if we hadn't seen each other in class at all. I walked with her for blocks and blocks through the middle-class streets of Adrogué, without even being able to make some bourgeois comment such as, "What beautiful houses around here. I wonder how much they cost?" From time to time she would look at me and smile. I felt like I was suffocating, and secretly blamed her for not helping me out, or — as they say in Hungarian — for not at least dealing me into the game. To make matters worse, she took off her coat; her breasts stood out against her blouse, and her hips were accentuated by the plaid skirt that fit tightly around her waist. Later I would learn, almost as a secret, that the colours were those of her mother's clan. There's also a saying in Hungarian that whatever's meant to happen eventually will, one way or the other. As we got closer to her house, I was finally able to utter a few questions: "Do you like classical music?" Yes, Chopin and Schubert. "What have you read lately?" A few authors and books in English that I didn't recognize. Ah yes, she mentioned Somerset Maugham and *The Razor's Edge*. We said goodbye.

As the weeks passed, I continued to walk her home after school. They were real strolls together. My efforts to talk about teachers or mutual friends didn't lead to much. "Yeah, I like that one," or "No, I don't like the other," were the only answers I got, accompanied by a smile in which her beautiful teeth shone. She had been educated in an English environment in which discretion was the norm. I bought a copy of *The Razor's Edge* in Spanish and read it through in order to have something in common with her, but it didn't help much. She had read it long before and couldn't remember much about it. Languidly, with a touch of indolence, she told me, "I don't really feel like reading it again."

The streets were turning into tunnels; our strolls were becoming boring and spiritless.

The free concerts at the Law Faculty in the evening, at which they played Chopin and Schubert, and the Sunday matinées at the movie theatres provided pretexts for going out together. Her father kept close watch over her, to ensure that the virginity he'd never honoured himself — with the ensuing consequences — would be respected for his daughter; she had to invent all sorts of stories and lies just so her parents would let her stay out till ten at night. The concerts had now given way to park benches, pounding heartbeats, caresses that went progressively farther, deepening desire, and a mutual accord. And then, one Sunday afternoon, instead of the movies, there was a bedroom where, without saying "It's the first time," she lost her virginity.

Note: I look out the window once more. What makes me wish so much that this snow-covered field were in southern Argentina? Yes, I also travelled down there in order to earn enough for a small nest egg, to do a little very Argentine "business," and the snows of Patagonia reminded me of those of my childhood in Hungary. Where am I? I come to myself again and overcome the impulse to get up and go into her study and tell her that, in her own way, she also lied to me when she was young. No, by this time she must already have left the house and be at work. The impulse to have her near me continues. Yes, I know, it's useless to call her on the phone and tell her about it. If I remember right, I already did that in the past. And she, with great sadness, told me, "Yes, but I did it for you," or "for our love," or "out of love."

Entry 7
The End of the Romance

Whether romance or engagement, it was long. High school ended and it was time to choose a career. Ana, whose father had always wished had been a son to carry on the family line, went into medicine, as had her older sister. I did the same. My own father, who was progressive and proud of his independence and culture, had never obtained a diploma; for him, a professional degree was the only way to become somebody and move among other men with dignity, and he wanted me to be a doctor. My true career in those days was simply being with Ana and making love in some park in Buenos Aires or in a friend's apartment or, when I used to walk home with her in the evenings, in an evergreen bush. I soon tired of a medical career and gave it up after failing my exams at the end of the first year. I was also to fail in another career: the following year I enrolled in the education faculty to become a teacher of mathematics and physics. I only lasted a few months. It was a lot easier to forget about textbooks and ensconce myself in a corner of some café to read about the universe and travel through the stars to infinity.

I ended up helping out my father in his workshop, where I earned enough pesos to take the train to Buenos Aires, have a pizza, keep myself in cigarettes, and drop by cafés to talk with my friends, who were disappearing one by one into their own careers. But in those days a cup of coffee still bought you a comfortable nook in a bistro, an orchestra seat from which to contemplate the world as a stage. I would sit alone and smoke, chatting with friends who were no longer there, fantasizing vaguely about doing something great in life or becoming a famous novelist and making up for the failures that, without my realizing it, were already beginning to gnaw away at me. The characters in the café — the old retired guy reading the newspaper, the couple talking in the corner, or the man sitting alone like myself, who had only stopped in for a minute or was waiting for someone else — were the raw material from which I would weave stories or lose myself in reveries about the lives of others.

I know, Doctor, that I'm taking too long in getting down to what's essential in the story, but my thorough training in the sweet art of doing nothing at all, a kind of nirvana, must certainly have been essential. Cafés at dusk with rain at the window, filled with incense-like cigarette smoke, were pagan temples for me, places where I could sit quietly in front of an empty coffee cup. Perhaps there would be a moment of illumination as the world flowed calmly and serenely around me and I sat there without the least stress, filled with vague, floating reflections, waiting for Ana, who would come in with her lab coat and case of surgical instruments that always proclaimed her arrival like a rattle. Yes, Ana, who had only once told me she loved me yet who, reserved as ever, had given herself to me unconditionally. Her body, her abandon, spoke for her eloquently. She didn't ask anything of a man other than that he be one. Never a reproach or question or wretched plan for the future. A refuge, someone to lean on, was all she wanted — or so I wanted to believe.

One day I waited for her in a café near the medical school. I heard the tinkling of her instruments and she came in with a red-haired man with freckles, impeccably dressed and carrying a leather briefcase: an exemplary human being. With great poise — Oh Ana, I never thought you could do that — she introduced him to me as an ex-boyfriend. As soon as he opened his mouth to say hello, his accent and his name, Robby, told me that here was the model, the ideal that her father would agree that she marry. I became jealous. He'd barely sat down, taking great care not to get his clothes dirty, before I shot at him, "Are you English?" "Yes." "English from England or were you born here?" "By chance, I was born here." "And you don't speak Spanish any better than that?" "Isn't my Spanish good enough?" A smooth, delicate irony insinuated that I probably didn't speak English.

He was a man of importance, the exclusive South American agent and representative for the famous BAC One-Eleven airliners, with Rolls-Royce engines, which were then the top-of-the-line aircraft for domestic flights. To my surprise, I found that planes could be sold like candies and cookies; the only thing different was the price. It was like discovering an unknown world. It prepared me later to accept the sale of Exocets, bombs, poison gas and intercontinental missiles. Either out of an effort to piss me off or to impress Ana and show her the type of man she was missing out on, Robby opened his briefcase and took out a folder. After calling the waiter over to clean the table and ordering coffee, he unfolded a multicoloured brochure in which there was a diagram of a plane cut open diagonally, filled with arrows and names. Rather than enter into technical details, Robby expanded on Rolls-Royce's prestige as one of the largest British companies in the world, and described the aircraft's speed, comfort, cruising altitude, and price. If I remember rightly, each plane cost eleven million dollars, 4% of which went to Mr. Robby as commission. It didn't seem like much. I knew that some commissions went as high as 10 or 20%. In order to be friendly, I refrained from asking him why he kept glancing at his watch every thirty seconds, and instead inquired, "How many planes have you sold?" "None so far," he replied. "Not a single one?" I exclaimed, with satisfied envy. "No, not yet," he answered. "But if I do sell one, and I think there's a great chance I will, I'll earn four hundred thousand dollars, enough to buy myself an *estancia* and never work again."

That night, after we emerged once more from the evergreen bushes and kissed good night, Ana whispered to me, "If you were an agent for an aircraft company and sold just one plane, we could buy a house and live together and have children."

It was the end of the romance.

Note: I realize that in this file I wrote, "I'm taking too long in getting to what's essential in the story." I must admit that, frankly, I don't know "what's essential" and what isn't. Although it's true that my old trembling has disappeared or at least diminished, the other feeling, that our son is still in the hospital and that we — and even he, albeit unknowingly — are still expecting a miracle cure before he dies, has returned. In any event, you asked me to write down "everything," so I'm including "everything" that seems necessary. You also said that you would skim through it first to select the material you found most important. You can do so, if you like, by going straight on to Entry 10, in which I describe how, having inherited two different ways of dealing with life, Ana and I conceived our son; or you can jump over to Entry 14, which describes the accident Ana had when she was pregnant and what a medical doctor decided to do to cure her, another fact that is probably "essential." I haven't put in anything about the three abortions Ana had while we were going out together, since in terms of objective, scientific facts, they only added an element of guilt. But let me return to what's "essential": What have I really been writing? Is this the book about our son's story that Ana asked me for and which she was sure would make me famous, or, inevitably, is it a strange love story?

Entry 7 (continued)
Attempts

Ana's dreams began to fence off the endless pampas over which I had always galloped. We didn't really seem to have any reason to hurry. She was just entering her third year at medical school and still had three or four more to go. Something, however, had changed: when we saw each other, things did not feel quite the same, and although she never again alluded to the years ahead in the same way as she stopped telling me she loved me, the question of the future had now been raised and I was bolted to it. I can't really say the idea displeased me, or that I liked it, either. For the time being, the idea of freeing myself from my father's endlessly repeated stories, as well as from depending on him financially was reason enough. I had tried a hand at selling books, dictionaries, and collections door-to-door as a travelling salesman, and had ended up spending my travel allowance in bars and failing completely. It was time to look for something more important.

Robby already had the BAC One-Eleven account sewed up and someone else was evidently taking care of things for Boeing and Douglas. Selling safes and strongboxes wasn't really quite the same thing, though it seemed to have something in common. If I were to sell a safe or vault system to every bank in Argentina, I could certainly think of retiring. Vironia Scandinavia was a company that was internationally known for its safes, somewhat like Rolls-Royce for its engines — or so said the sales professional who gave the course on how to sell them. The first rule of salesmanship was to believe more in what you were selling than you did in God Himself, which in this case meant having a perfect faith that Vironia safes were the best in the world. They were the only ones that could survive fires, earthquakes, and tidal waves. They were indestructible, even immortal — the very altar of security. Armed with my new faith, I learned to instill fear in people, to frighten them with stories of robberies and fires and the ill-fated futures they might face without the security of Vironia. I also picked up other sales techniques, such as answering a customer's question about the price with, "How much is a human being really worth?" I learned how to explain that, if a dead person's body were reduced to mush, dried out and had all the water squeezed from it, what would be left? Nothing but a bit of powdered calcium, plus a few minerals and salts, which of course wouldn't be worth anything. My conclusion: The higher your station in life, the more you needed a Vironia safe. Unconvinced of my own worth, but eager to prove it, I would set forth onto the street, equipped with a miserable travel allowance and a company briefcase filled with brochures, bills, and receipts. My assigned zone and destination: the wealthy suburbs and country houses of El Tigre. I would take a book along on the journey, though I would carry it in my hand instead of putting it in the briefcase, so as not to contaminate the sacred texts inside.

In three months I read many books, without discovering the mysteries of infinity or the universe, both of which seemed to be receding farther and farther away, but still with dreams of better worlds on other planets. I never understood why I had those dreams. Things weren't going that badly for me: I was completely free to do as I wanted. Like a tourist with time on his hands, I got to know new towns and neighbourhoods, stopping off in unknown or familiar cafés, with an ever-decreasing circle of friends — and I never sold a single safe.

Freedom has its price. Since I hadn't paid it, just as had happened before with the book company, Vironia showed me the door. I landed on my feet in the street.

Ana was wiser than I. "You need a job with regular hours," she said.

Entry 8
May He Rest in Peace, and the Wedding

Without considering that my turn might, in fact, come first, it's quite probable that I frequently wished that my father-in-law would die — a most human desire. I never asked either God or the Devil to make it happen, but a cancer that wasn't diagnosed early enough finally sent him to the hospital. His breastplate of European culture was unable to save him from death.

He died because we're all mortal. Ana loved him, despite her disgust with his alcoholism. Someone had to stay home on the day of his funeral, and she offered to do so. She hadn't failed to inform me. As soon as I saw the cortège disappear around the corner, I ran up to her house, hesitating as I neared the gate: no, my father-in-law was not sitting on the front porch. I went up the path across the verdant lawn and, for the first time, crossed the threshold of Ana's beautiful home and went in.

Life is strange: I don't know how death can be celebrated, nor what obscure forces came into play at that moment. The door closed. We didn't exchange a single word; she began to step back and I to advance. Both of us were nervous: a corridor, a cry, a limit: "No, not in that bedroom!" And so it was to be in hers, where she said she had dreamt of me so many times. Tears came to her eyes and then she cried, holding me tight without letting go, her body — which was always more expressive than her words — demanding me a second time, openly, desperate to frighten away death and fill up the void it had left behind.

Life is not born from death. "We didn't choose it," she told me. It was her last abortion.

The worms and the lawyers went into action almost simultaneously. Ana had always been quiet, and she became even more so now. I was full of suspicions and fears and wanted to help her with the procedures, but, according to the law, I had nothing to do with it at all. Six or seven months later, when the lawyers finished their task (as if to refute the theories of Vironia — as well as sales techniques — Ana's father was worth more dead than alive), the question arose of what to do with her part of the inheritance. When I told her we could buy a house and get married, she answered, "Yes, all right. I've thought of that too, but it's not how I wanted things to be." My question, "And how exactly did you want things to be?" was futile and absolutely stupid; I'm afraid it even hurt her. Her blue eyes, looking steadily into mine, spoke for her. I remembered the BAC One-Eleven and the Vironia strongboxes.

Ana received her part of the inheritance with a comment in English from her sister, which Ana translated for me: "You're on a fast track to nowhere with that gypsy. He'll take you for all you're worth." She didn't answer. I thought of the worms that, like the lawyers, had probably already finished off my father-in-law and were hungrily rubbing their little hands together, waiting to begin on my sister-in-law.

We bought a house with an overgrown backyard in the town where I'd grown up. There wasn't enough money left for anything more. The house's only advantage was that it wasn't out on the edge of the pampas, but in the town itself, not far from the train station, so that Ana wouldn't have to walk far at night when she came back from medical school. It had a large kitchen — big enough to live in — but instead of the purring and crackling of the wood stove, we would hear the continual hissing of gas. We fitted the house out with the furniture Ana inherited, which turned out to be the worst, most worn-out items left over from her old home, with the exception of a beautiful antique wall clock that her mother and sister thought didn't work any more. All I had to do was wind it up properly and it ticked away like a charm. We were able to buy a few more things, and Ana had a room for her study.

Two friends from town, one from secondary school and the other from childhood, acted as witnesses at the county clerk's office, after which we had lunch at my parents' house — that was our wedding.

Home Sweet Home

The new house, although it was ours, was not like the one I'd grown up in. Although it felt strange for the first few weeks, Ana's presence as she moved about, doing and undoing things as if her life's destiny had been to establish a home, awoke me to a new reality. Certain feminine touches, such as a tablecloth, a vase of flowers, a serving platter with a soup dish (even though there was no soup), napkins, wineglasses, the set of cutlery she had inherited for everyday use (the silver one had gone to her poor mother) — in short, the leftovers of a rich man — all let me play at being a *nouveau riche* or an apprentice *petit bourgeois*, and were both a novelty and an agreeable surprise. For my own mother, who had gone through the war and lost her silver service, as well as a brother and other relatives, such details and "little touches" had lost their meaning. My family had had a miscellaneous assortment of knives, forks, and glasses, along with the same deep-bottomed plates for soup and all the rest of our meals.

Although by then nothing much was left of my childhood attachment to the house I'd grown up in, I still to this day miss the purring of the wood stove. People who grow up next to a wood fire, with its flames and crackling as it burns, travel back through human history. The hiss of a gas stove, though it's a bit of a solace for loneliness (much more serene, for instance, than the racket from a radio), is unlikely to evoke legends — and nostalgia idealizes legendary kitchens.

Be that as it may, I was clad with a breastplate of civilization and humanity had not evolved in vain. Although I had lost all religious faith, the resonant chimes of the clock as it told the hours in the silence made me imagine I was in a cathedral, in the midst of a mystical union or encounter that perhaps I'll never really know.

Note: My suspicions were gradually confirmed as the years went by. At the last family meeting with their lawyer (which was basically a tender and very understandable human story), Ana's mother wept, accusing her of being ungrateful, and Ana ended up signing a sheaf of papers and losing a large part of her inheritance, including a valuable piece of land in Miramar, to the defenceless woman. A few years later we found out that everything, even the things that were supposed to be passed on to Ana after her mother's death, had been left to her sister Jackie. And, according to Ana, that wasn't all. There had also been a romance between her sister and the lawyer, which was certainly quite probable — even taking into account such details as the fact that Jackie's figure was slightly swollen from alcohol, that foam always formed around her mouth, and that large quantities of spit would fly from her lips when she spoke — because after all, she wasn't a bad-looking blonde.

Entry 9
Looking for Work; The Manger

During the soul-searching I used to indulge in when I frequented cafés, I often used to ask myself whether man was made to be free or whether he preferred to be a well-fed prisoner. I didn't put it quite like that, of course, but would say to myself: All this running around in different directions isn't getting me very far and, despite my dreams of glory, I don't really have any driving ambition pushing me along. It must be better, as everyone says, to work like a horse or a mule but to have a reliable manger where the boss makes sure you're well watered and fed, no matter what happens. In other words, as Ana had told me — a steady job.

Although the great economists haven't yet given much proof of wisdom, you don't have to be too clever to figure out that any money you can count will eventually run out. The middle-class lifestyle that let us be somebody, Ana's studies, her desire to fill the new house with children, even my own pallid dreams and yearnings to do something important in life, all had to be fed to be kept alive.

As soon as I set out in search of work again, I realized that I was one of those people known as a good-for-nothing, who's useless at everything. I didn't even have a commercial diploma from secondary school, which would have let me start a career as a pencil-pusher behind a desk somewhere. Nor did I have enough muscles to lift boxes and heavy sacks. Go back to sales? Not on your life.

Doing sweet-bugger-all had become my main occupation, but it had also lost its attraction, if it had ever had any. I would return home in a bitter mood, without daring to confess that, after going through the help-wanted columns, I had spent the rest of the day reading a book in a café. Ana didn't say anything or ask me any questions, but even though she gave herself to me unconditionally and seemed prepared to keep on waiting, I now began to interpret her silences as a reproach.

Whatever's meant to happen eventually will, one way or the other. It was late fall, and winter was coming on. I was walking down Viamonte Street, gazing into one display window after another of carpets. I stood looking into one that was full of Persian rugs and had a few oriental touches added to it: a hookah, a brass scimitar, and a kind of large bronze plate. Dreams are free, and I found myself thinking back to the *Thousand and One Nights*, imagining an oasis where my camels could rest, or meeting up with the Thief of Baghdad and his flying carpet, and I was soon flying off myself. I didn't hear the first shout.

But the second one I did. A tall blond man (I didn't think it could be an Englishman or a German, because they're not effusive enough and certainly wouldn't be yelling my name in Hungarian) rushed toward me, embraced me, and kissed me on both cheeks. Then, as he shook me by the shoulders, he asked me in Spanish:

"Don't you remember me? Listen, think back a while, eh? You bum, the problems you caused me in Villa Gesell. I'll never forget you."

"Aram!" I recognized him.

The road to hell is long and sometimes covered in carpets, and that day I began my journey along it. Aram Kalpakian was one of the brothers of the Kalpakian Brothers' carpet company. He was also an Armenian-Hungarian-Argentinean. Some ten years before, when my father was still polishing his suit of European armour and trying to make me one too, he had sent me to a Hungarian boy scout camp in Villa Gesell. They eventually threw me out for reading Nietzsche (which they never found out I couldn't understand) instead of the *Lives of the Saints*, as well as for retelling the stories of the *Thousand and One Nights* to the younger kids around the campfire at night, without adapting them to Catholic morality or straining them through the filter of Disneyesque puritanism. Aram had been my group leader.

He asked me into the store. Almost the whole Kalpakian clan was there, including old Don Garabed and his sons Ohan and Artim, Aram's cousins. Don Hagop, his uncle, was out at the moment. There were questions, lots of questions, a whole interrogation that you could never be sure came from real interest or was just a dialogue that ran along fluidly, in true oriental fashion, and then finished off with a sale at the greatest possible profit. Whatever the case, it was a custom that could easily pass for genuine interest.

I told them briefly about myself and my search for work, and they did the same. As chance would have it, they were about to open a new store; the busy season was coming up, and they needed a salesman whom they knew and could trust. Better the devil you know than the one you don't. Would I keep on reading Nietzsche and telling depraved tales from the *Thousand and One Nights* to the children? Maybe I was rebellious and a bit of a bum, but deep inside I was a good kid. And, what's more, I might have changed, matured, and settled down now that I was married, especially since Ana and I were thinking of having children. I could sense reservations and hesitations; the long, heavy noses of the Kalpakians traced lines in the air as they exchanged looks with their dark eyes (all except Aram); their thick black eyebrows rose and fell in a kind of clan dialogue in the presence of an outsider, as if they were asking me, "What do you know about selling carpets, or more important still, about the secrets and tricks ... not to say lies ... of salesmanship?"

Every inhabitant of Buenos Aires carries around a brilliant little ego inside, an alternate self who speaks on his or her behalf in order to construct a façade. I still don't know where all my wisdom and knowledge came from, or whether I actually learned more than I thought during my two-week course in selling safes. Yet when I made my pitch for the job, I spoke of "modern sales techniques," of "needing to believe in what you're selling"; I talked about "learning the customer's name and repeating it as often as you can, because it is the sweetest music of all for his ego"; I told them about "taking the deal's temperature" and "gauging the customer's genuine interest by asking questions such as 'Where can you envision the safe, or rather, the carpet in your home? Can you imagine it in your living room?'" I assured them I could "communicate enthusiasm, inspire and transpire honesty and confidence"; I spoke of "normal", "pleading", and "forced" sales techniques. Finally I brought out, "What is the real worth of a human being?" — an argument to which all of them gravely assented, nodding their heads as if it were a philosophical principle. They gave me the job. They congratulated me on becoming a part of a company in which I would have a great future and might someday even become a manager if I worked hard and was an honest man.

It was a Wednesday or Thursday. I was to begin work the following Monday. I thanked them, and just as I was going out the door, the elderly Don Garabed, who up to that moment had remained seated in a chair, running his worry beads through his fingers without once opening his mouth, called me over and, taking me warmly by the arm and looking at me out of a face furrowed with wrinkles and filled with beatitude, said to me in Hungarian, "Son, I only knew you from hearsay. You speak like a snake charmer. I like you. But you don't know anything about sales. You play the flute like a real conjurer, but the snake doesn't come out of the basket, and if it did, you wouldn't know what to do. It's easy to talk, but I'll teach you how to spellbind the customers. Good luck."

Aram accompanied me to the door. "Be on time," he recommended. "Never forget your identity card. Oh, and don't waste time on old Garabed; he's getting a bit doddery and likes to talk. See you Monday."

I waited for Ana in front of the university. Crazy with happiness to have finally found a place for myself in the world, and ignoring an inner shadow, I announced, "I'm what I swore I'd never be again, a salesman, but this time I've got a manger."

Entry 10
Pedro Begat Pedro and Pedro Begat ...

I knew, yes, that I had achieved stability, a place in the sun, and that Monday I would begin a new job. Ana was also aware of the change. Dare I say it? A steady income — stability — revitalizes and calms a woman, although often, faced with the tastefully arranged merchandise in a store window, it can also throw her into emotional chaos. Oh, yes, I've seen it all as a salesman. But this didn't seem to be the case with Ana.

Ana and I have different mentalities. She likes precision, exactness, order. I find that disorder allows me to have my dreams of grandeur without asking if I'm really destined for them. My source of theoretical training in matters of love is the *Kama Sutra*; Ana's is *The Perfect Marriage*, by a German or Austrian essayist, Von Something-or-Other. The *Kama Sutra* is poetic: it speaks of the "lingam", the male battering-ram of various proportions, such as those of the "hare," "bull", or "horse." On the feminine side, there's the "yoni", the woman's warm nest, which also comes in different sizes: the "deer", "mare", or "elephant." There's also no shortage of expressions such as "bow", "arrow", "target", "bamboo waists", and "nests." The German text, on the other hand, is scientific; it speaks of the vagina, penis, moistenings, and centimetres, and is illustrated with graphs and anatomical sketches.

Nevertheless, on that day (I don't remember the date), the truth — indeed, the only true thing — was the final sentence of the *Kama Sutra*: "When passion is unleashed, neither Kama nor Sutra is of use any longer"; to which I would add, at least in reference to Ana, "nor is *The Perfect Marriage.*"

The weekend arrived. Ana was transformed; her blue eyes shone, her body vibrated, she rubbed up against me as soon as we were within a metre of one another; her smell enticed me from the other room; she had become the most beautiful and attractive animal on the planet and I, like those insects that are guided by vibrations and scent (or like a dog), was right behind her. Sometimes she waited for me; at others, she took the lead.

I, a man of no particular faith, knelt before my only true altar, the face of God, and prayed to you, Ana. You prayed to me. You prepared the target and I the arrow for the bow that would take us to other worlds. How did you manage not to break when you arched your body like a bamboo bow? It was the last warm days of autumn, maybe Indian summer. The open window, moonlight and clouds, the gallop of rain across the tin roof: you vibrated and I did too; a lightning bolt flashed and the sky thundered, drowning out your cry, even as your body said, "Now." And your body arched, and I let the arrow fly; I saw it cross the sky, skirt along a lake bordered by ancient trees and come to rest, white, on the golden sand of a serene shore.

It was life that was born from life.

Sunday night, exhausted, I sank down into the bed. You came in. "It's getting cold," you said and closed the window.

You came over to the bed, covered me up, and told me, "It will be born next summer. Look."

I peered out of the corner of my eye. It was a piece of paper — a graph, I suppose. "Why not in the spring?" I stammered. "Isn't that more romantic?"

You kissed me and went back to your studies. Yes, we were different. That night, in order to sleep better, more deeply, I would have liked you to caress me. You didn't notice, but then I never asked you. And maybe I made a mistake: regardless of that graph, summer can also be romantic.

The heirloom clock struck midnight. I had gotten used to it, and it no longer used to wake me up, but that night it did. I reached out my arm; you still weren't there.

Entry 11
Settling into the Manger

Who or what am I? A pseudo-gaucho who once lived among gauchos, drank *mate* with them, and inherited the illusion of freedom that lies in following the weary trail behind the cattle. The order is given to drive them to the slaughterhouse along overgrown trails, and the gaucho is free to veer off a bit to the left or right if he likes — that's all the freedom he has now. The horizon, the limit of the pampas, gradually widens as the herd advances, fueling the illusion of liberty. It's preferable to the illusion of the manger, which, if truth be told, is a little too much like a slaughterhouse.

The following Monday morning I set off earlier than I had ever gotten up before to take the train or even go to high school, on the mission of my life. With a book under my arm, I joined the throng of other people — and was amazed at how many of them there were — wondering whether I was really a human being or just a steer, and boarded the train almost without realizing it, as part of a collective shove, as if we were being herded on by a gaucho, all in the hope of finding an empty seat, which of course I couldn't, because I was too out of practice.

Nevertheless, despite having to travel standing up, squashed against the other passengers, I was happy to finally have a mission, a destiny, to be useful at least to Ana, who was my one true reality — or at least the only person who, without saying it, made me remember there was a reality. Ah yes, and to be useful too to that new being who would be arriving the following summer, though I'm not sure whether I already had his image in my mind or if he had yet become part of my reality. Perhaps he was, vaguely.

I don't remember which book I read on the way into Buenos Aires. I do know it wasn't about sales techniques. Constitución Station, and then the subway to Lavalle Street. The store was already open when I arrived. There was an impatient bustle outside as rolls of carpets were being loaded into a delivery truck.

"You're late!" Aram remarked sharply and a little hysterically, without saying hello.

"Sorry," I replied, "but you told me to be here by eight and it's ten minutes to."

"Yeah, OK; the truck has to be loaded up first. Watch them and learn how they do it."

I watched, but I don't know if I learned anything. Or perhaps it was so easy that there wasn't much to learn, except how to do things without getting excited. The truck drove off. I went into the store and walked all around, looking everything over, and then searched for old Garabed. The comments and observations he had made had given me the feeling, without really knowing why, that he might be a threat and that I should win him over. I didn't know at the time that no one had ever been able to sway him in the least. Like most of the other Kalpakians, his thirst for money was as infinite as numbers themselves, something like the horizon of the pampas that forever recedes as you approach it.

He wasn't there. He used to arrive around eleven in order to deposit the morning's earnings in the bank when it opened at noon.

After the truck left, Aram came over to me and led me to a desk.

"This is your desk. Take care of it; it's new. We're thinking of getting an adding machine, but you won't be allowed to use it, except for checking your figures. A lot of the sales are made in customers' homes, and if you get too used to a calculator, you might get stupid and make a mistake. If it were in our favour, that would be all right, but if it weren't, we'd lose money. Come on, I want you to meet someone else we just hired."

He introduced me to Erminia, a pleasant Armenian woman with wide black eyes.

"Erminia's very reliable. She takes care of phone calls, orders, and payments. You hand in the stubs of the carpets you sell to her … and I hope there's a lot of them. And don't get any ideas about her. I want speed and efficiency, not problems. Oh, before I forget. From now on we aren't Kalpakian Brothers anymore; we're Kalpakian Limited, incorporation pending. Now get to work."

He disappeared, leaving me standing next to Erminia. I looked her over: there were dark hairs on her arms and beneath her stockings. I remembered having asked Ana not to shave any part of her body. My tastes in women are somewhat like those of monkeys. I raised my eyes slowly as they followed the line of her breasts, and when I got to her face it was red, and she hid her eyes from me, lowering her lashes and turning her head.

"Are you married?"

"Separated, with a son. I won't ask if you are; I've already seen your ring." She'd raised her head and was smiling.

She seemed a bit out of it. I decided to call her "Sweet Erminia," and, inevitably, I'll come back to her later.

I went over to my desk, my place in the manger, and she stayed at hers at the back of the store.

The fall shopping season was drawing near, but there weren't many customers yet. I sat at my desk, learning the prices of the carpets; occasionally I would get up and, with the help of Enrique, a dark little guy from the Chaco, would match the prices and marks on my sheets with the reality that surrounded me: rolls and piles of carpets of all different sizes. Enrique also deserves a few words, because, after all, I saw him every day for almost three years. He was quiet and slow, with an innate unhurriedness that was ideal for surviving in the subtropical region he came from. He never gave me what you could really call a lesson, but only answered my questions and then remained silent, as if exhausted by the effort or knowing that it was useless to say more. From time to time I would go back to the rear of the shop to talk to Erminia, the receptionist-secretary-bookkeeper-administrator, but would find her buried in paperwork, as absorbed in her job as if she'd been born to it. Any move in her direction, if there were to be one, would have to wait.

My first steps in learning the trade weren't all that noteworthy. The main thing to be able to do was to tell the difference between authentic carpets that were made by hand and knock-offs that were made by machine; the manufactured ones, in turn, were subdivided into roll-up carpets for the living room, sets of rugs for bedrooms, and wall-to-walls, more elegantly called "fitted carpets." The basic merchandise consisted of two or three brands of machine-made carpets that came in several different grades and thicknesses: five to six millimetres thick for the hard-up and fourteen for the sybarites, all dispensed in rolls one to three metres wide. My job was to go to the customers' houses to take measurements, give an estimate, call them back, explain it to them, speak politely and knowledgeably, flatter their vanity, be at first understanding and then insistent, lower the price when necessary, go after the ones who didn't pay, and comfort the others about problems and great dramatic questions such as what to do about certain dogs and cats that, without the least respect for their master or mistress, relieved themselves on the new carpet, leaving stains from their pee-pee and caca that were impossible to clean, just like those from Coca-Cola and coffee.

Not so much from my readings or sales apprenticeship as from the information that came from customers who read glossy magazines with beautiful photos, I found out that there existed faraway worlds, veritable El Dorados of carpeted bathrooms and fabulous multicoloured nylon rugs that added life to a home, and, what's more, had extraordinary, magical qualities, such as being impervious to pee-pee and caca and easy to clean afterwards. "No ma'am, no sir, we don't carry carpets like that," I would tell the customers. But I knew that one day they would also be available in Argentina; people were looking forward to them with the same zeal they would await a Messiah or Redeemer or a colour television set.

I spent that first day, like the novice I was, in a state of semi-paralysis, watching the infernal level of activity that Artim and Ohan deployed in their two branch stores, which had different names but were on the same street. They would come in and go out, argue with Aram and then take off. Aram would shut himself up in a kind of box at the back of the store, next to Erminia's desk, from which he commanded a full view of Kalpakian Limited, incorporation pending. Finally, on one of his short trips outside in order to inspect something or give a few shouts to get people back to work, he invited me for coffee in a café on the corner that had a stand-up counter.

"Aram, I've been meaning to ask you: am I the only salesman?" I asked.

"Why would we want more?" he replied. "We used to be able to do it all ourselves, but now, with one of my cousins in charge of the new branch store, we need another person."

When they'd hired me, I'd been so overcome with enthusiasm and happiness at finally having a manger that I had forgotten an important detail.

"How much will my salary and commission be?" I asked Aram.

"What a question! There's no commission and the salary is of course the minimum specified by law. We always abide by the law, as far as possible."

"You mean you're legally exploiting me and sucking my blood."

He looked at me as if he were asking himself, "Is this guy ever going to change?" His answer to my observation was dry and clear.

"Whatever you say. I don't care what you think just so long as you sell. But let me tell you that we don't want any revolutionaries around here. So keep your trap shut."

Note: I already have the next entry propped up against the box, ready to be copied. It's called "Moral Lessons from the Master." I think there's another one around here titled, "Authentic Carpets and Erotic Lessons from the Master." Let me point out once again, Doctor, that you're free to skip any files you like — just as readers of novels do with the boring parts — especially since I still haven't reached what's "really essential." Should I include the next entry or not? Is Don Garabed really that important? Despite already having the entire nation and its worthy representatives as a model for corruption, I'm quite sure that without Don Garabed's contagiously warm teachings on Middle Eastern morality, which was as slippery and elastic as that of all the other Kalpakians (old Hagop, Aram's father, whom I will speak about later, was a rare exception), I wouldn't have been able to make it over the last hurdle and put together the small nest egg I finally did. My father certainly wasn't much of a role model. What's more, his later conduct toward our son so enraged me that I ended up thinking he was a spineless coward, without once realizing, as I do now, that he simply wanted to help me out in his own way and see his descendants flourish in a land that, after all, was still foreign to him. In that sense, amidst all the ambiguous and twisted attitudes that surrounded Ana and me, his was one of the few that was truly human. I'm not fully convinced of this, but I'd like to be.

Entry 12
Moral Lessons from the Master

The two or three customers who came in that morning limited themselves to asking about prices. I consulted the list, told them how much, and they left. A bit exhausted from racking my brains thinking up questions to ask Enrique, I sat down at my desk and had a cigarette, watching the ebb and flow of people and cars along Viamonte. I wasn't in a café, but I still felt the pace of life slow down for a few minutes. It occurred to me that experiencing life as it goes by is equivalent to living longer or more intensely, fully aware and without fear, though knowing it will someday end.

Don Garabed appeared in the doorway, wearing a raincoat and hat, with his hands in his pockets. He came over to me; I stood up to greet him and he asked, "Have you sold anything?"

"No, Don Garabed."

He frowned, lowered his head, his face hidden by the brim of his hat, cleared his throat and went to the back of the store. I sat down again. Neither he nor I had asked how the other was.

Five minutes later, he was back, minus the raincoat and hat. He moved a chair over to the desk and sat down next to me. He took out his Arabic rosary of worry beads made of green stones — jade, I suppose.

"Are you a Muslim?" I asked.

"You're as much of an idiot as all the other Argentines," he said, with a gentle smile and without a trace of anger.

"Why?"

"Because of what you infer. Running these worry beads through my fingers is a custom I picked up in Turkey. I do it to calm my nerves. It's a lot cheaper and healthier than taking tranquilizers. I'm an Orthodox Christian, though not much of a believer. I can see you don't know much about Armenians."

"Other than that they have two feet, two hands, and a head, no, I don't," I replied. "I suppose that they also drink, eat, reproduce, and sleep like other mortals, Blacks and Jews."

Garabed leaned his head back, narrowing his eyes so that the crow's feet stood out, and studied me; then he shifted his head forward again slightly, and his hooked nose seemed to lengthen.

"And you want to sell carpets? Hmm. I don't like comparisons. Let's leave the Blacks out of it: they don't matter. As to the Jews, yes, they're clever and intelligent, but they also don't count for much. In business, an Armenian can easily screw a dozen Jews."

"And who can screw an Armenian?" I asked, a bit falteringly.

"The Greeks, my son, the Greeks. One Greek is worth ten Armenians. They're the most dangerous people in the world." He sighed with sorrow and began telling his worry beads again. "Yes, if a Greek customer comes into the shop, be careful, very careful. You never know how he's going to get you. They're all dangerous. It's true, though, that Christians in general are rather stupid and gullible. The Jews, because of our noses, think we're Jewish too. Just let them believe it and the sale will go through. But with a Greek — what are you going to do with a Greek?" He sighed again. "Last week you spoke very nicely, like a typical smooth-tongued Argentine sharpster. It's all very well to build up the customer's trust, but there's also a limit; a Greek, for example, is never going to trust you. He's going to take you for a thief right off the bat."

The worry beads spun.

"A bit like Armenians do?"

"Well, yes, of course. Buying and selling carpets is basically nothing more than an arrangement between thieves: a battle with a lot of blather in which the smartest thief is the one who wins, and the conceited idiot who actually buys something gets to keep the merchandise. It's an art, one that I've been actively engaged in since I was fifteen years old. But all this is changing now; educated people like you are coming along and pushing sales techniques. And of course they don't know the first thing they're talking about. You know what I mean?"

"Not really. Give me an example."

"The price list, my boy, the price list: in addition to being nothing but pretense and simulated honesty, it's death to the art of selling. When you sell something with the list and then knock down the price, the only way you can keep from losing anything is to give them a product of inferior quality."

"I think it's more a question of making money than losing it. I understand, though: what you see is not what you get. I can't say it sounds very moral."

The worry beads stopped and his eyes widened.

"Moral? Moral? Oh no, I was afraid of that, exactly that. You'll never be a good salesman if you think like that. Listen, my boy, once and for all: Nobody comes in here to buy bread or meat or medicine. None of the poor come in here unless it's to beg; they usually stand there humbly at the doorway, which keeps customers away, and I feel bad about having to drive them off. And the customers who come in here don't do it because they're called; they enter the shop to satisfy their vanity or make their friends jealous. Get one thing into your head: this place isn't a church or convent or charity organization. If you have moral problems, go into the priesthood. There's still time. Ah! I've got to get to the bank before it closes. We'll continue our talk this afternoon."

The afternoon lesson was much shorter than the morning one. There were more customers, whom Aram also waited on, and Don Garabed never let me out of his sight, which made me nervous. In one of his free moments, after finishing up with a customer, the old man came over to me and, almost as a scolding, pointed out, "Son, you're too quiet with the customers. Remember that carpets don't have tongues, so you need to make them talk through yours."

I stammered back something about being new and not knowing much about carpets. But I remembered a phrase I'd once read somewhere: "The merchandise speaks through the salesman's mouth."

The secret was to transform myself into a talking carpet.

Note: I have fond memories of those first few days on the job. Ana's happiness added to my own, at least until the first shadows began to appear. I see I'm skipping a lot of details. I'll come back to some of them. Except for a few unusual events, work had become monotonous within the first two months, and then, finally, even the unusual began to repeat itself. Later on, with the birth of our son and my own precarious state, everything became out of the ordinary and even somewhat pathological. In the meantime though, as I started out at work and then continued on during Ana's pregnancy, perhaps thanks to a regular paycheck and the inevitable necessity of buying bread and meat, I accepted and learned to live with monotony. I compensated for it and survived it through my imagination: whether seated in the shop listening to Don Garabed or old Hagop (who came in less and was more laconic), looking after the customers, taking measurements, or drawing up estimates, every once in a while, if there were still a tiny corner of my mind that was free to imagine, I would think of our new home, a manger where I was king, and of how Ana would be waiting for me, of how the chimes on the clock would strike five, six, and then seven in the evening — seven bells that coincided with my getting off work and coming in the door just as they struck nine, and then kissing Ana and sitting down to dinner. I didn't even miss my friends any more, and with a regular salary coming in, I ended up losing them.

Entry 13
Ana's Pregnancy

Whether it happened that weekend or the next, I'm not sure, but the truth was that Ana became pregnant. She told me she was sure it happened then, because her basal temperature indicated that she was ovulating, and insisted on showing me the indications on a graph. It didn't really matter much to me. Maybe I hurt her. I should have shown more interest, but I wasn't selling her a carpet.

Ana's smell changed and her breasts grew, and I soon found I had a different woman in the house. This did matter to me — and to her, too. Within a few months her breasts were brimming over, and she asked me whether I would still love her as much when her body was deformed by the pregnancy. She explained to me that, according to her books, a husband always finds his pregnant wife distasteful and looks for other women.

I never cheated on her during her pregnancy, though. A bit abashed, perhaps, by my past sins or hidden desires, I asked her if all this stuff about the sweetness of motherhood, the joys of the future dad, preparing the nest, matrimonial faithfulness, and the mother-to-be needing her husband more than ever was really nothing more than poetic invention.

"A lot of times it is," she said.

There wasn't much need for her to worry about me. Working for the Kalpakians didn't leave much time for adventures, except for those that, according to other salesmen, sometimes occurred by accident in the homes of debauched or insatiable female customers. In spite of my failure at selling books and safes, I turned out to be an excellent carpet salesman: that is, instead of remaining a human being, I transformed myself into a talking carpet. I'm not very proud of this: any idiot can do it, as long as he's insensitive and a fast talker. Perhaps in my case there was also a touch of humour, a different sort of style that gradually turned more bitter, but never stopped bringing in sales. My talent for salesmanship became increasingly evident as I grew ever more willing to sell myself so I could rot away in a luxury manger.

An Entry That Has Already Been Mentioned but is Unnumbered: Authentic Carpets and Erotic Lessons from the Master

The Kalpakians never allowed me to sell genuine handmade Persian or Arabian carpets. I didn't know the first thing about them, it was true; they also cost too much (I compared their prices to my salary and found that the cheapest of them cost more than I earned in a year). More than any other kind of merchandise, their sale depended on the customer's face. You practically had to be born into selling them, as some people are born into the aristocracy. In order not to waste time, you had to know right off, from the first glance or whiff, if the person interested in them — whether it be a diplomat or an impeccably dressed member of the leisure class (who might well have bought his or her outfit on time and then skipped out on the payments) — actually had the cash in hand or were there simply to prove their good taste or parody (or experience a little) the life of the rich. They would usually end with a whimpering, "Ah! If only I had the money! You can see I have the taste!" and go off bemoaning the injustices of life, which kept them from buying things they obviously deserved much more richly than others.

No, I never sold any of the legitimate carpets, but I soon learned to recognize who was who. Don Garabed continued his lessons as to how "We don't sell carpets, we stuff vanity with wool." For better or worse, I accepted him as my teacher and he no longer made me nervous. With a slight shake of his head he would tell me that a customer wasn't serious and would never buy anything. A wink would mean that a real customer had come in, and he would discreetly signal me to start preparing an invoice; he urged me to always get a deposit out of the customer as fast as possible because, he said, "Son, with a down payment, the enemy's beard is firmly in our hands." Once, during a short break in activity — as soon as I sat down he would immediately be there by my side — I asked him why they bothered to print up a price list which, besides being the death of salesmanship, was a presumptuous simulation of honesty.

"Because you're selling them garbage," he replied. "Even the most expensive machine-made carpets are basically junk; one wash and the glue and body of the carpet are gone, and all that's left is a rag."

"Does that mean that only the authentic hand-made ones are really carpets, Don Garabed?"

"Well, I wouldn't go so far as to call them 'authentic.' You've actually got to lie more about them than about the others. Sometimes even I, who am an expert, can't be sure if a certain carpet with Persian motifs was really made in Iran, as we say it was, or if it came from Pakistan. I don't really know what's authentic anymore. But I am sure of one thing: you aren't really selling the carpet, even if it's from Bukhara, Isfahan, or Tehran. You're selling myths and legends: 'My dear sir, the carpet that you see here once belonged to the Shah of Persia, who used to make love to his seventy-second wife upon it.' Or perhaps: 'This one has a long history behind it. It was stolen from the harem of the Emir of Kuwait by a eunuch who sold it to a diplomat, who then ...' 'You don't like it? I have a very special one I think may interest you. Wait here, it's in a locked case. It was taken from the palace of the Sultan of Baghdad when it was sacked after his death a hundred years ago. The Sultan was old and impotent, and just for the pleasure of his eyes he would make a couple of his favourite dark-eyed and slender-waisted young girls perform the belly dance for him. To the music of sitars and tambourines they would remove their seven veils one by one till they were nude and then continue dancing in each other's arms, right here, on this very carpet.'"

I smiled as I listened. Don Garabed suddenly fell silent, as if returning from faraway worlds; he looked at me, blinked, and asked, "Do you understand what I'm saying?"

"Perfectly, Don Garabed, perfectly. The oriental forerunner to modern striptease. Let's see, maybe we could add something like, 'My dear sir, sexual potency declines with age, especially with a man's own wife, but if you buy this carpet and, for a little variety, fantasize about your favourite girl or secretary, your potency and pleasure with your wife will ...' et cetera. Or, 'I assure you, Madam, that in order not to continue crying and lamenting the solitude of the harem, uselessly waiting for the genie from the lamp to change your eunuch into a lover, it would be much more effective to buy this carpet and then, dressed as an odalisque, invite your husband to recline upon it with you. His indifference, which you believed to be that of a eunuch, will be transformed, and your pleasure, madam ...' et cetera. What do you think?"

"Yes, something like that. Throw in whatever you want: poetry, legends, fantasy, money, power, status, sex, or illusion."

"And how about you, Don Garabed? Which do you prefer: carpets from Bukhara, Isfahan, or Tehran?"

The old man knitted his thick grey eyebrows, looked at me, and laughed.

"Don't you think you're a little young and out of line to be asking me questions like that?" he replied.

My feeble and unfulfillled fantasies of being a writer, inspired as they were by the teachings of Don Garabed, found a practical outlet with the customers. I would laughingly tell them, "Madam, this set of bedroom carpets will change your life. Its design is based on a Persian carpet that was much loved by the Shah of Iran. He would use it in the most sublime moments of his life. Believe me, with this set, your husband will feel his desires rekindled and will recover his youthfulness; rather than getting angry about the cost, he'll thank you for it. Buy it and your life will change completely." A lot of them would look at me dubiously and didn't seem to believe me, but just when I was thinking that I'd gone too far, they would smile and some of them would ask, "Really?" With the men the spiel could be even more outrageous.

Without any real financial worries, other than the insatiable desire to make greater and greater amounts of money, all the Kalpakian brothers had families and children. I had the feeling they were happier about the news of my wife's pregnancy and my coming fatherhood than I was. In their own way, they were quite human. They knew, as I did, that being a father would not only make me settle down, it would bind me to my job — and to them. There are thousands of ways of nailing down the future and living your life in a coffin.

Entry 14
Ana's Accident

"Madam, it's all been fully researched and proven. There's no danger. On the contrary, the anti-tetanus shot will mean one less vaccination for the child once it's born," the doctor said.

Brandishing the chart, Ana would assure me later on that the accident occurred exactly two months after the beginning of her pregnancy, during the time in which the fetus's spinal column was still forming.

Every second Sunday or so, we would go to my parents' house to have lunch and spend the afternoon. My father would launch into his customary round of complaints and self-justifications, which I only grew to accept years later when the reasons for them had become real. It was useless to tell him that his theories about how the diesel motor and penicillin would bring about the future happiness of mankind were a little unrealistic now that everyone was talking about atomic engines and the inexhaustible, eternal, and (above all) cheap power they would provide, and that people still went on dying, despite the discovery of penicillin.

His talk about his personal happiness and his married life with my mother used to spark a certain interest in me as to what I could expect in my own marriage. According to my father, if my mother had loved him as much as the chickens she fed, talked to, and fussed over, his life would have been quite different. In any event, he had long since resigned himself to his present condition, especially since no matter how hard he tried, he would never be able to lay an egg or be as useful as a hen, in accordance with my mother's wishes.

At times I would ask Ana if our conversations in Hungarian were boring her, to which she would always reply that no, ever since she had lost her own family the minute they had all signed at the lawyers' office for the disbursement of her father's estate, she had always felt at home in my parents' house. She added that, perhaps out of her affection for my mother, or some indefinable sense of solidarity, or pure boredom, or just basic curiosity, especially since her own parents had never raised chickens, she took a genuine interest in chicken farming herself.One Sunday she offered to collect the eggs, and my mother gave her a basket. A short while later she returned with a half-dozen eggs and her tennis shoe and foot punctured by a rusty nail that had been sticking out of the wood floor. She took off her shoes; there was a little blood and a bit of dirt around the wound. Perhaps out of a desire to stop my father's shouts of, "Those goddamn chickens are going to be the death of me," or my mother's, "You ... you shut up! If you were half as useful as they are ..." my sister and I smiled and remained silent, and, in order to calm herself down, Ana said, "It's nothing."

We went home with her limping.

Two days later, when I got back from work, the infection could no longer be ignored: a red line was working its way across her swollen foot, and she could barely walk.

There wasn't much to discuss: at nine o'clock that night, I went out to look for a doctor. I knew all of them in the village. Mazzulo, who used to faint at the sight of blood, only made house calls three times a week. He was getting on in years and didn't do much anymore besides cure colds with aspirin and gonorrhea and other infections with penicillin. Chiesa, renowned for his bone-cracking abilities and proficiency in straightening out hunchbacks, wasn't in. Neither was one who used to teach and could diagnose so precisely that he was known as "The German." Luckily, I found there were still one or two patients waiting in the office of Dr. Giela, a pleasant, fat little Italian, who "kills you without your even noticing, so you die happy, singing about your victory, like Cabral." I spoke to him, and he said he'd drop by the house around ten.

He arrived at eleven. He was in a hurry. He listened to our story of the accident, glanced at Ana's leg, and spluttered, "A henhouse, eh? Have you had an anti-tetanus vaccination?"

"No," said Ana, a slight tremor in her voice.

He sat down and wrote out a prescription: anti-tetanus serum and vaccination and penicillin for injection. If he thought it would be over in a jiffy and a "thanks so much" with the money in his hand, he was wrong.

"Doctor," Ana said, "I'm pregnant. Won't the tetanus shot be harmful for the child?"

"Where did you get that from?"

"From books about vaccinations," she replied. I think she even cited the source, but I'm not sure.

"Why would you want to read those books? They just upset and confuse people who don't know about these things."

Ana hesitated.

"Yeah, Ana," I said, "like the Bible does for ignorant Catholics. She's studying medicine, doctor."

"Ah," he answered, "that's different. Of course it could … How many years of medical school do you still have to go?"

"Three," she said.

"Well, it's a long time yet till you get your diploma — if you ever do. Anyway, don't worry about it, all right?"

"Doctor," she said, with a vehemence that startled me, "if the tetanus shot can harm the child, I would prefer not to have it and to take my chances."

It was getting late. Standing with one foot forward and his head thrust back, the doctor looked as if he were levitating as he declaimed, "Please, madam, do not do that under any circumstances. The mother comes before the child. But let me allay your fears by assuring you that it's all been fully researched and proven. There's no danger. On the contrary, the anti-tetanus shot will mean one less vaccination for the child once it's born."

I was just as surprised by Ana's rapid acceptance.

The whole affair was becoming urgent, especially the tetanus shot. Small towns have their own ways of doing things: Dr. Giela gave me a ride to the local pharmacy that was on night duty.

"The worst thing about medical students," he said as we drove along, "is that because they get more up-to-date information, they think they know more than doctors themselves … if you don't mind my saying so."

I looked at him in the darkness; he smelled like a hospital.

"I don't think that's the case here," I pointed out. "She just wanted to express how worried she was about it."

"Yes, of course, but like all medical students, she thinks she's caught all the diseases she's studying. The same thing happened to me."

That didn't seem to me to be the case, either, but I didn't say anything. He dropped me off at the pharmacy. I thanked him and wished him goodnight.

"Goodbye, and if there's any problem, just call," he said. He accelerated and the car disappeared.

The pharmacy that was open that night belonged to "The Uncle" who used to sell us — apart from condoms — the nitric acid we used when we wanted to make nitroglycerine and, like sorcerer's apprentices, blow up the world. We talked for a while and I asked him if tetanus shots were harmful for pregnant women.

"Who knows, kid; there's a lot of different theories. Every quack's got his own little book. Some say yes, others no."

47

It was one in the morning before Dr. Giela's nurse finally gave Ana the vaccination and penicillin shots.

When I got into bed, Ana pressed up tightly against me and hugged me. She was slightly trembling.

Entry 15
Ana's Fears

Mid-winter, with a lot to do at the store. After being crammed into the subway and then the train, I would come home from work exhausted, trampled on, burnt out — and, without knowing it, deeply frustrated. Ana would have dinner waiting for me; something different almost every night, because she didn't really know much about cooking and got everything out of cookbooks. The kitchen had become a laboratory. This also irritated me; I reproached her for it several times, but, in my calmer moments, I also told her in all sincerity, "Ana, a steak and a couple of eggs are enough. Let's break the monotony: would you rub my back?" She insisted on being the perfect wife and the recipes continued. In order to please me, she asked my mother for recipes for Hungarian dishes (which my mother supplied, with lots of "a pinch of this" and "about a cup of that" for measurements), but after being processed in the laboratory, they tasted like products from outer space. I'm not one of those people who go on and on about how good Mama's cooking was, and I told her so. But she persevered. Finally, one day, I exploded: "Listen, I'm not some guest that's trying to earn points by lauding the junk you serve up."

That night she stayed in her room and I ate alone.

Aside from the accident in the chicken coop, her pregnancy went wonderfully. She never vomited, except after gorging on a few cravings, which she said were actually organic, physiological needs intended to supplement deficiencies in her own body and strengthen that of the child. By the fourth month, her condition was already very noticeable and she had to walk with her body tilted backward.

It couldn't have worked out any other way: being a medical student, she not only converted the kitchen into a laboratory, but the pregnancy into a scientific event. In those days opinion had turned against the idea of suffering being God's punishment for original sin, and techniques for "painless birth" were all the rage. Ana had a book on the subject that would periodically crop up next to her Doña Petrona cookbook on the kitchen table and then keep appearing and disappearing on the bedside table or in the bathroom. I looked through it at least once. The introduction was called "Birth Can Be a Sporting Event." It was written in the United States, and translated and published in Spain. The Peninsular vocabulary and expressions gave a strange sound to that typically American style that is at once free and direct, light and familiar, assuring you that nothing is impossible if you want it enough. Ah yes, and practical, too: "You can give birth during your daily exercise routine at the gym," or "while washing the dishes or scrubbing the kitchen floor or during whatever activity you may find yourself in: it all depends on your own creativity." According to the prologue, it had originally been based on Russian techniques that, after exhaustive and thorough research, had been improved and adapted to the needs of the American woman so that she could "give birth with a smile on her lips." I didn't ask her if it had also been adapted to the needs of the Spanish or Argentinean woman, or what the difference was between women of the different countries. I kept quiet. It was her world, and I couldn't say much of anything, except to keep her happy.

Nevertheless, when a textbook on embryology, a course she had taken, reappeared open to a page of photos of the various kinds of monsters and birth defects that could occur, I couldn't stand it any more.

"Ana, this is horrible," I said, thumping the page with my finger. "Why don't you read the Bible or pray or something? I doubt these photos are good for your mental state, which is already 'dizzy from the happy experience,' as your birth manual says."

"You're always talking about the Bible, which you've never even read yourself," she shot back. "Why do you say these things?" I could see she'd been biting her lips.

"I've read it, and I should go back and read it again. I tell you these things because I can't see what good it's going to do you to keep looking at this collection of deformities that I'd never have been able to dream up even if they'd paid me. What's going on? Is something wrong?"

Out of pride or fear, she hesitated, as she always did when I raised my voice. She lowered her eyes.

"I'm … I'm afraid. And I'm not superstitious."

"I think you are. Who isn't? When you're faced with the unknown, one superstition's as good as another. Let's follow the old Hungarian proverb: 'Once it's fallen, listen for the sound.' We can't do anything about it for the moment."

A moist film appeared on her eyes.

"I just want to make sure …" Her mouth was closed so tightly that her words sounded like a grunt and I could barely hear her.

She couldn't take any more. But instead of throwing herself in my arms, which I thought she'd do so I could comfort her, she turned around abruptly, went into her study, and closed the door.

And while I looked at the monsters out of the corner of my eye, I sighed and wondered what had just happened, how I had hurt her, and how deep were her fears — and her pride.

Entry 16
An Ounce of Prevention is Worth a Pound of Cure

Five months into her pregnancy, Ana had become a kind of flying fortress, you might say. Compulsively biting her lips, to the point of even disfiguring them, she hardly ever spoke, and when she did so it was with her head bowed. My questions as to what was wrong were futile.

Besides the books on child-raising theories and the layette, we had to get ready for the birth and plan out the budget and place. I wasn't in Longchamps during the day, but she didn't need me to accompany her on her visits to the midwife, whom we knew from the abortions she had given Ana in her small clinic. The midwife was a genial, tender-hearted Bulgarian woman, and, due to the abortions, had almost become a friend. Ana went on her own.

That night, as we were eating croquettes made from a Doña Petrona recipe — and that I called "Japanese" because I never knew what exactly was in them — I asked her how the visit had gone.

Ana lowered her head over her plate. "Oh, fine. The first thing she said when I saw her was that I was much too far along for an abortion. I told her we'd gotten married. She congratulated me. She checked me over and said that, judging from the number of months and the size of my tummy, it was probably twins."

"Twins? Identical ones?'

"I don't know if they're identical or not, but two of them, anyway."

"Is she sure?"

"How could she be? She's not a medical professional or a doctor, just a midwife."

Her contemptuous tone surprised me; or perhaps it just seemed that way because she was biting her lips. My eyes narrowed.

"Maybe so, but listen: it could be precisely because she's not a doctor that she knows more about pregnancy than the doctors themselves. My sister and I were delivered by midwives, without any doctors being there … at home, too, in the same bed we'd been conceived in."

There was a long silence. Finally Ana spoke, still looking down at her plate.

"It's not the same thing. And what if there really are two of them? I asked her what would happen if I needed a Caesarean. She said they'd take me over to the local hospital in her husband's car. Can you believe how dangerous that would be? Everything's so primitive there. They still use forceps, even though it's well known that they can do a child serious damage. And she's rude, too. My questions made her impatient. Can you imagine that?"

I had a premonition that I should be imagining a lot of things, more than my tired mind and body could take at that hour of the night. She had such scorn for the Bulgarian midwife, but none for the surgical and technical arsenal of the medical profession. And reason can be as indulgent as love.

"OK," I said, "I agree. What are you thinking of doing? And what can I do to help?"

She had already spoken to a few friends at medical school who understood and shared her fears. One of them was going to give her the address and some information about a private sanatorium.

There wasn't much more to say. Before going to bed, my eyes roamed over the kitchen counter and came to rest on a bottle of thick pills.

"What are those?" I asked.

"What? Oh, those. Nothing, really: they're extra strength calcium pills for the baby's bones."

"For both of their bones. Aren't milk and cheese enough?"

"Not always. When …" She fell silent, biting her lips again, which was beginning to irritate me, and blushed.

"Did the midwife recommend them?" I asked.

"Well, yes. But the book also advises taking them."

I closed my eyes. "The book" was all books. I didn't insist. A month later she couldn't hide it any longer; she had to go to the dentist. Her teeth were being devoured by the little one or ones on the way and were on the verge of falling out of her mouth in bits and pieces.

Entry 17
Two Ounces of Prevention Are Worth Two Pounds of Cure, or Private Care is Always Better

The busy season continued, with far too much work. Perhaps because of that, or because Ana's worries constituted another reality that was knocking at the door, the creative salesman in me began to languish. Faced with the major human dramas that I spoke of earlier, such as the perverse insistence of certain cats and dogs, or diaperless toddlers, in staining carpets with their pee-pee and caca — stains which then became tinged with a vague and indefinite guilt, often ruining the harmony of tastefully decorated living rooms in which the carpeting had cost a fortune and had sometimes entailed considerable sacrifice — I simply was no longer capable of coming up with some clever way of soothing the hearts and souls of the discomfited customers. Nor did I feel up to repeating the same stale jokes, like an elderly professor: "Thank God it wasn't your husband, Madam," or "How lucky you are to have a dog or cat during this time of loneliness, defencelessness, and ingratitude," or "In the same way that the Buddha gazed at his navel, look upon the stain and meditate; it may be an omen of destiny." I couldn't even give them a bit of hope: "Try a little vinegar or lemon: that sometimes works." All I could do was comment, "No ma'am, there's no way to get it out, even if your maid is a hard worker."

But I kept on selling, and that was what counted most. It may have been around that time that I discovered and began to apply, almost without wanting to, another sales technique that I called "The Horror or Fear of the Void," based on an emptiness that already existed. Now is not the time to explain it; let's just say it got excellent results.

Those were the first symptoms of my vague unease. I didn't know what was causing it — though I had my doubts — until everything suddenly fell into place one Saturday afternoon.

The yard out in back of the house didn't amount to much because I never took care of it, nor did I ask Ana to do so. She, however, was from a family and social milieu given to the cult of the meticulously cut lawn, which was seen as a symbol of order, peace, serenity, and well-being (and probably of love and happiness as well), and she never tired of pointing out that "Spring's on its way now. Wouldn't it be nice to fix up the yard? We could clean it all up, mow the grass, and have a beautiful green lawn." I told her what I thought of the idea: "Hmph, a beautiful green I suppose to go with the flowers and trees." She sighed. "Yes, we do have three trees. Can you imagine how delightful it would be in the summer for the baby to be out there nice and cool in his little carriage in the shade? He'd love it."

One Saturday afternoon, after getting home from work, I got out the rake, a shovel, the pruning shears, and everything else I could borrow. I was in the midst of raking up the old leaves — generations of them — when I heard someone call at the front gate, which was open.

"Ana! Could you see who it is?"

She went out and then came back.

"It's a man I met last week, an agent from the Metropolitan Sanatorium."

"The Metropolitan Sanatorium? What the hell's he doing here? Did you call him?"

"No, I didn't, but the sanatorium was recommended for births and I went to have a look. He's the one who showed me around; he asked for our address and now here he is. It's an excellent hospital, believe me: everybody says so."

I tossed the rake aside and went to the front door. Ana followed. A washed-out face smiled at me from a sickly body encased in a tie and jacket. His hand clutched one of those executive briefcases that the dynamic set is partial to. I ignored his greeting and opened the screen door.

"Come in," I grunted, hoping my surliness would wipe away his smile.

It didn't. What's more, his smile became even broader when he shook hands with my wife.

"How are you, ma'am? Everything's going well, I hope?"

"Yes, of course, thanks. And you?" Ana smiled tautly without showing her teeth.

I didn't shake hands with him or ask him his name. I invited him into the living room. The three of us sat down. He placed his briefcase on the table, opened it, and took out a folder that, as if by magic, overflowed with photos of babies and twins, all beaming and gurgling with health. As people say about their dogs, the only thing they couldn't do was talk.

"These are my twin sons," he proclaimed proudly. "They were both born at the Metropolitan."

"Whoaaa! What cute kids get born there!" I exclaimed. "Ana, did you by any chance tell the gentleman that we were expecting twins?"

"No, I told him the chances were good we might have them."

"Hmm. What a coincidence. But listen, I think we're going to have triplets or quadruplets. Do you have any pictures of them?"

He looked a bit taken aback, but the smile didn't fade.

"Do you mind if I ask," I went on, "if you've ever taken a course in sales as part of your job?"

"Well, yes, if that's what you want to know. But the truth is we don't sell anything … we provide a health service."

"Oh, yeah, of course. I don't sell carpets either; I provide a sexual potency service. And tell me, have you ever thought of showing your customers photographs, like the companies that make safes do, comparing the happy prudent customers who bought the product with the unfortunate wretches who didn't?"

"I don't know how I'd be able to do that," he answered. The undeviating smile had now become ironic, like a challenge.

"Hey, it'd be easy. You just take one of the photos you've just shown me of one of those model babies, blond with blue eyes, and another of a little black kid all covered in dirt, starving, rachitic, and half-dead, or maybe completely dead. And then you say, 'This baby was born in the Metropolitan Sanatorium and this other degenerate creature wasn't.'"

For the first time his smile constricted, but returned immediately.

"Pedro," Ana said softly, beseechingly.

I looked over at her; she was biting her lips.

"I know. Just one last question. Why come here on a Saturday afternoon when you could be home with the twins and your wife, doing things with the family, taking them out for a walk or maybe to visit your mother, who makes such good ravioli?"

"What can I do?" he answered. "It's a different kind of job. It's about health. We're a bit like martyrs and missionaries."

"Really? They don't pay you?"

"Of course they do. I don't see ..." He stopped short cautiously. The perennial smile was twisting.

"Well, how much do they pay you, and how? A travel allowance, a bit extra for Saturdays, or is it by the number of births or cancers or heart attacks you sell? I'd like to know because I'm also ..."

"Pedro, please," Ana begged, gently but reproachfully, her voice fading into a moan.

I sighed.

"OK, you're right. Let's get to the point. How much will it cost and where do I sign?"

"Don't you want to know more about the hospital? Look how interesting ..."

"If my wife likes it and trusts it, that's all I need."

He began filling out an application form with a special price for births, which were considered an introductory offer by the hospital, a booming enterprise whose owners — in order to carry out their mission — were doctors themselves. Thanks to the sanatorium's seriousness of purpose and efficiency, there was an ever-increasing number of customers.

"What you mean is that there's an ever-increasing number of sick people and that the world is worse and worse off."

"If you want to put it that way." His smile grew imperceptibly.

He handed us the form. I looked at the price and let out a whistle.

"Tell me, please: I know the sanatorium is the best in the world, but do you mind if we think it over a little and check out a few other prices before we sign?"

"Of course not, but don't take too long. I should point out that the deadline for our special program is not later than six months into the pregnancy."

"Why's that?"

"Because in the past, people have tried to take advantage of the company's generosity. When they find out they'll need a Caesarean or have other problems, they come running to us. If, on the other hand, you come to us in the first six months, we, uh ... how shall I say ... share the experience and difficulties."

"You're so brave and generous it makes me feel like crying. What happens if it's twins?"

"They're welcome too, at no extra cost." The smile was spreading again now, as if from real happiness.

"And if there are complications?"

"The Metropolitan Sanatorium takes responsibility for everything. Our standard is that neither the baby nor the mother leave the hospital unless they're in perfect health," he declaimed.

"Yes, I am going to cry. That's what you call 'creating a positive image.' The dead must get carried out in gilded coffins and the little angels in white ones ... or maybe they just fly away."

I looked over at Ana and asked her if she agreed. She nodded her head. We signed. The sanatorium's generosity was limitless: all we had to pay was the first installment, or part of it. I went to get the money; the missionary counted the bills as if each one were a consecrated host.

He rose to his feet.

"Let me congratulate you on the excellent decision you've made. You can sleep easy now. You can count on us."

He shook Ana's hand. I held out my own awkwardly, but he only gripped my fingers.

Ana saw him to the door as he sang the praises of the sanatorium and all the advantages it offered, including the most advanced technological resources available, the doctor's guaranteed presence during childbirth, the immediate attention we would receive without having to wait in humiliating lines, the freedom to see whichever doctor we wanted, and a litany of other things.

I went back to raking the leaves.

A little while later, Ana appeared.

"Well, at least you must feel better now that you know the baby will be looked after by experts," I said.

She didn't want to risk a confrontation. I'd already learned that about her, but there are exceptions to everything. When she spoke, her voice was calm.

"Yeah, I guess so; I don't know. Why did you treat him that way?" Her body was thrown back and she held her head to one side.

I stopped working.

"Treat who?" I asked.

"The representative from the sanatorium."

"Sales agent, Ana: a common salesman. You think I was hard on him?" I asked, pretending surprise.

"Are you kidding?" she replied.

I thought it over for a moment.

"You're right, I did treat him badly. I just couldn't help it, but now I know why."

"And?"

"It was because he was a salesman."

"But you're a salesman yourself."

"I know, but don't you see? It's not the same. Even though we're in the same line of work, he's worse, because he passes himself off as a guardian angel and lies and plays on people's fears. He makes it sound like the babies born there never piss and shit or dirty a carpet."

Ana was silent. She gave a deep sigh.

"Maybe I don't understand. It *is* your job, but you tell me so little about it ... as if it didn't really exist. Or as if ... you were ashamed of it."

I looked at her tenderly and smiled. We rarely had this kind of conversation. I also sighed, in response to her.

"No, Ana, it's not that. Or at least, not just that. It's something deeper. This is the first regular job I've had in my life; the first time I've looked out on the world and felt useful. Yet the more I find out about it, the more demeaning and empty it seems. It's as if ... How can I put it? Ana, tell me truth: Do you really think the birth is going to be a sporting event? You see? You're holding something back from me. Dr. Giela, and then this shill disguised as a promoter, and, at the same time, there are so many things that suddenly seem useless: books, conversations with my friends that I never see anymore, my dreams ..." I stopped.

"Yes, it's true: you don't see your friends much anymore. You should get together with them more often. It wouldn't matter to me; quite the contrary."

Should I also have explained to her that, for some reason, I didn't feel like seeing them? I took a step toward her and tried to say something, but it was she who spoke next.

"I don't know: you've changed, maybe too much. Please don't treat people that way again: it scares me. It makes me afraid that ..." She bit her lip, turned around, and went back into the house.

I stood there, leaning on the rake. Fear. Yes, a diffused kind of fear:

the insecurity and doubt we live with among other beings that seem human but who think the sky is falling because a baby has soiled a carpet. That wasn't living. I didn't feel that kind of fear.

The sun was setting. I continued raking away with a shadow of a doubt that grew and spread along with that of the bare branches that would soon be sprouting leaves once again.

Entry 18
Being Somebody

I haven't said much of anything so far about the other Kalpakians: Aram's cousins, Artim and Ohan — Don Garabed's sons. Both of them were chubby and dark-skinned, with the same long nose as their father. Artim was almost a head taller than his brother. Ohan was a bit thick-headed — not my opinion, but certainly that of Aram and Artim, who yelled at him constantly, getting him more confused than ever. He was also the only one who smoked — a pipe, no less. Aram maintained that he wasted so much time running around cleaning, filling, lighting, and generally fiddling with his pipe that he was not only dense, but a freeloader as well. It was precisely for that reason that I found him likeable. He was in charge of another store, so I saw little of him and we talked to each other even less, but sometimes we went out for coffee or ate our sandwiches together, and I discovered that he differed from the others in other things besides the pipe. In fact, he was the only one interested in things beyond the carpet trade. His dream was to travel the world and become more cultured. Yet, despite all his money, Ohan had neither the courage nor the character to become the true black sheep of the family and was incapable of ever leaving his job to travel. It was much cheaper and more convenient to simply skip out of the store when business was slow in order to browse through second-hand book shops and buy beautifully illustrated works about far-off civilizations. Several times I suggested that he avoid his relatives' recriminations and show his originality by donning a turban and sitting in the show window on one of the authentic carpets, smoking the hookah that was part of the display, and flying off as far away as possible. Thinking of my own dreams in life, I assured him that it was the cheapest way to travel.

His brother Artim, on the other hand, liked to think of himself as a grand bourgeois or even aristocrat, a man of taste and refinement. He always came to work impeccably dressed, with a tie of raw silk held in place by a golden clasp, and was the only one who used cologne. He certainly had the money to play out his role — far more so than the genuine Russian, Hungarian, and Polish aristocrats running around Argentina at the time. He had a fleshy mouth and the chubby-cheeked face of a spoiled child and, like my sister-in-law, sputtered when he spoke, sending out a fine rain of saliva toward the listener as he held forth contemptuously and glibly on everything from the "good-for-nothing mestizos" to the "degenerate toffs" who had immigrated to the country with nothing more than haughty poses and "underwear so threadbare it left their asses exposed to the elements." I suspect that, deep down, like any well-heeled plebeian whose pedigree doesn't go back any farther than his shopkeeper grandparents, he secretly envied the bluebloods he disdained. I don't know if he would have dared spend the money it took to buy himself a title if he'd had the chance; you either become a shopkeeper or you're born an aristocrat, and the road to majesty begins in the cradle. Apart from the denigrating opinions he literally spat out, he had a fault that would undoubtedly not have been tolerated in any royal court: whether it was a nervous habit, a reaction of some kind, or who knows what, when talking to a customer or to anyone else, really, he would suddenly stick his index finger into his nose and poke around quite deliberately as far as he could, as if turning over the ground with a spade. One day I told him I'd figured out why Armenians had large noses. He asked me what I'd discovered.

Every morning when I arrived at work I always found the Kalpakians talking together at the back of the store. They would wave their hands about, argue, and shout themselves hoarse, as if they were in a market or tenement house. Unmoved by great passions or ideals, they would remonstrate about rugs or who was selling the most.

After signing up for the Metropolitan Sanatorium, I realized that I would be needing more money and spent the weekend devising a plan: I would wait till I found them all gathered together before asking them for a raise, so they couldn't use the excuse of having to consult one another in order to keep putting it off. I came in on Monday morning and told them the news about the hospital.

They congratulated me warmly: "That's wonderful" "Bravo" "Couldn't be better." Then came the comments.

Aram: "You made the right decision in choosing a private hospital."

Artim: "Yes, that's right: you couldn't let your wife give birth surrounded by grimy mestizos."

Ohan: "Yeah, private and grimy mestizos."

Artim: "You've shown your true style and quality."

Pedro: "I'd like to, I mean, ask for a …"

Aram: "It's all taken care of. We'll talk later. Go on now and get back to work."

Artim, Ohan, and Aram: "Yeah, get a move on. We're busy right now; we've got to settle an important deal, and we don't have a moment to lose."

My intention of asking them for a raise remained just that — an intention.

Later, around noon, I spoke with Don Garabed.

Don Garabed: "Yes, son, you made a wise decision. If in the end there are problems, well, there are problems everywhere."

Pedro: "And do you think …?"

Don Garabed: "What? Your salary? A raise? My boy, those questions are no longer my domain. Besides, sales have been going badly lately, very badly."

Erminia came back from lunch, walked over to me and said, "Hey, I've been meaning to ask you: Is that sanatorium place a luxury hospital?"

Entry 19
The Cows of the Field

"Yes, it's certainly luxurious," I would later tell her. Ana had made an appointment with a doctor that she'd had the right to choose from a list. I can't remember what method she used to select him — whether by recommendation, age, experience, or wisdom — but that's how we ended up in the carpeted waiting room of his private office at nine o'clock one morning. (I'd had to get special permission from the Kalpakians, with corresponding remarks such as, "Can't your wife go there alone?" "Is she all right in the head?" and "What's the matter: Is she afraid the doctor will bite her?") We sat waiting beneath a speaker that played music by Ray Conniff: "functional music" they called it, still a novelty in Argentina at the time. The municipal sign posted on the opposite wall, in direct refutation of the musak, declared that "Silence is Healthy."

The sanatorium's promoter was right: we didn't have to wait in line. We were the first to arrive and still were (they had already taken care of two other pregnant women, accompanied by their mothers or mothers-in-law, who had come in after us) when, an hour later, the doctor called Ana's name.

He seemed to be a pleasant old man, kind-hearted and serene; since it was we who had been waiting for him, he didn't feel obliged to apologize for the delay. He asked the usual questions about the pregnancy, and we had to repeat our answers progressively louder. He listened to Ana's chest with a stethoscope, felt her body from head to foot, measured some kind of dilation, and declared, "Everything's fine. The baby is well positioned, though it could still change place — unless there are two of them, of course."

"Is it twins?" asked Ana, a bit pale and with her mouth closed.

"Excuse me, I didn't hear you."

She repeated her question.

"Judging by the size, I would say 'yes,' without a doubt. But I only hear one heartbeat, which doesn't really mean anything, of course."

"Is there any way of knowing for sure?" I asked.

"Sorry, what did you say?"

I repeated the question.

"Yes, with an X-ray. But why expose the mother and child to that kind of radioactive poison?" He smiled. "We'll find out just how many there are when they're born."

"Do you think there's any danger?" Ana asked, swallowing her saliva.

"What's that, madam? Danger? For Heaven's sake, what danger? You're in good health and your hips are flexible, with plenty of space for the baby, or babies, to pass through. I understand your fears, but think about Nature and observe the fields. How did the Indians used to give birth? Who's there to help the cows and mares? Everything'll be fine, don't worry. A few routine analyses, just in case, and you'll be all set. If there's anything that worries you … any problem at all … give me a call. If not, I'll see you the day the baby's born."

We went out. As we walked away from the building, Ana turned toward me. "What did you think of him?" she asked. "He's certainly wise, isn't he?"

"I guess so. He was a little deaf, but then learned men are always deaf, mute, or blind by definition. Maybe the only heartbeat he heard was yours. But I've got to admit that the comparison with the Indians and the cows was fantastic: he almost had me convinced that childbirth was some kind of sport."

Ana stopped suddenly. She looked at me, and her eyes filled with tears. "Pedro, is there anything on earth you're actually capable of liking or accepting?"

I returned her gaze.

"I'd have to say there isn't," I replied. "Not even my name, which always makes people think I'm Polish, or my moustache, which gives me a bit of the air of a Hussar but makes my lips look deformed if I forget to comb it. Maybe my being a foreigner makes me more authentically Argentine than the perpetually cynical, ironic, native-born variety that always bets in order to lose ... or else win sadly. All the same, there is one thing ... perhaps the only thing ... I like: you."

"And you want me to believe that?"

"If it were just for one day, it wouldn't be bad."

She took my hand and we went on. I walked her back to medical school.

Entry 20
Becoming a Bulldog

What fears do you have to overcome in order to be born and grow up? Thanks to my Christian upbringing, Aram's incredible ability to control people made me feel guilty about everything, including leaving my desk to go to the bathroom. The Monday I was going to ask for the raise, thinking that the busy season was over, I not only walked Ana to medical school, but stopped off at a café with her to have coffee and talk about the course in "Painless Birth" that the sanatorium was offering at a reduced price. Of course I told her she could take it, just as I said "yes" to her for everything. I'd figure out how to pay the bills later.

When I came into the shop around eleven, I was greeted with a shout from Aram.

"Where the hell have you been? Was your wife having the baby?"

I continued the birthing steps I had been practising and that had now begun to afford me a glimpse of the outside world I was nearing; stepping forward (a bad idea in birth), I answered, "We're going to have twins, so I'll need two pesos for every one."

"Twins? You're kidding."

"No, I'm not."

Aram followed his own advice of always looking before you leap, or some old quote from a famous Argentine worthy who said to always count to ten or turn your tongue around three times before speaking.

"Congratulations. When they're born we'll raise your salary to the official family level, so don't worry about a thing."

"You always obey the law, don't you. I'm talking about the birth. My wife has checked everywhere, and twins always cost more, and that's not including the cribs, clothes, and painless birth ... the course she's taking, I mean."

Don Garabed joined in.

"Son, children always show up with bread under their arm."

"All right, Don Garabed, but at the moment we're just trying to get them born."

"A customer, a customer!" Aram cut in, pushing me toward the showroom. "Come on, before he escapes!"

I was in such a state of fury that, when he saw my face, the customer scurried out before I could bite him. I went out on his heels to get some air and have a coffee.

When I came back, Aram was in the back with Don Garabed, preparing a bank deposit. By now I'd become a bulldog; I came over to them to growl, but as soon as they saw me Aram started growling at *me*. "Don't bug us. We're busy now."

Erminia's big eyes followed me, and I went over to speak to her.

"Ah, yes," I told her in a loud voice, "in answer to your question about the hospital: it does seem pretty luxurious, but I'm not sure I'm going to be able to pay for it." My voice was getting progressively louder. "Listen, Erminia, don't you ever take a break for a leak, or do you use a bag the Kalpakians give you? Oh yeah, of course: I suppose you buy one with your own money."

I went back and sat down at my desk. A few minutes later Don Garabed went out to the bank; the shop was quiet.

"I want to speak to you."

It was Aram. He drew up a chair for me and shouted, "Enrique! Look after anyone who comes in!"

I sat down. He started speaking to me in Hungarian.

"I've thrown people out of here for a lot less than your behaviour today. I can see you haven't changed much since the days at camp when you used to read Nietzsche and tell the kids dirty stories. We don't want any barking revolutionaries or rebels here. We'll talk things over; if in the end you still can't get along, it'll be because you simply don't want to. I'm telling you, once and for all ..."

"Cut it out, Aram. I'll clear out if you want."

"And your wife will give birth surrounded by a bunch of grimy mestizos. You, with your willfulness, won't ever find a job anywhere that lasts more than a day. That's why I'm telling you ..."

"Aram, Aram, for God's sake, lay off. Can't you see I'm desperate, that you're paying me next to nothing, and that every time I try to talk about it you avoid saying a word?"

"I'm paying you what I'm supposed to."

"Yeah, according to the law, Aram. And the law's on your side."

"But you live like a lush." We'd changed back to Spanish. "You smoke, go out every half hour for coffee, and I'm sure you're ..."

"Knock it off, Aram. You're driving me nuts."

"OK, I'll speak to my cousins. But, all the same, don't get your hopes up."

I got up and stood in front of him.

"Aram, don't try to con me anymore with stories about talking to your cousins. Those meetings and consultations every morning are just a parody: you're the one in charge here. Listen. Am I a bad salesman?"

"No, I wouldn't say that."

"Do I cheat or rob you?"

"I hope not!"

"Then tell me how you can be such a son of a bitch? If I had all the money you have ..."

He jumped up.

"Oh no, you don't! I won't let you start in on that. Go find out for yourself how much of a son of a bitch you've got to be to amass the money we have. You don't have the guts for it. You want proof? You haven't got a peso. And I've got things to do."

He went off a few steps and then came back.

"Oh yeah, a word of advice. Don't ask sons of bitches for favours."

After that incident, there was a long empty space. Even Enrique looked at me distrustfully. Old Garabed didn't give me any more lessons that afternoon. He left at four o'clock, as usual, but without saying goodbye on his way out. Artim and Ohan stopped by and glanced over at me the way you'd look at a mangy dog. I knew all of them talked together on an internal phone line.

I didn't sell anything that day. At six-thirty in the evening, Aram called me over. He took me to the pay window and asked me to sit down.

"How much do you need?"

"Are you going to give me a raise?"

"I asked you how much you needed. Stop arguing about it."

"Ten thousand pesos, at least."

"Ten thousand! That's two-thirds of your whole year's salary!"

I started to get up. He pushed me back onto the chair.

"I'll lend you eight thousand and dock your salary eight hundred a month till it's all paid back."

I smiled. I knew they were also moneylenders.

"How much interest?"

"For you, in spite of inflation, just two percent a month."

"How generous. I'm so happy and grateful I could cry. Should I thank you?"

He thought for a moment.

"No, it's not necessary. But I will ask you never to call us sons of bitches again. Maybe that's what we are, like all merchants. But it's not very pleasant to hear."

"All right."

He opened the drawer and counted out eight thousand pesos in notes of a thousand. He also took out an IOU form, filled it out, and pushed it over to me.

"Sign it."

I looked at the paper: eight thousand pesos, and no date.

"How does it work?"

"When you've finished paying, we tear it up."

I took the money, counted it, and put it away. Then I picked up the IOU and tore it in two.

"You told me not to call you sons of bitches anymore. I want to keep my word, no matter what you do."

I stood up and walked out.

Note: As I reread this today, I realize how pathetic it was to think I was tearing up an IOU out of honour and dignity, in order to be someone.

Entry Without a Number

This entry, Doctor, which is as yellow as the rest — all of them are fading more and more, especially if you look at them in the light — only contains a few headings that act as reminders: "Spring, or the First Days of Summer", "A Bedroom on Santa Fe Street", "The Dyed Blond", "Feelings and Worries: Freedom, Ana's Teeth, and Money", and several others.

I don't know, Doctor, what's actually making me write up this episode now — whether it's out of a desire to purify myself, enjoy a few memories, or confess. I told you that I never cheated on Ana while she was pregnant. Did I deliberately lie, and was the episode in the bedroom a deception or an adventure — the only one possible for the bourgeois I myself never was?

There's a saying in Hungarian that "God's zoo is grand and varied," and the following interlude would generally be nothing more than one among many that salesmen run into and then end up boasting about in some bar — without ever once doubting that their own wives are saints. But in my case, there was another reason: a difference of eight millimetres, one that can also be the measure of a bank account — or of a human being. Later on, in the bedroom of a house in Palermo Chico, the memory of this episode would help me free myself from the Kalpakians.

Over the next few months, with my freedom draining away and Aram's cries still echoing in my ears, I did everything I could to win back my dignity. I would leave the shop with my briefcase, tape measure, paper and pencil, running along with my tongue hanging out to take measurements and try to grab the enemy's beard with a deposit and then, without slowing down or losing a second, would return to the shop, my tongue dragging on the floor by now, all in an effort to make good, to be an exemplary salesman, to draw up estimates and chase after customers.

I had been working for the Kalpakians for eight months now, and Ana was in about the eighth month of her pregnancy. It must have been near mid-summer. The Kalpakians buzzed about as desperately as horseflies, but nobody was buying. Don Garabed would have torn his hair out if he'd still had any.

One morning, about eleven-thirty, Erminia appeared with a customer order for me to go over immediately to a client's house to measure a bedroom for a carpet and then make up an estimate. I got up and put a block of graph paper and a measuring tape in my briefcase; I told Aram where I was going and he gave me bus fare. Before leaving, I said goodbye to Don Garabed.

Selling is a mechanical art. As time goes by, and without giving it much thought, a mere address is enough to prepare you mentally to grab the enemy by the beard. In this case, the indicated battleground was near the intersection of Santa Fe and Callao Streets, an area of middle-class flats for people who think they're on the way up. Fourth floor apartments are cheaper than those on the tenth, and the "B's" at the back aren't as nice as the "A's" at the front. The last name, Anchorena, was of no special interest, except that I remembered seeing someone by that name marked down in the files as never paying on time — one of those clients with holes in their underwear that, as Artim would say, must have left his (or her) ass exposed to the elements.

Strangely, though I'd left the store with the usual dynamism, I found myself walking down 9 de Julio Avenue without having taken the bus. And I kept on, without thinking much about the coming combat with the enemy or planning how to grab his beard.

My thoughts oscillated between the approaching birth and Ana's teeth, half of which were now gone. The twins were giving signs of charging their fee before they even appeared. It had been her teeth, those lovely teeth, glowing in her soft, relaxed smile, that had played an important part in conquering me — as they would have conquered anyone; they had been her insurance, even against me, and now they were gone. According to the dentist she had seen, it was better not to do anything for the moment and wait till the babies had been born before

67

deciding which teeth could be saved and which couldn't. And I, like an idiot, hadn't thought of the cost or included it when I'd asked Aram for the loan.

When I arrived at the address, it was already noon and the main door to the building was locked. Since there wasn't a doorman in the flesh, I pressed the electric one: a voice asked who I was and buzzed me in, and I took the elevator up.

When I arrived at apartment 4B, a tall, scraggly maid opened the door. There was a smell of stale cooking odours and I entered a large living room filled with the kind of bric-à-brac that passes for antiques.

The lady of the house was resting. Could I please wait.

I swallowed my opinion of the lady of the house's easy living. The maid disappeared down a hallway and came back right away.

"She says it's all right, to go on in anyway. She's very tired. It's the last door on the right."

I stepped into the hallway: a first bedroom, a second, and shadows at the entrance of the third. I hesitated.

"Come in, come in," a voice said.

I did.

"The light's not too bright in here," I said, and realized I was getting nervous.

There was a little laugh.

"Is it all right if I raise the Venetian blinds?" I asked.

"No, please don't. I'll turn on the lamp."

She switched on a lamp on the bedside table. I looked at her, as she must have intended — and kept on looking.

How can I describe her, Doctor, without being vulgar? If God or Nature hadn't provided her with certain proportions and protuberances, she would have ended up a common servant and would have been the one who opened the door for me. You could see it in everything about her, from her face, smudged with makeup from where it had rubbed against the pillow, with prominent cheekbones and dark eyes, to the dusky or sun-tanned skin of her legs — or at least of one of them, which protruded at an odd angle from the sheets — and her black hair, dyed with streaks of blond.

The rest was what you would find in a photo of a fashion model in a layout for lingerie or mattresses.

She was young. She smiled. Her tongue emerged from her mouth and licked slowly across her upper lip. I don't know which magazine might have told her that this was a particularly provocative gesture — perhaps it was the one of life. I felt a bit nauseous but, spurred on by my fantasies or some unconfessed wish for variety, a shudder passed through me.

The human mind works in strange ways. I remembered my father telling me that my hard-working mother used to make his underwear herself in order to save money, using a coarse, rough material so that he would be ashamed to take off his pants in the presence of another woman.

Before I began measuring the bedroom floor, I asked her, "What kind of carpet are you thinking of putting in? The six millimetre Classic or the fourteen millimetre luxury Tafter?"

"The Classic."

With my heartbeat accelerating and wondering which pair of underwear I'd put on that morning, I placed the briefcase on the bed, opened it, took out the pad of graph paper, drew a square representing the carpet, and began to measure the bedroom.

When I had finished and was putting the papers and measuring tape back in the briefcase, I realized that both her legs were now completely uncovered; she seemed to have somehow wriggled out of her negligee and most of the sheet, so that her shoulders were now bare.

I wondered whether she might not be some kind of hysteric who would end up causing trouble. I'd heard about cases like that. With laboured breath, she kept watching me and I, her. I know now that if she had licked her lips one more time I would have told her, "Thank you very much," and gotten out of there as fast as I could. But no: instead she smiled and her eyes came to rest on the door.

I went over to it and looked back at her before closing it: she nodded her head slightly and I pushed it shut.

I came back and stood over her bedside, and she turned off the light.

Once outside, I was overcome by a desire to relax even more, to let go completely, to take it easy and reconcile my feelings of satisfaction and distaste, and I went into the nearest café.

I took a seat next to the window and ordered a coffee. I stirred it slowly and reviewed what had just happened. There's no accounting for taste: I had barely put down my briefcase before she was already weaving a handmade rug — an authentic one in its own way — without a single loose thread.

I smoked a cigarette and loafed, without worrying about Aram's shouts when I got back. Outside the window, I rediscovered the street and the world again, far away and yet right there next to me. Happily, I thought that it was freedom.

I had a second coffee, paid with my bus fare, and began walking back to the store, my pace as weary as a cow's. That afternoon I drew up an estimate and called the telephone number on the order form. No one answered. I didn't call again, but sent out the estimate by mail. I never got a reply.

Both the satisfaction and the distaste soon disappeared.

I know now that there is no such thing as freedom, though perhaps there are liberties. Or maybe not. And now when I look into Ana's eyes and then at her wineglass, perhaps I feel bad for another reason.

Entry 21
The Longest Day of the Year Begins

I thought I heard the chimes from the wall clock.
"Pedro?"
"Yeah, what?"
"I'm losing my water."
"Turn off the tap."
"I tell you I'm losing my water."
"What water?"
"The liquid from my uterus. I think it's burst."
I opened my eyes.
"Liquid? Burst?"
Ana's voice was soft and gentle, imploring.
"Pedro, Pedro, wake up! I think the birth's begun."
"At this hour? What time is it?"
"Pedro, please. There is no right time."
I sighed.
"I guess kids are like the police: they come without notice at any time, day or night. How long do you have?"
"Three or four hours. I'll check in the book."

Ana dragged herself out of bed. I lay there fighting against sleep. I reached out my hand to where she had been lying: it was soaking wet.

With an effort, I got up to make coffee.

While I prepared things in the kitchen, Ana consulted the book, searching for arcane secrets or "the word." She had a towel between her legs; a sickly-sweet smell floated out into the kitchen. I served us both coffee.

"Yes," she announced, "it'll be within three to five hours."

"We've got time, then." The clock on the wall marked four-thirty. "We'll be there by six-thirty or seven. I'll tell Don Tomás. We've also got to notify my parents and your wonderful relatives."

I drank my coffee and smoked a cigarette, then got dressed without washing or shaving. God, it's funny the things you remember at the most unexpected moments: I thought of Aram saying, "Before going out I always shave, shower, and put on a tie and jacket because I could be chosen cabinet minister at any moment."

Ana would be ready in twenty minutes. I went out to get Don Tomás. It was summer. Mist floated up in long strands out of the darkness. Hardly a star was visible. It was strange, an odd time to be about. Ever since I'd given up going out with my friends and getting back to my parents' house at dawn — an era that seemed far distant now — I hadn't walked through the town at this hour.

My hand still had that sickly-sweet odour which had adhered to it when I'd touched Ana's place on the mattress. I'd had as little faith as that saint who'd wanted to see Christ's wound.

Don Tomás, an elderly Italian who was now retired from the Union of Tramway and Self-Propelled Railcar Drivers, was sitting against a tree next to his truck, drinking *mate*. He often talked about how in the countryside back in Italy he always used to get up at four in the morning. Over here, he'd continued rising at that hour in order to travel to work. He was always in bed by nine at night. He said that way he got a few hours of peace, far from the chatter of his wife and three daughters.

After retirement, he'd taken the driving exam to become a trucker and had failed it three times: he kept confusing the truck with the tram. "But, since in a dis a-country, everyting can be a-fixed up," he'd paid a bribe, gotten his licence, and now earned a few extra pesos doing freelance hauling "becausa wita tree daughters, da pensione isn't a-wort a goddama ting."

71

"Good morning, Don Tomás."

"But a wata happen? Dey trow ya out, ya bum?"

"No. I need a ride into Buenos Aires. You remember what we arranged?"

"You wife's a-gonna give a-birt?"

"That's right. Are you free?"

"Ofa course. Disa tinga neva stop. Wata time you wanna head a-out?"

"I can't speak for the baby, but we want to get going as soon as possible. I'll just tell my folks and be right back. OK?"

"Sure. No a-problem."

My parents' house, at the back of town, was on the edge of the pampas. There hadn't been much progress since they'd bought it: a few other homes had been built, but that was all. Five minutes after leaving Don Tomás, I was knocking on the blinds of their bedroom window. I stood there and told them what had happened, but it wasn't enough. My mother asked me to wait and came to the door in her dressing gown with her eyes filled with tears, asking me for more details.

"Mama, don't get so dramatic. It's not a funeral. And it's better for me to be back there with Ana than standing here giving you details about things I don't really know about. Her water broke, that's all."

"You seem to be taking it pretty lightly."

"No, Mama, I'm not taking it lightly. Should I be groaning, wailing, pulling out my hair?"

She began to cry openly: "Poor Ana, poor Ana." I hugged her and told her to go back to bed. I'd come back afterward and tell them how things had gone.

I don't know what made me take the long way around and go by the field just beyond the village. The cows, which belonged to Don Pedro, the old Polish farmer, were standing in line along the barbed-wire fence. It was the last under-the-counter milk you could get in the village. Don Pedro treated his cows better than his own family and had completely domesticated them. I'd known them for years; I stroked their muzzles, and their saliva, moist breath, and animal warmth comforted me a little.

Yes, I was definitely worried about the whole thing. I left the cattle and went quickly back to get Don Tomás. As I walked away from the animals, the odour of the barn diminished and my fears grew. The mist continued.

When I got back to the house with Don Tomás, Ana was ready, waiting there with a towel between her legs. As I picked up her suitcase, I told her, "You're even prettier with the towel. Just the right touch, as they say."

She smiled wanly. Before getting into the truck, she doubled over with a contraction and we had to wait till it was over. Don Tomás went pale and made the sign of the cross.

Don Tomás and Ana got in. I ran back to lock the house. We were abandoning it at that moment, but I thought about how, within just a few days, we would be returning with a baby girl or boy — or a couple of them. I wondered what it would be like. I sat down next to Ana and hugged her.

"Please, Don Tomás, drive carefully," I asked.

"You wanna teacha me howda drive after tirty year a-drivin' da tramway? Donta you worry."

Don Tomás took the road to Buenos Aires. He murmured something about the Madonna. Every so often, Ana had a contraction and ground her teeth. Don Tomás accelerated a bit. I put my arm around her and smelled her hair, holding her close and trying to put her inside of myself. I don't remember any more of the sickly-sweet odour. It must have disappeared, or perhaps I couldn't smell it any longer because of the blackened cigarillo that Don Tomás was smoking and chewing on as he drove.

Ana was sweating and trembling. I don't know if that was the same trembling that eventually spread to me — and that I still have — or if there were others that were even worse.

The mist was disappearing; we could see the lights of the city and probably of the dawn that never really came. I remember it was raining.

We finally pulled up outside the Metropolitan Sanatorium on Lavalle Street and got out of the truck with relief. As I reached into my pocket, Don Tomás said, "No, wea settle upa later. Look afta youa wife. Be a-strong. Ciao."

At the reception desk, Ana laboriously took out her hospital card. Even then, she didn't let me take care of things for her. Her purse was sacred territory, which I would later often violate in my search for an answer to an unknown question — an answer I would never obtain.

They sent us up to the third floor. A smile came through a swinging door and took Ana away with it. After a while, the same smile came back, shuffled through some papers, and announced like a trumpet: "Dilation of five centimetres. Take care of the paperwork."

I run downstairs. The smile dances along in front of my eyes like that of the Cheshire Cat in *Alice in Wonderland* ... another reception desk ... no ... over there ... I enter a tiny office ... the cat smiling at me from every angle reappears in the face of the guy who attends to me ... I leave a deposit on the down payment and go out, I don't know where ... Ah, yes, I remember: "Call my mother," Ana had told me ... I look for a telephone and have to go outside to call from a café on the other side of the street ... no change ... I ask for some ... put in the coins and dial ... My mother-in-law answers ... oh's and ah's ... She passes the phone to my sister-in-law ... more oh's and ah's ... They live in the city now and will be over in half and hour; I hang up ... dial again ... this time the carpet store ... No one answers ... I remember the time ... a night watchman ...? "Night watchman, son? Everything's insured: why waste money on a guard?" I hang up, forgetting the coin ... and then go back to get it ... I order a coffee ... It burns my mouth ... The reception desk again ... Where do I have to go now ...? Fourth story, the nursing mothers' room ... I climb the stairs ... ask the way ... They don't know where it is ... Several women are giving birth ... "Wait next to that window over there" ... I look ... There's a large window in which a nurse appears every so often, like a machine that works miracles, with a baby in her arms, and picks up a microphone through which she announces what sex it is ... the happiness show ... There are other men seated waiting, smoking, pacing the floor ... I sit down and light a cigarette ... My legs are shaking ... I get up and walk around ... I sit down and smoke ... half an hour ... forty minutes ... an hour ...

Entry 22
There Inside (Ana's Story)

They took me away on a stretcher: white ceilings, voices, an elevator, metallic sounds.

"Mommy, what's wrong with that lady?"

"Please, son, be quiet and don't stare."

Harsh lights. I was in pain, but calm. The book said it would seem unbearable, but that it wouldn't really be so; if it were, I would pass out. I felt like a heroine.

The doctor came in. He felt and measured me.

"Six or seven centimetres' dilation. Blood pressure and information. Enema. Shave her."

He left. I asked the nurse, "Where's my husband?"

"He's taking care of the paperwork. What do you want him here for? Breathe deeply each time you have a contraction."

She took my blood pressure. She didn't shave me or give me an enema. She disappeared.

I lost my sense of time. The ceiling filled with colours: reds like burning coals — the lights danced about with each contraction — grey, black, they disappeared and came back as red again. I had trouble getting my breath. I began to feel dispirited, the way the book said.

A nurse with dyed red hair appeared and pulled away the covers.

"Open your legs. Easy, easy, come on now, madam, relax."

She put her hand inside me. Hard, bony hands with long, sharp fingernails.

"It's just that ... Wait a second ... I'm having a contraction ... Please ..."

"Come now, let's not waste time. There's a lot of other women here and I've got to attend to all of them; you aren't the only one, you know. The doctors leave us all the ..."

She pulled away her hands; her fingers had blood on them — or maybe it was nail polish.

"Take her away."

Two nurses, one fat and the other thin, pushed me into a room and put me on another stretcher; the lights were even stronger, and there were faces among them. They tied my legs down.

"Can't you ... do that ... slower ... please?" I begged them.

"Don't be such a baby. If this hurts you now, how are you going to take what's still to come? Other women don't make such a fuss. Open up now! It's starting ... Cotton!"

They put a mask over my face.

"Push! Your child's starting to come now. Breathe!"

I breathed deeply. But I didn't feel anything. I remembered the book: "Oxygen is odourless." I pushed hard. I couldn't get my breath;

I was suffocating. I shook my head from side to side in desperation. The mask came off.

"I can't believe it. She tried to bite me!"

"What's all this? Showing us your teeth now, are you?" The redhead got up from her seat. "If you're going to be like that, we'll just leave you here alone; you'll soon be screaming for us to come back and help you."

"I didn't want … didn't want … just air … air …"

"Air? It's right here. What's the matter with that oxygen?"

"Don't you put it on like this?" The mask came over my face again.

"No, not like that! The tube's still closed; open it."

"OK now, push! But watch out, because if you don't, you know what'll happen!"

The oxygen soothed me. I pushed.

"See how you could? Push harder now, harder …" The colours danced about again; something split open. "Harder … relax now … Don't scream … Quit screaming!"

A pause.

"Now look what she's done! Clean it up before … If the doctor comes he won't even look at her. It's disgusting!"

"Turn on the fan. I can't stand it."

The colours came down and danced next to me.

"We've got to cut her open. Syringe!"

The needle went in and out. Something gave way. I think I murmured your name or asked for you.

"It's a good thing we didn't let her husband in; otherwise, can you imagine? These modern childbirths …"

"Come on now, come on. You're not just some ignorant peasant who doesn't know any better; act properly now."

I squeezed … nothing … pushed … nothing …

"Forceps!"

I got frightened. The child! I felt something hard and cold.

"What's the matter? Won't it come out even with them?"

Red … red … the fat one's on top of me … I can't hold back …

"It doesn't hurt now … Come on, what's the matter, madam? Quit screaming! QUIT SCREAMING! Your child is trying to be born and you're not letting it. Let it come out! Do you want to kill your own child? Come on now, both of us, let's go!" Both of us … I was breaking apart ... the colours ran together ... a white explosion ... I felt it ... a liquid ... blood? ... I heard it gushing to the floor ... like a wave ...

I opened my eyes. The book said the baby had to cry. The silence distracted me. I searched for it. The three of them looked down at me silently, as if from a distance. One of them held it in a cloth. I could just barely hear a feeble whimpering. They brought it over to me.

"It's a boy. Give him a kiss. We'll have to take him away now because he's cold and we have to wash him."

The midwife started to sew me up. Maybe she'd only had a bad day. I smiled at her.

"I'm sorry if I gave you a lot of trouble."

"Oh, it's nothing. The first time's always the same. Get some rest. It's over now."

"And the other one?" I asked.

"What other one, madam?"

Note: It was only one night three or four months later, when we were lying in bed together, that Ana finally told me the whole story of the birth. Before she could do it, she had me turn off the light. When she had finished, we made love, but without turning on the light again. It was one among many other (not all) sad acts of love, more than ever like a gentle death.

Entry 23
Here Outside

A loudspeaker repeats my name ... Me ...? I stand up like a sleepwalker and look for ... Someone touches my shoulder ... Others point to the window ... I go over and wave my hand ... A nurse wearing a mask brings a microphone up to her mouth; her cheeks suggest a petrified smile; she holds up a diapered baby with a red, wrinkled face and closed eyes ... I calm down a bit ... Ana: where's Ana ...? I walk off like a zombie ... A woman runs after me ... With a slight, authoritarian pressure on my arm she drags me back ... The nurse is still there, waiting ... Her smile has disappeared, and there are frustration and rebuke in her eyes ...

"Is something the matter?" I ask the woman who's dragged me back.

She sighs as if she knew every man alive.

"You men, always asking, 'Is it a boy or a girl?'" She has a strong Jewish accent.

I had forgotten to ask the classic question; the classic scene had been too perfectly set. I'd altered the ceremony. All I can think of is to trace a question mark in the air. The nurse's smile returns. She forgives me, blows into the microphone and says through the loudspeaker, "It's a boy."

She disappears.

"Those fathers," the lady who dragged me back reproves me softly. "Congratulations."

"Thanks." I try to be funny. "He's ugly."

"That doesn't matter. It's a boy. May he be rich and intelligent. Especially rich."

Ana … I look for her … "She'll be right out, sir …" "They're sewing her up…" My sister-in-law and her mother arrive … Unwillingly, I tell them … The swinging doors open … They're bringing Ana out … She's pale, so pale … paler than the most beautiful women lauded by the poets … My sister-in-law and her mother rush forward … They irritate me … We follow Ana's gurney and enter a room with three empty beds … They lift her off onto one of them … The nurse leaves … Ana opens her eyes and looks at us as if she's dead or looking inside herself … Her eyes are swollen … mouth dry … lips cracked … My sister- and mother-in-law question her; they want to know … Ana tries to speak; she opens her lips, tries to wet them with her tongue, but can't … I bend over her and wet her lips with my tongue … "Oh's" and "ah's" of disgust from my sister- and mother-in-law, who move away … Ana looks at me … We look at each other … There are tears … hers, mine …? She closes her eyes … Two drops of glass hang suspended … I realize she isn't strong enough even to cry … I lick the drops away with my tongue … I take her hand … It's icy … She tries to raise it … I help her … She wants to touch my face … I bend down over her … She wants to caress my head; just a few strokes and then her hand becomes still. I'm not sure whether she's collapsed or fallen asleep.

There is a reading, the reading of silence. Ana had read the silence, heard it and seen it. It wasn't the silence of the firing squad before the final order is given, nor the silence of the explosion before hearing the shots, nor the silence before pulling the trigger for the *coup de grâce*; it wasn't the silence of the burial, nor the silence a second before an earthquake, nor the silence of some monk in search of illumination trying to listen to nothingness in order to lose himself in it or in the breath of God. She heard it and saw it in the silence that fell over the midwife and the nurses when her son was born. It was the silence that seized her and in that silence and in all those to come, she would continue looking for the other one, without knowing it, for the twin that spilled out in a pool of cephalorachitic liquid.

We were surrounded by silence.

Entry 24
Meningo Celly

The silence was interrupted by a nurse who came in: the pediatrician wanted to see me.

"Is something the matter?" I whispered, so as not to wake up Ana.

"It's routine. Room 403."

And, following the routine, I went out to look for the pediatrician. In the corridor I ran into my mother- and sister-in-law, who hurled themselves at me. What in God's name did they want? They followed me. I found Room 403. Later I learned that this eminent professional was one of the sanatorium's principal shareholders. At the moment, I hesitated at the threshold of the open door of 403; I supposed that the man in a white lab coat, with his back to me, was the pediatrician. I cleared my throat.

He turned his head, got up, and came over to me, and when he focused his crossed eyes on me, I wondered how someone who so closely resembled an ogre in a fairy tale could be a person who treated kids. Perhaps he cured them by fright.

His eyes moved ceaselessly about from top to bottom and right to left, so that I couldn't tell whether he was inspecting me — unshaven, disheveled, and tieless as I was — in order to ascertain what calibre of person I was, or whether he was staring me in the eye.

He looked, or seemed to look, at my mother- and sister-in-law, who understood immediately and stepped back as if they'd seen a ghost. Right there, without asking me to come in or going through any introductions, he said, "The sooner you know, the better. These things shouldn't be put off. It's incurable. A small wound in the spine: it's meningocele together with spina bifida."

I didn't know what to say, what to ask. The tremor.

"For his whole life, you understand … if he lives. But let's wait for the specialist. We've already sent for him."

Bells. Trembling. Faraway bells creating a vacuum, echoes. Waves of trembling. Walt Disney, you who paint life as being so happy, help me.

Besides being an ogre, he was an evil genie who immediately vanished, closing the door behind him. I suppose I'd turned completely white. I suppose. My mother- and sister-in-law fell upon me.

I told them without knowing what I was saying. Explain? What more could I explain to their: "What'd he say?" "It can't be!" and "Is that all?" Jackie, my sister-in-law, commented, "Ha! Now I get it. I thought you were too quiet."

I closed my eyes.

"And that's it? Didn't he say anything else? You didn't ask him to explain?" Whenever she was either happy or in a rage, Jackie's mouth would fill with foam and — perhaps either from thinking about food, or becoming angry, or just as a lubricant — she would spray saliva as she spoke. "Ah no, no, no. Thing's aren't just going to end like this. How did it happen? Why? This isn't any old hospital. Here you pay for them to take care of you. It's private. You can't just let them do whatever they want. You've got to stand up for your rights."

"My rights!" I thought.

"Jackie," I said, "stop spitting at me or move away a bit. And get off my case. If you want, you can go in yourself and ask him to explain. I authorize you to."

She hesitated. I told her I wanted to have a cup of coffee and smoke a cigarette.

"But … but how can you drink coffee in a situation like this?"

"You're right. I don't know how I'm going to be able to swallow," I told her. I was sincere. "But I'm going to try, anyway." A sharp pain: I didn't know which one, but only one: maybe Ana. Should I go see her right away? What should I tell her? My stomach tightened and my throat constricted.

"We'll go with you," Jackie said; it sounded like an order.

Life is strange, and so are human beings. I don't know why, but, even though I knew her well, I wanted to believe for a moment that her offer was what I felt it to be — a gesture of solidarity.

I needed some air. The three of us went over to the café across the street.

I ordered a coffee; they each had a gin and tonic. After a few minutes, my mother-in-law's face — red, fat-cheeked, and furrowed with blue veins — lit up like a traffic light. She only spoke Spanish haltingly at the best of times and hadn't said a word the whole time. Now she began to speak rapidly in English, with an elegance usually reserved for those who exchange bits of good news at five o'clock tea. No, there'd never been any solidarity. I thanked God for this corner of solitude and freedom. I moved my chair and with it my body in order to look somewhere else.

Note: That day, Doctor, twenty or twenty-five years ago, was just four or five days before I met you during our first get-together, or dialogue, or interview. You will notice over the next few file cards that I have left out several entries. I haven't done so in order to jump ahead to our meeting or because I have forgotten about them, but rather because they've become irrelevant. Entry 25 is the story of the efforts of my sister-in-law, charged up and propelled by alcohol and spraying saliva in all directions, to make an appointment with the pediatrician she chased after all over the sanatorium, and of how the doctor in question categorically refused to see her. It also tells how he finally dispatched a nurse to let her know she needn't worry, because the child's problem was easily curable. The entry ends with my sister-in-law standing in front of me, with froth at the edges of her mouth and alcohol on her breath, telling me, "You see? What'd I tell you? Things can be fixed up. It's just that with you, they do whatever they want."

Entry 26 is about the call I made to the shop to tell Aram I wouldn't be coming in to work that day, and of how he in turn notified me that the law only allowed me three days off for the birth of a child; of how he asked me if it was a boy or a girl, and if it was sound and healthy and not a jerk like me. In response to the latter question, which I considered most significant, I told him a tale I believe I'd first heard from an old woman in my hometown, turning it, of course, into my own: that the baby's umbilical cord had gotten tangled around its neck, almost strangling it and coming within a hair of preventing it from being born. I confided all this to him in a worried and distressed voice, and the story was a remarkable success. Later on I would complicate it, complicating my own life in the process.

Entry 27 is shameful. Although I still hadn't been able to see the specialist, I visited Ana in the hospital and, pressured by all her questions, I refused either to be silent or to tell her the truth (which, in reality, I couldn't pin down myself exactly). Perhaps I should have simply said, "Let's wait for the specialist." In any case, in order not to raise her expectations, I talked in circles about the umbilical cord which, in some way, would explain the problems she'd had. Luckily, her mother and sister, probably fresh from a few drinks across the street, burst in on us like a couple of crows.

Entry 28
The Specialist Speaks

I was with Ana and my mother- and sister-in-law when a nurse informed me that the specialist had arrived. If I remember correctly, he was a neurosurgeon.

I followed the nurse down the corridor. Jackie bounded along behind me, stepping on my heels.

"Jackie, please: you're wrecking my shoes."

We walked down a long hallway to the nursing mothers' room, where the pediatrician with the dancing eyes was standing at the entrance to a small cubicle. We waited there for the specialist while he examined the baby, who still didn't have a name.

Finally he appeared: tall, thin, and with glasses, followed by a middle-aged woman with a smooth face.

"Are you the father?" he asked.

"I guess so," I replied.

"Come in." He gestured toward the room.

I entered, as did he and the woman. My sister-in-law, who had been sticking to me like an octopus, withdrew her tentacles as the specialist closed the door. The pediatrician didn't enter either.

The specialist took off his glasses and looked at me. I'll never know whether there was any feeling in him or not — or perhaps just a clear truth, without sentiment.

"There's not much to say," he began. "We could operate on him or let him die. If you want, we'll operate. If he survives, his head will grow disproportionately, and he'll be profoundly retarded all his life. If he doesn't either die or suffer from hydrocephalism ... which is all but impossible ... he'll never be able to walk: he has no motor reflexes. He won't be able to urinate and he'll have to live with an unnaturally formed anus. He won't be able to have sexual relations. In short, his spinal column is open at the tenth vertebra, and he's paralyzed from there on down. What do you want to do?"

Bells. Tremors. A freezing wind.

"Do? It's not hard for me; I don't feel anything for him."

"That's natural. You'll feel nothing at all for the first two or three years. That's the way we fathers are. I don't think his mother feels much either. She probably hates him for the difficult birth she must have had: that sack of cephalorachitic liquid. Well, what do you want to do?"

"Will we be able to have other children?"

"Without a doubt; and healthier than this one. A baby like this, if it survives, can destroy a family. What's your decision?"

"What caused it?"

"Who knows? The lesion usually develops within the first two or three months of the pregnancy. There are so many possible causes: it could be a vaccination, some medication."

"A tetanus shot?"

"Quite possibly. Well then, what's your decision?"

I had to speak with Ana, who would ask me for a thousand explanations. As for me, my next question was a type of decision.

"Doctor, couldn't you give him an injection to make him d—, make him go to sleep?"

"That would be a crime. Let's let nature take its course. With the wound left open, in three days, a week at the most, he'll get an infection and die of meningitis. In order to avoid any kind of problem and facilitate things, see if you can find a nurse who'll take care of him. I'm sure you'll be able to find one here in the sanatorium. We've had several cases like this in the past."

He smiled.

"Or don't look for one; she'll appear. They're like vam— ..."

He shook my hand, opened the door and went out. The woman, who hadn't uttered a word, closed the door part-way; then she looked at me with a bitter, or perhaps philosophical smile, and said, "Tell your wife that ..." She fell silent. "No, don't tell her anything; it's not my business. She'll have to decide. But let me assure you, there's nothing more horrible than having a child like that; than caring for it and wishing and praying to God every day, every minute, for it to die as soon as possible."

She left the door ajar.

Entry 29
The Day Continues

I stayed in the room, taking deep breaths, trying to recall what I'd just heard and fix it in my mind. A pair of crossed eyes appeared at the door and focused on the walls on either side of me.

"Everything all fixed up?" it asked.

I seemed to hear a sniffing and nosing around.

"It looks like it," I told him, without knowing how wrong I was.

He disappeared.

I couldn't stay there forever, and stepped gingerly outside, right into my sister-in-law's tentacles.

Although I know I asked myself many times that day how the things that were happening to me could actually take place in this world, I'm sure I also wondered how people like my sister-in-law could exist. She was deeply offended that the specialist had not invited her in when he'd talked to me. She was, after all, a former medical student who had made it to fourth year, an English-speaker who had studied the latest medical texts from Britain, texts so new that she had actually failed several exams simply because she didn't know the names of things in Spanish.

"That doctor's just rude. I can't imagine why he would want to speak with you when you obviously aren't qualified and don't understand a thing about all this."

The spray flew. I still hadn't found out what our misborn son's disease or defect was called and had to limit myself to telling her what would happen if he survived.

"He was too hasty and categorical about it all," she spat out. "And the guy's a liar: he spoke about monsters and we've never had monsters or anything like that in our family. I don't trust him. Nobody's had the last word yet. We've got to consult a real professional, someone who's capable and well qualified. Then we'll find out what's what."

I didn't have the strength left to ask her what she'd just said really meant. I just wanted to get away from her. Fortunately for me, she had a dentist's appointment that afternoon.

Note: Although I wasn't aware of it at the time, I'm surprised now that all those decisions fell on my shoulders, making me the central figure in the whole drama — and also the one responsible for everything, the criminal of the tale. This intrigues me so much that I've consulted a lawyer at the local Argentine consulate, Dr. Jorge Blanco, who's been kind enough to reveal the mystery to me: in those days, by virtue of the law of paternal authority, the father was responsible for family decisions.

Entry 30
It Must Be the Humidity

Mercifully, Ana was sleeping. I spoke with the nurse on duty, who told me they had given her a powerful tranquilizer and that she would sleep till nightfall. I also asked her if Ana had eaten; she wasn't sure, but she did know that she couldn't seem to get enough water. Her thirst was and would be infinite.

A heavy task lay ahead of me: telling my parents. I didn't feel an ounce of gratitude toward God for the gift with which He had blessed our matrimony, but I did think He could at least send the Holy Spirit or some angel to my parents to tell them the news.

I got off the subway at Constitución train station and, as if from afar, the great dome of the building sent back the echoes of the throngs below, the whistles of the locomotives, the noises and cries of the newspaper vendors. A feeling of detachment and isolation had begun to take hold of me. In an attempt to grab onto something, to go back to before, I bought a newspaper to find out what had been going on in the outside world.

I got on the train. There were still a lot of empty seats at that hour. I picked the last one on the right, the one the door opened up against, and hid. I couldn't read the paper. My eyes closed on their own. I attributed my disinterest and detachment to my profound tiredness.

I dozed fitfully. The swaying and the clanging of the bells kept me from sleeping. I was sweating; it must have been the humidity.

Over the years you learn the sound of the rails on the open stretches and then the small familiar changes that signal the delights of the approaching home station, especially if someone's waiting for you — even if it's just with Japanese croquettes and the possibility of making love. The train stopped and I got off. Yes, it was Longchamps. I'd left the paper on my seat. It didn't matter.

It was still cloudy; perhaps it would rain. The absence of sunlight helped and relieved me. The heat increased the weight I was carrying with me. For the first time in my life, simply walking through the town, meeting people I knew, saying hello to them, talking to them and explaining things, all seemed a titanic task.

I decided to take streets that were less travelled. The weariness was sucking out my energy. My head drooped and dragged me down with its weight, and I didn't try to stop it. As I walked by our house, it took an enormous effort to resist going in and throwing myself down on the bed to sleep. The duty (or obligation in this case) to tell my parents what had happened, as well as the overwhelming desire to get it over with, spurred my steps along.

Don Tomás's flatbed truck was parked next to the door of his house. The old Italian wasn't sitting next to the tree. He liked taking long siestas.

I could smell the odour of the Pole's stable, but his cows were nowhere to be seen. They were probably out to pasture in the fields.

I walked around to the back of my parents' house and went in through the kitchen, as I always did. A smell of cooking lingered in the air. My mother jumped out of her chair and stood looking at me, perhaps reading my silence, without even saying hello. I couldn't say a word. But I wanted to get it over with as quickly as possible.

"Where are Dad and Veronica?" I asked. My mouth was dry and I had difficulty swallowing.

"Your father is out making a delivery, and your sister's at her photography class."

I hesitated a few seconds, and then continued on in one breath.

"Mama, I've got to tell you everything, once and for all. But for God's sake don't ask me any questions, at least not today." I swallowed dryly again. "The baby's umbilical cord got tangled around its neck when it was born. It's very weak. It could even die. They've put it in an incubator."

Did I run out the door? I don't remember. Did my mother offer me something to eat? Did she ask me anything I didn't reply to? I don't remember that, either. I was already on my way home when I realized I'd unwittingly added a technological detail to my "natural" story about the "natural" birth.

Note: I see that both the conversation with my mother and the entry itself end too abruptly. Yet I remember (or is it simply a feeling I have now?) that my gently aggressive behaviour, if you can call it that, left me with a shadow of guilt and self-reproach as I walked back to my house. I'd escaped my mother's tendency to theatrics, to over-dramatize even the smallest incident. I don't know if I wondered at the time, as I do now, whether or not I could have stood a full-scale emotional reaction from her, at least under those circumstances. What I do know is that the technological detail about the incubator seemed a highly appropriate touch that made my story sound a bit more believable.

Entry 31
Our Home

They say that the house, the refuge for the family unit, where a man can be king, is a fortress protected by doors, iron grilles, and the law. That's what they would have us believe, and we like to hear it. When I got to our front door, I had a sudden desire to ram my head right through it in order to get in faster — or perhaps simply to break my skull open. My hands were shaking so much I couldn't fit the key in the lock.

Once safely inside, the very opposite of what I had expected occurred: I found the silence frightening. It was not the customary time or day of the week for me to be home; I should have been at work, doing my part to increase the price of shares in Kalpakian Ltd. Despite Ana's warnings, which she'd probably gotten from some book — "He'll be crying at any time of the day or night during the first few months, you know. Won't it bother you? Do you think you'll be able to get used to it?" — I had always assumed the baby's cries would fill the silence just like any other kind of family din. Now, however, I felt a deep suspicion — a certainty, really — that everything would be completely different, and that the rooms of the house would be peopled with phantoms and shadows rather than a child's cries.

The clock chimed four times — a small relief.

The blinds were closed. I went into the kitchen and turned on the light. In order to do something, almost out of habit, I looked in the refrigerator: eggs, meat, a bottle of milk. I wasn't hungry. The task of cooking a meal for myself seemed futile; the effort, gigantic. I poured a glass of milk and drank it as I nibbled a cracker from a box I found next to the sink.

The clock struck again: a quarter of an hour had gone by and I was still turning around in circles without even sitting down. I had the unpleasant feeling that the house had become another café in which to idle away a few minutes and then move on.

Suddenly I was overcome by the urge to go back to the hospital and be with Ana again. I don't know whether it was because I needed her or she needed me. We had embarked on a ship that was leaking badly and, I knew now, there were just the two of us on board. The idea of going back outside into the sunlight kept me from leaving — as did the possibility of meeting my sister- and -mother-in-law. In any case, according to what the nurse had told me, Ana would sleep until nightfall.

More pacing. I went into the bedroom and turned on the light: the stain on the bed was still there. I touched it again; it was still damp. I sighed: Buenos Aires, the whole metropolitan area, the country itself, were damp.

I smelled my hand. Where does guilt begin, and who is the guilty one? My reflection in the mirror looked horrible: unshaven, dishevelled, my shirt and jacket wrinkled. My shabby appearance oozed neglect: as Aram would say, I'd never be named cabinet minister looking like that.

I felt an urgent need to clean up, change clothes, look presentable. I shaved, undressed, and stepped into the shower, with the vague intuition that the water would somehow purify me from some of my long list of sins, stretching back from the original one to those I had already or would eventually commit. I turned on the hot water; the noises the water heater made in the kitchen as the gas burners switched on were also of some comfort. I listened to them, but had to imagine the hiss of the gas.

Entry 32
Dusk

A chime. I opened my eyes and counted the ones that followed: eight of them in all, unless I'd missed one. I jumped out of bed. Eight o'clock. Without remembering the tale about the umbilical cord, without considering that I'd have to tell her the truth and nothing but the truth, my desire to see Ana seemed as natural, light, and agreeable as a visit to any convalescent who was now completely out of danger.

I opened the blinds. The sun behind the other houses would soon disappear below the line of the horizon. The sky, with its threads of cloud, was beginning to be stained with red. It had rained. Once again I thought of water as purification and lamented having missed the rain. The toads and crickets were already fulfillling their duty of reminding us we were alive. After the shave, the shower, the nap, and now the clean clothes I was putting on, I would be back on a more civilized track. As I finished dressing, several questions without answers floated through my head: Do toads croak, or is it frogs? And if toads don't croak, then what do they do?

Ten minutes later I was ready to be named a government minister. I finished adjusting my tie in front of the mirror, closed the blinds, and sallied forth from the house like a well-heeled gentleman ready for a formal visit and dinner. And, like such a well-to-do gentleman, I carefully locked the door to the castle, the better to safeguard all I had so deservedly earned, and then proceeded to inspect my domains, just to check that everything was as it should be. I walked out to the back yard that Ana had asked me to clean up and found the three trees full of leaves under the red sky — just common *paraíso* trees, but the sight of them hit me like a blow to the stomach, knocking me back to reality.

Yes, they would offer their shade, just as Ana had dreamt of, but to whom?

At eight-forty, having successfully avoided running into any neighbours or acquaintances, I arrived back at the station. The train was due in twenty minutes. Still feeling that punch in the stomach, as well as a lump in my throat, I stepped into the bar across the street to get a coffee. Pepe the railway man, who had introduced me to the face of God through the graces of The Turk, was seated at one of the tables, drinking a glass of vermouth.

"Hey, Little Polack! Come on over and have a seat." If he hadn't noticed me, I wouldn't have spoken to him. I walked over, though. I found him changed, almost transformed. He sported long sideburns and had a thin moustache, something like an anchovy, perched above his upper lip; he was wearing a dark suit with tight-fitting pants and a white shirt and had a bandana around his neck and a carnation in his buttonhole. But something was missing from the tango image. I started to sit down.

"Watch out for the fedora!" he cried.

That was the missing touch. He watched worriedly as I picked his hat up off the chair and placed it to one side on the table. Even that wasn't the right spot; it might still get dirty. He dragged over another chair and hung it on the back.

"Why don't you put it on?" I asked.

"I'm not Jewish."

"We're not in church here."

"Yeah, but I'm eating."

"Nibbling and tippling, Pepe."

His body and hands moved about in short, angular motions. He smiled at me from under his tiny moustache while spearing a square of cheese with a toothpick. He wore two thick rings on his fingers, and his nails were long, not quite like those of a Chinese mandarin, but enough to show he didn't do any manual labour.

"Did you stop working on the railroad?"

He took a drink of vermouth, wiped his mouth with the back of his hand and then cleaned his hand with a napkin.

"I got promoted." He sniffed his carnation. "From crossing-keeper to guard. No more breaking my back. A gentleman's job. And you,

Little Polack, what are you up to these days? Are you working? Judging by your face, I'd say you'd been hired by a funeral parlour."

"Nothing special. I sell carpets. And as of today I'm a father."

I felt myself blushing. I discovered I had an impulse toward normal life. A bitter, acid taste rose up from my stomach.

"Heyyyyy, congratulations, man. We've got to drink to that. It's on me. What'll you have?"

"A vermouth." I thought it would help get rid of the acid taste in my mouth.

"Hey waiter, a vermouth for my friend and another one for me, too," he yelled, and then:

"A boy or a girl?"

"A boy."

"A little guy. That's great. Ah …" he exclaimed, as if he had just thought of something.

He waited for the vermouths. The waiter brought them over, put them on his bill, and we drank a toast. There was a brief pause. He smoothed down his clothes, looked from side to side, and brought his face closer to mine as he spoke in a low voice.

"Listen, now that you're quarantined and have to keep your nozzle dry, let me offer you my services. Remember The Turk? The old days are over, far behind. You should see her now, the poor thing: it's pathetic. Well, that's life: everything has its day. But as I was saying, I've got a twenty-something for you, homegrown meat, export quality. What d'you say?"

Without getting into nausea or morality, I felt a deep revulsion.

"Thanks, Pepe. I knew you made a few bucks off The Turk, but I never realized you were a pimp. If I need anyone, I'll give you a shout."

Pepe stiffened. His hands moved, and I thought he might be reaching for a knife in the back of his belt. Maybe he was only straightening his clothes, adjusting his shirt cuffs and lapels. He put on his hat as he spoke, biting his words.

"I'm surprised, Little Polack. Ha. Calling a friend a pimp. A professional, you mean. Or, since I spend my time negotiating on behalf of my clients, an entrepreneur, a businessman. Each girl is a branch plant."

He looked at his nails and then at his rings. I sighed.

"I'm sorry, Pepe. The birth went badly."

He looked at me, his bony face questioning.

"I'm talking about my son."

He took off his hat.

Note: The entry ends here, and I was thinking of deleting it. Other than having offered me The Turk's services — and I remember how her dark eyes never even glanced at me during the entire ceremony — Pepe has nothing to do with this story. In some way, however, he was a friend. I'd known him since childhood and though he was a pimp (and perhaps because of it), he knew life better than most psychologists and psychoanalysts. I soothed my soul that night, as the drinks continued and I gradually forgot about the appetizers and, without avoiding or covering up anything, I told him the truth. He didn't say much or tell me what he thought, except to ask questions such as, "What do the quacks say?" or to throw in a few less than extraordinary comments — "Whatcha gonna do?" "Life's like that." "Even if it hurts, it's probably better for the little guy to die." and "You'll have other kids." — as he speared tidbits on toothpicks, sipped at his drink, and made sure that his mandarin nails didn't trip and fall over anything. It felt good being with him. I let a couple of trains go by without getting up. When we finally said goodbye, he offered me his friendship and a present: "I'm sorry, Little Polack: I'm a little short of cash — and don't take this wrong — but the girl's yours free for the asking whenever you want her." I thanked him. I didn't find it necessary to give him a lesson explaining to him that friendship never gets you very far and that you've got to be a son of a bitch if you ever want to make any real money. He probably knew that better than I did.

Entry 33
Privileges

The doors of the sanatorium were locked. The night watchman said he'd open them for me when I showed him Ana's identification card, and then held the door for me as I went in. It was like entering a private club.

In order to save money or provide a more restful nocturnal atmosphere, half the lights had been turned off. I took the elevator to the fourth floor. The halls were deserted. I turned the corner, found Ana's room, and put my hand on the doorknob.

"Sir! Where are you going?" The voice was low but commanding.

Without taking my hand from the doorknob, I turned my head irritably and saw a nurse.

"I'm the father of the child that ..."

"Oh, yes, yes; I'm sorry. I'm the nurse on night shift. They've informed me about your case. If you need anything, let me know."

"Thanks."

I opened the door. The night light had been dimmed by partially covering it with a towel. Ana's mother was dozing in a chair at her bedside.

"Hello," I whispered to her.

She gave a start.

"Ah, you finally here. It's late."

She picked up her purse and coat. I sat down on one of the empty beds, closed my eyes, and rested my face in my hands. There were no "good nights." I heard the door shut and, relieved, uncovered my eyes. Ana was looking at me.

"Have you eaten?" she asked.

"No, not yet. How about you?"

"Just dessert."

"Was it good?"

She smiled weakly and nodded her head.

I looked around the room. The third bed was also empty.

"Haven't they brought anyone else in?"

"No, no one. The nurse told me they wouldn't be bringing in anyone until I was feeling better."

"A private room at no extra cost: a real privilege," I said. "How thoughtful of them."

"You think so?"

"No. Polishing the company's image is the 'in' thing right now."

Ana's smile was as faint as it was bitter. Perhaps I was afraid that, as in marriages gone stale, it meant, "You never change, do you?"

My fear increased during the long silence that followed, in which neither of us had anything to say. I looked at her and then turned away, and she did likewise. Finally she broke the silence.

"I'm thirsty. Could you get me some water?"

Service should be called when it's provided. I started to buzz for the nurse.

"No, no. In the bathroom."

I took her empty glass from the night table and went to fill it.

I sunk my hand into her thick blond hair and held her head up as she drank. Then I put the glass back on the table and sat down at her side. I looked down at her breasts, which were overflowing with milk. I'd never seen them so large. The milk from her nipples had stained her nightgown. I laid my head against her chest, and she caressed my hair. From beneath her breasts, as if from a cavern, came the sound of muted sobbing. Then a wail went through her. The cavern was filled with storms, thunder, winds without rain to purify her. I hugged her, held her tightly, and kissed her until her spasms ceased.

Entry 34
Dollars

Exhausted, Ana's body finally stopped its convulsions and her moaning became calmer, more deeply sorrowful. I caressed her, kissed her, and cleaned the tears from her face and eyelids with my lips.

At last we looked into each other's eyes, searching for a way to speak again and for something to say.

There was a soft knock at the door. We (or at least I) heard it clearly. Though it sounds absurd, it was as if someone were knocking directly on the door of my consciousness.

"We've got a visitor," I said and opened the door.

An unknown nurse was standing in the corridor, suspiciously close to the door; she stepped back and waited. I went into the hallway and closed the door behind me. Her platinum blond hair and her bony, overly made-up face, which was now contorted into a grimacing smile, gave her the air of a maternal hooker. I didn't ask what she wanted. It was she who spoke first.

"Are you the ones?"

"Are we what? Ah, yes … We're the ones, all right. How could we not be? It's gotta be us."

"The pediatrician told me it was. I'm the nurse who can take care of things and solve the problem."

What a kind and speedy pediatrician. The nurse lengthened her grimace, trying to force the smile wider; her teeth were black and full of cavities. I sighed. Certain dark, parallel worlds, full of filth and loathing, which I'd read about in fiction, were now becoming reality.

I had my doubts about her. She took a step toward me, and her red nails felt like grappling hooks as she squeezed my arm. Somehow, however, I again thought I sensed warmth and understanding.

"What … What will happen?" I asked.

"You simply give it to me; neither you nor your wife need to see it. Your prior authorization is enough. I take care of it till … And then I'll get it a death certificate. The poor little thing: you're making the right decision."

Was this a humanitarian mission? I remembered Don Garabed's remark: "Son, only idiots work for free."

"How much will all this cost?"

"Thirty dollars a day while it's alive and a hundred and fifty for the death certificate."

"Dollars?"

"Please understand, sir. It may take some time to die and inflation keeps going up every day. The peso's falling and life's getting more and more expensive."

Don Garabed had spoken to me of life, buying, and selling: "Son, you're naive. You've got to learn how to buy." I sighed. I didn't need to calculate anything before I replied.

"Listen, I simply don't have the money. Couldn't you do it for a bit less?"

Her answer was quick and vehement.

"No, absolutely not. It's too risky. And you or your wife might regret your decision and make trouble later on. You've got to understand my position: I've had too many problems in the past. I don't make anything off the certificate. Doctors don't work for free, you know."

"Yes, I understand. No one works for free. I'll think it over and try to come up with the money."

"She's got the right to a three-day stay here in the hospital. Think about it and let me know. Or, what's better, I'll come by again on the last day. See you then."

"Yes, all right. See you then. But I …"

Entry 35
Decisions and a Christening

I never knew whether it was because of my own brusque character or the more withdrawn personality of Ana, or the combination of the two, that certain questions were neither raised nor asked, or only would be later — or never. In any event, I was thankful to her at the time for not asking who it was that had knocked on the door.

Or perhaps her blue eyes — and the reddish tinge to them — were themselves the question as they followed me back into the room, and I either didn't realize or refused to understand so I wouldn't have to answer.

Nevertheless, when I came over and sat down next to her, an aspect of her character that I had already noted surged up in her — a soft explosion, muffled as always, but this time with an energy and vitality that I'm sure took an enormous effort.

"I may not know exactly what's going on," she said, "but I do know it's something serious. The baby's not well. I knew it as soon as he was born. I can see it everywhere among the people around me here: in their looks, gestures, attitudes, and whisperings behind the doors. My mother doesn't even answer my questions in English. And now you ... even you! What are you afraid of ... hurting me? Or are you ashamed? What's wrong with the child? Is it that bad? What's all this about his umbilical cord? It's too much: I can't stand it. Tell me, please; I've got to know the truth."

I felt as if I had suddenly stopped pushing an enormous weight. I trembled from head to foot with nervous relief and had to get up and walk around to calm down. Then I stopped and answered her.

"He's got a breach in his spinal column. If they operate on him and he lives, he'll be paralyzed and profoundly retarded his whole life. If they don't operate, he'll be dead within a week."

The impact registered on her face. After a while the colour began to return to her cheeks.

"In that case, it's better to let him die. I don't want him."

"Love him or leave him, eh? Are you sure?"

"Yes, if it's the way you say it is, I'm certain."

"I didn't say anything. The doctors spoke through me."

"Have you seen him?"

"No, I haven't."

I had to tell her everything. A dozen university professors couldn't have answered all her questions: causes and reasons, the gravity of the case. When it came to the diagnosis, I couldn't remember much more than "meningo celly." But she, who had read and reread and scrutinized the photos in the book on embryology, remembered and filled in the rest. Again she turned pale.

"No, I don't want him," she repeated. "This is horrible, Pedro. If we have him operated on, we're creating a monster. It's better to let him die."

I told her that I agreed with her and that I'd already told the neurosurgeon not to operate. Ana's accord lightened my heart a bit. Nevertheless, the baby was still alive. I tried to think.

"What shall we do, then?" asked Ana.

"I'll throw him out the window if you like, and then jump out myself so they can't put me in jail."

"Don't joke about it. You're always the same."

"Yes, Ana, I never change."

Her eyes filled with tears. I also told her about the proposal the nurse had just made to take care of him till the end. She dried her tears.

"Doesn't that seem like a good solution?" she asked.

"Yes, but how can we pay for it?"

"Maybe my sister will help."

"Your sister? She'd open up her own spinal column first. But I'll speak to her all the same."

Silence. Could I ask the Kalpakians for another loan? Would I have to explain why? Of course I would; they only lent money for good, logical reasons that would pay them dividends later on.

"What'll we name him?" she asked.

"Who?"

"Him: the child."

Whether twins, a girl, or a boy — we hadn't thought much about names. The only thing I was sure of was that he wouldn't be called Pedro.

"Is it really necessary?" I asked. She hesitated.

"Well, if he's going to die, maybe we'd better not," she said, biting her lip.

I thought for a while.

"If you want, at least in order to know who and what we're talking about, we could name him after what he is: Meningito. The '-ito' sounds affectionate."

"That's a horrible name, Pedro."

I sighed.

"You come up with one then."

She didn't propose any. She shut her eyes.

"For the first time today, I'm hungry," I said.

I called the nurse. The kitchen was closed. I'd have to go out to get something. I didn't feel like going home. I asked the nurse as nicely as possible if I could spend the night there.

"Regulations allow for a single seated companion. If you want to lie down, you'll have to pay. Well, seeing what you've been through ... and since no one else is scheduled to be brought in here ... but we've never had this conversation, eh?"

I gave her a tip, wondering how long our privileges would last.

I asked Ana if she wanted anything. She asked me to get her some chocolate. I gave her a kiss and went out.

Entry 36
A Summer's Night in Buenos Aires

As I left the sanatorium I looked at my watch. It was one in the morning.

I walked along Callao Street and then turned down Corrientes toward downtown, wandering through nighttime Buenos Aires, the city so many writers, poets, musicians and essayists had written about, and were to write about in the future. Like all cities, I suppose. Whether I liked it or not, I was a pseudo-gaucho, a country boy who knew his neighbours and would say hello and stop and chat with them. But that night I learned to love Buenos Aires: no one waved or stopped to talk to me and ask me awkward questions.

The restaurants, the late night bookstores, the crowds: no, nobody would recognize me or ask me anything. Life is strange. I still had two more days by law before I had to go back to work. Ana and I had agreed to let the child I'd christened Meningito die. The sensation of relief and freedom was almost infinite, but it was tinged with a sinister gloom and a recurring sense of guilt that were much more intense than the feelings that follow an abortion.

I continued on as if walking under a giant bell or dome: the sounds of the city, its conversations and honking, came from another, faraway world. At times the crowds around me disappeared or melted away and the buildings folded in on themselves, or shrank, or stretched, or bounced around as if on springs; doorways opened like mouths and sang. It was an animated world, as funny and enjoyable as a Disney cartoon, with a soundtrack of sensual saxophone music by Ray Conniff or Fausto Papeti. From time to time Daisy and Donald Duck or Minnie and Mickey Mouse would appear, without ever once making love, as pure as ever, followed by Scrooge McDuck, seated on top of his mountain of gold, who would tell me, "Don't worry. Don't be sad. Look on the bright side: things will somehow turn out all right. You know how kind-hearted I am deep down inside. I'll always be there for you to help you out."

I went by the bars and cafés I used to haunt. Maybe all I needed was some company; perhaps I could stop by one of them and find someone who still hung out there from old times. But I didn't go in.

The feeling of freedom grew and threatened to explode. Its price was directly proportional to my infinite solitude. I missed Ana and felt guilty for not having stayed with her. She'd spoken so — How could I put it? — so precisely and scientifically, but inside she was writhing with sorrow and pride, impotence and failure. Probably like me.

I crossed the immensity of 9 de Julio Avenue. The obelisk had eyes, a nose, and a mouth. All that was missing were ears.

Too many hallucinations. It occurred to me they must be caused by hunger. Next door to the Cine Rex was one of the first self-service restaurants in Buenos Aires. It had been vehemently criticized when it opened, but it did have acceptable food at modest prices. I wouldn't even have to talk to a waiter there: no one to cut into my freedom or the feeling it gave me. I never gave a thought to being a victim and martyr or to the costs involved. All I felt was a growing rage and frustration that I feared would lead me to do something crazy or, even worse, something stupid. That could happen. Or had it happened already?

The restaurant was packed. Shoving ahead, like everyone else in Buenos Aires, I also wanted to be the first in line. I needed something with a strong taste: I ordered marinated pork chops and, remembering the comfort I'd found in talking and drinking vermouth with Pepe, I also asked for a half-litre of wine, and then rushed over to a table that had just become vacant.

I picked up the dirty plates myself and gave them to the busboy. My kingdom had been readied for my arrival; my domain was the tabletop. I sat down to my feast.

I devoured rather than ate. The half-litre of wine disappeared. When I was finished, I lit a cigarette and leaned back against the wall. The people, the tables, and the enormous long counter were all becoming misty. I felt nauseous.

"Excuse, this place is free?" a woman's voice asked me, in a strong foreign accent.

Maybe the time had come for someone to speak to me. I looked at her. The summer had forced her to wear a low-cut red sleeveless blouse or halter-top that revealed half her breasts: flaccid white skin and flesh with a sickly tinge. She should have really covered them up. She had dyed-blond hair, too much lipstick, and a load of trinkets that jingled as she sat down.

"I know here, in Argentina, you doesn't like sharing table," she said. "Are individualistic."

"I wouldn't have invited you," I thought. I recognized her accent and switched to Hungarian.

"But that's what they do in Hungary?"

"Ah, yes. I thought so," she replied in her native language, looking at me intently. "With a moustache and face like that, you look like a sergeant in the Hungarian cavalry."

"Just a sergeant?"

"Well, a lieutenant in the Hussars if you prefer."

"A gaucho, madam. Let's say a gaucho lieutenant."

After the obligatory questions as to when she had arrived and what she was doing in Argentina, I let her talk. She had the corrosive way of speaking of someone who was unforgiving even to herself. That comforted me. She was a street-walker, a cheap one by the looks of it, or perhaps her face had been marked by nothing more than the miracle of age. During the Hungarian Revolution of '56, she had "happily moved her ass" out of the country, escaping through the barbed wire along the border to liberty and the Free World, El Dorado. Besides all the dyes, perfumes, and makeup items she could buy here, she had misguidedly thought she would stand out in her profession. But the West, the Free World, with its laws of supply and demand, had many more and much younger prostitutes than she had expected. Thanks to Argentina's contribution to Western democracy, she'd been allowed entry to the land of promises and opportunities that my country still was in those days, via the shadow of a dream. Now, though, just to practise her profession and make a living, she had to travel continually all over the country, especially in the South, where she had gotten as far as Tierra del Fuego, the last place El Dorado had ever been imagined. Luckily, she had also learned a few dance steps in her youth, which stood her well down in the miserable nightclubs and bars of Patagonia, where she could shake a little this and a little that and earn enough pesos to keep from opening her legs all the time. She didn't know what fate had in store for her. Soon she wouldn't even be able to work in the whorehouses that serviced army bases. I bought her a drink and, before leaving, found out everything I could from her about the South.

It was four in the morning when I got back to the hospital. I heard someone moaning as I walked down the corridor. Ana was sleeping. I lay down on one of the beds fully clothed and fell asleep immediately.

Note: This is another entry I was thinking of leaving out: the encounter with the Hungarian woman whose name I can't recall. It's strange, though: it took a Hungarian from Puszta to make me discover the land beyond the pampas — Patagonia, and beyond that, the vast silent world, waiting to be peopled with fantasies and illusions, despite the miseries she described. I felt driven by a desire to move away and escape the whole situation. One day in the future I would indeed travel South and return with money but without glory, and without having learned what that Hungarian woman had tried to tell me: that there is no El Dorado.

Entry 37
The Hunt for Money Resumes

Noises.

"Why you rascal! Don't you know it's against the rules to use the bed?"

I sat up. It was the day nurse with a cart, come to change Ana's dressings. I got ready to leave and then realized I hadn't given her a tip. I thought she might not look after Ana properly if I didn't. I offered her a few pesos. She smiled.

"That's not necessary, especially for a case so … Well, all right, then. Thanks."

I looked at my watch. It was eight o'clock in the morning.

"I'll be right back," I told Ana, and went out.

My sister- and mother-in-law were waiting outside in the hall, both dressed in black. Yes, really: a couple of crows. I said hello and added, "Jackie, I've got to talk to you. Could we go over to the café across the street?"

She followed me. We took the elevator down and walked over. I decided to be generous, like someone in public relations.

"Let me treat you to a gin and tonic."

"No, thanks. With all that's happened … a coffee will do."

She must have already had her dose. I ordered two coffees and croissants. Hmm: "With all that's happened." Maybe she did have a human side, after all. I'd always considered taking refuge in alcohol to be an understandably human reaction. The waiter brought our order. Judging from their aroma, the croissants were freshly made. We ate in silence. I finished my coffee and lit a cigarette.

"Jackie, I know your family has never liked me much."

"That's not true!"

"Jackie, I came here to talk, not argue. In view of the circumstances, let's make peace. If I say things like that, it's because I want everything clear and out in the open. No, I've never been much appreciated by the Petersens. But this isn't about me; it's about your sister … and you, too, in the end. I'm talking about the Petersen family line."

I waited, but she didn't reply. I went on to tell her about Meningito, about the nurse who had offered to take care of him, about how much it would cost, and then I asked her for the loan. Her face went pale and then red. She ordered a gin and tonic. We were both silent.

"Well, what do you say?"

"I'll have to ask my mother." She took a long swallow from her drink.

I bit my tongue.

"Jackie, let's not use the same ploys as the Armenians. You're the one who calls the shots and has to decide."

"You're always talking off the top of your head," she answered. "Most of the money belongs to my mother. What did Ana do with her part of the inheritance, anyway?" Another swallow from her drink.

"Well, despite what you all said, that I was going to lose every penny at roulette or blow it all on drunken binges, we put it into the house."

"Yeah, and half of it's in your name, right?" Foam was beginning to appear at the corners of her mouth.

I made a superhuman effort.

"Jackie, will you lend it to me or not?"

"I'll think about it." She drained her gin and tonic.

I paid and we went out. I asked her to tell Ana that I'd gone to the shop to see how things were doing. As I walked away, it occurred to me that I hadn't been very humble with her, that I hadn't whined and cried enough. Bah, things would have turned out the same.

I didn't take the bus or the subway. I walked all the way, enjoying my freedom. I knew it was a mistake to ask the Kalpakians for a loan. All I hoped was that they wouldn't insist on more than five per cent interest a month.

I walked down Santa Fe, the avenue that someone had once called aristocratic. Its wide sidewalks were relaxing. I didn't pass up the opportunity of dropping into a café and treating myself to another coffee and a couple of cigarettes.

As I stepped through the doorway into the shop, I was sure that everything was all over before it had even started. The story about the umbilical cord had tied my hands, and I didn't have the energy to tell them about my misshapen son and refute the original version. I also knew that the Kalpakians would be reticent about investing in death, though it wasn't as if I were going into weapons production. The best thing to do was probably to dramatize things, to draw out the umbilical story, invent some special life-saving treatment that would be a sound investment. Ah yes, the incubator.

"Well, here comes the great lord and grand duke himself! And about time, too!" It was Aram.

Why did my face get so red that I felt it burning?

"Bad news, Aram. The kid didn't have any bread under his arm after all, or maybe it fell out somewhere along the way."

"Well, bad news for you then. What's happening? How did things turn out? How's the baby?"

I put on a sad, remorseful face.

"Bad, really bad. But ... there is still some hope ... not much, but some."

Erminia came over, kissed me on the cheek, and congratulated me.

The winds were evidently not blowing in the right direction; it looked like I'd better retreat and take shelter somewhere. My reaction to Erminia was curt but quiet, serious, but with a sad smile from time to time. Instead of being a hurricane of sorrow, I was a well that gave off a few noxious gases.

How much humanity did Aram have? Could you define it as limited to anything that didn't cost money?

"Let's go have coffee," he said.

A shout to Enrique and we were on our way.

"I expect you to come in tomorrow," he told me as we walked along.

"I don't think I will. The law gives me four days off."

"That's for government employees. In business, it's three."

"Isn't there an extension or some kind of exception for problem births?"

He looked at me. He was going to say something, but we were already in front of the café on the corner. He went to the counter and ordered.

"Let's sit down at a table," I said. "We'll be more at ease than at the counter."

"Sure, since it's on your time," he grumbled, but he followed me over.

We stirred our coffee.

"I'll tell you the truth," I began, "but I ask you to save any commentaries, observations, or discussions for afterwards."

"All right. Go ahead."

"The birth went badly. With the umbilical cord all knotted up, the baby didn't get enough oxygen. He was blue when he was born. They'll have to put him in an incubator and they don't know how long he'll need to be there. But even though his brain may have been damaged from lack of oxygen, there is a slight chance he'll be all right."

"Listen, if it's that bad, take him to the Children's Hospital. That's where I take my kids when I think they've got something serious. Don't waste any more time. I don't know what you're still doing here."

"The Children's has a good reputation, it's true. It's also free. You want me to take him with the incubator on my back?"

"He's already in the incubator?"

"Isn't that what I just told you?"

"No, you said they'd have to put him in one."

I sighed and let my face sadden.

"Aram, do you know how much an incubator costs over at the sanatorium?"

"I can't imagine. How much?"

"Thirty dollars a day, and that's not counting the doctor's fees."

"That's why I say you should take him to the Children's. What's more, I know an Armenian doctor who works there. I could put in a word for you."

Aram's eagle eyes studied my face intently from over his hooked nose. I felt myself getting red again.

"All right. I'll have to talk to Ana. I'll think it over. If I can't convince her ..."

I fell silent.

"Whatever you want. Let's go."

Entry 38
A Discreet Salesman

I went back with Aram to the store. As soon as we came in, sweet Erminia came running toward us waving a piece of paper.

"It's an emergency. They need a salesman ... someone who's discreet."

"Discreet?" asked Aram. "It's the first time in my life I've ever heard that. What are they doing, carpeting a cathouse?"

He took the paper from her hand, read the address and let out a whistle. It was on a street in the elegant district of Palermo Chico, and the eminent last name tallied with the neighbourhood. They needed to have a stairway carpeted — the golden goose of the business. Stores had been known to charge more for that than they did for authentic carpets.

But it was also a bit complicated to measure, estimate, and act as a mouthpiece for the carpet and staircase all at the same time. Aram turned toward me.

"Since you're the only sales specialist in this company, there's nothing to do but christen you discreet. If you measure everything right and get the contract, I'll give you an extra day off."

"Whoever can't make a deal with us, can't make a deal with anybody, eh? My wife's waiting for me. If you pay for a cab, I'll go."

After a short discussion as to how much a taxi would cost, I packed up my briefcase and left.

To show how pressed I was for time, I hurried down the street as if to flag a taxi and then, as soon as I'd turned the corner, changed my pace to the relaxed amble of a free man. I headed back along Santa Fe, then down to Plaza San Martín, past the English clock tower, which struck eleven, toward the Retiro train station. Suppressing an impulse to go into the station, sit down in the coffee shop, and imagine I was travelling off to faraway lands, I crossed the plaza and continued down toward the port.

Once I reached the waterfront, where the sky opened up and stretched out to the horizon, I felt my problems recede into the distance. I walked past an open-air grill frequented by the dock workers and stevedores; I wasn't that hungry but the smell of barbecued meat was tempting, and I had to do something with the taxi money. I went over to have a look. A large tree and an awning shaded the counter. A massive steak and a variety of sausages were hissing on the fire, watched over by a heavy-set guy in a T-shirt. There were only one or two customers.

"Do you have any sweetbreads?" I asked.

"Hey, buddy, you've got the wrong restaurant. This isn't La Cabaña," he replied quickly. "What you see is what we've got."

"It's good to see sausages that are the real thing, instead of overgrown hot dogs."

"Yeah, well, these are pedigreed."

"Give me one."

"Bread or board?"

"Both."

He tossed some bread on the counter and brought over a juicy, sizzling sausage on a wooden board.

"Wine?" he asked.

"Yeah, I'm on holiday."

"You're lucky."

He poured the wine.

"Tell me, is eating sausages with your hands a popular thing these days?"

He swore softly.

"Sorry. I should have realized how refined you were, especially after asking for sweetbreads. I'll get you a knife and fork."

He cleaned them on his grimy apron before giving them to me.

"I'd wash them better for you, but it hasn't rained yet."

He laughed.

"I'll take them like that," I said.

He poured himself a glass of wine and we drank a toast. I smeared the sausage with *chimichurri* sauce and continued talking with him as I ate. I told him about a friend who had had a deformed son. You had to be careful with those doctors — a lot of them were quacks. He too had examples to spare: "Yeah, yeah, it's better when they die." By the time customers started piling up for lunch, we'd arrived at the conclusion that nothing ever mattered much and everything always turned out the same in this country. I paid and said I'd be going.

"I hope the sausages don't make me bark," I told him. "I'm supposed to be discreet today."

"Don't worry about it. If they do, it'll be in C major. I told you they were thoroughbreds."

I walked back the way I'd come, stopping off at the café in the train station for a double espresso. The second glass of wine had gone straight to my feet, and my mouth still tasted of *chimichurri*.

Entry 39
The Discreet Salesman Goes into Action

I took a bus down Libertador Avenue and got to Palermo Chico about one o'clock, a bad time. No one ever won over a customer by barging in during lunch. That would be indiscreet. I decided to kill some time by exploring around a little.

The sun overhead beat down on the pavement. I tried to walk in the shade of the trees that lined the street, but the midday sun didn't leave any shadows. I reflected on how much I'd changed since the days when I used to walk Ana home through the streets of Adrogué: I'd become much more sociable, ready at a moment's notice to strike up a serious conversation worthy of a cabinet minister. I tried myself out: "Hmm, what a beautiful house. I wonder what it's worth? A good two hundred million pesos, I'd say. No matter. Enough to pay for Meningito's death many times over. Ah, what an elegant Mercedes-Benz. Does it belong to a diplomat, or some aging freebooter from a distinguished family, or to a nouveau riche Mafioso? That baby's gotta be worth at least ten million."

I don't know if it was the wine or the heat or my own impatience that had loosened me up, but I finally decided to get the whole thing over with, come what may. I quickened my pace, turned onto the client's street, looked for the house number, and found myself standing in front of a grandiose home with an open gate. I went up to the door and rang the bell; I couldn't hear it, so I rang again.

The door was opened by a butler in white gloves with a long, sombre face right out of a movie. I almost asked him if his name was Perkins. Though he seemed a bit peeved by my persistence, he showed me into an enormous, crepuscular hall lined with huge vases and tasteful furniture. Shadows seemed to scurry off into the nooks and crannies along the walls.

I bowed to him ceremoniously and waited motionlessly. He cleared his throat and solemnly announced, "The Master died this morning."

Buckling on the remnants of my European armour, I snapped my heels to attention like a lieutenant in the Hussars of the Austro-Hungarian Empire, and bowed lightly once more.

"He wanted the wake to be held in his bedroom. It's upstairs."

I clicked my heels and nodded.

"After the vigil we're to bring him down the staircase."

Behind him a beautiful white marble stairway ran from the main hall up to the second floor. The click of the heels was weaker this time. I turned my ear toward him.

"The Lady says it would be wise to carpet the stairway first."

I raised my eyebrows. He leaned forward and lowered his voice.

"The Master was rather stout, and the coffin, which will soon be here, is a rounded one made of oak. It's sure to be extremely heavy. The pallbearers might slip."

He fell silent. I thought it over. He pronounced "Master" and "Lady" with such respect that they seemed to be shortened forms of some title. I did the same.

"Would the Lady like a carpeted walkway or would she prefer to cover the entire stairway?"

"A walkway for the cortège. The Lady thinks it would be a crime to cover over such beautiful marble completely. It's imported from Italy. There's another problem, too."

"What?"

"The Lady believes a black carpet would be more in keeping with the gravity of the situation, but that, after the ceremony, it would no longer be suited to the rest of the decor, which would then require a red or burgundy colour."

I looked at him.

"Well then?" I asked softly.

"The Lady thinks the best thing would be to have some intermediate colour."

"Good idea. What would she like?"

He glanced up the stairs and shrugged his shoulders as if weighed down by decades of fatigue. He looked at me again.

"I don't know," he replied.

"Doesn't the Lady have something in mind?"

"I don't know that either. She didn't tell me anything."

"Could I speak to her?"

"Well, I don't know … She's in quite a bad state, but if you don't … Wait here a minute; I'll go see."

He went up the stairway as if walking on a mattress. A few minutes later he reappeared on the landing and signalled me to come up. When I reached the top step he whispered to me, "In light of her condition, she will receive you in the bedroom."

I didn't know whether he meant the bedroom where the dead man lay or the woman's own bedroom. When I got to the door he indicated, there was neither a dead man nor a bedroom. She was seated in an elegant robe at a dressing table, looking into the mirror as she daubed her wrinkled face with powder. I felt sorry for her: the state she was in went beyond bad — it was deplorable.

"Good afternoon," I said, touching my heels together and bowing again.

She nodded with a slight inclination of her head.

"What do you recommend?" she asked, without looking at me.

"Madam, the black carpet would be much more in keeping with the gravity of the situation. It would go wi— … It would have more solemnity."

She sighed, studied her face in the mirror, and applied a few more touches to the bags under her eyes.

"The problem," I said, "is what to do with the carpet after the ceremony."

She nodded her head several times. Judging from her reactions, something serious must have been occurring in the mirror.

"Madam, I advise you to put in the black one for the ceremony and then afterwards another one that goes with the rest of the decor. Not red, though, but a deep, rich, majestic burgundy — the colour of the finest Bukhara carpets."

There was no reply. Something had hidden or gotten lost in the infinite space of the mirror. Another sigh. She picked up a lipstick.

"In fact," I went on, "the only extra cost involved would be for the second carpet, because the price would already include the rods and installation. Though of course, one never knows what can happen. Someone else might …"

It seemed to me that she glanced at me out of the corner of her eye in the mirror. She began to work on her lips.

"The modern rods, or rather, the traditional improved ones, would allow you to change carpets with ease for any occasion. Just a quick call to the company, and the other one could be installed within an hour."

She threw the lipstick against the mirror and stood up. I was sure I'd lost the sale. She walked over to a closet in the wall, dug around a bit, and took out a black dress. She went back to the mirror and held it in front of her, studying herself. Her pitiful movements were more like contortions.

"Can you put it in tonight?"

Her question caught me by surprise.

"Pardon? Yes, of course we can. There will be a small overtime charge for the carpet layers. You know, ever since Perón, workers' demands have become insatiable."

She looked at me; her eyes were an expressionless blue. Perhaps despite her hatred of Perón, the mention of his name had taken her back to better times twenty years earlier.

"Install it," she said.

Heels and bow.

"No sooner said than done, madam. Unfortunately, though, the company cannot proceed without your specific approval. I know that in your case, of course, it would ..."

"Give him one of my cards," she told the butler.

After I left the room, I wondered whether I should have expressed my condolences.

I set to work measuring the stairway. I had just finished counting the steps for the rods when the butler reappeared holding a card.

"The Lady has already signed it. This constitutes her approval; her financial representatives at the firm will fill out the rest. They close at seven."

I thanked him and left.

I took out the card on the bus and studied it. There was an embossed bull's head in the upper righthand corner: whether it was a Shorthorn or an Aberdeen, I'll never know. In the middle was "Administrators of Country Estates," with an address on the Avenida de Mayo. On the back of the card, "For carpeting the stairway," and her signature.

A few blocks away from the firm's office, I ducked into a café to tally things up. Seeing that the Lady had not been very clear about whether she wanted both carpets or just the red or the black one, I generously included them both, added in enough overtime to carpet the Avenida de Mayo, and drew up the final bill.

Neither the firm's accountant — "She's going to go through that whole inheritance before ..." ("before they even bury him," I added mentally) — nor even Aram could believe the profit we'd made; when Aram saw the cheque he completely forgot to ask me where I'd been for so long. I left him with the papers and the job of getting the carpet installed that very night.

On the way back to the sanatorium, I realized that I'd forgotten to make one vital measurement. The carpet they put in would be a metre wide, exactly the width of the coffin. No matter how hard they tried, the pallbearers wouldn't be able to find the slightest bit of carpet under their feet.

I told myself I'd check the social pages in *La Nación* in a day or two.

For the moment, the vision of the coffin rolling down the hall or flying through the air offered some consolation.

Entry 40
They Open the Door

While still on the bus on the way back to the hospital, I suddenly remembered the chocolate that Ana had asked me to bring her the night before; I'd been too involved in my own misery and had forgotten to pick some up. I also remembered that I still hadn't had an answer from Jackie, though I hadn't been around to hear it.

I got off the bus at Callao Street, a few blocks before the sanatorium, and bought a couple of large bars of chocolate. It was five in the afternoon. I also got a copy of the evening newspaper, *La Razón*, and stopped by a café. With the exception of the comic strips, which I read with a certain queasiness in my stomach, I found my interest in world events had completely disappeared. But my hunger hadn't. I ordered two ham and cheese sandwiches and a glass of milk.

The queasiness continued. I went out and bought two more bars of chocolate on Callao. I didn't know what else to do to put off arriving at the hospital. I wanted to see Ana, but not her family. I had to find out Jackie's answer, though, even if it were "no."

I pulled myself together and headed down Lavalle Street. Ten minutes later I was at the sanatorium. I went in and took the elevator to the fourth floor.

At the open door to one of the rooms along the hallway stood a woman in a bloodstained nightgown, holding up her belly with one hand and gesticulating with the other as she shouted with indignation. Someone had sent her red carnations with a pink bow, the symbol for a baby girl, and she'd given birth to a boy. "How tactless can you get? It's always the same. She hates me and does it on purpose. And here's proof! Even though I've always ..."

I passed by her and came to Ana's room. She was alone. I went over to the bed, sat down on it next to her, gave her the chocolate, and hugged and kissed her. Her swollen breasts pressed against me, larger than they had been the night before.

"They wanted to bring in the child so I could breast feed it," she said in the same low voice she used when we made love — another kind of crime and sin.

"They must have gotten their files mixed up."

"My sister stopped them. She made quite a scene."

"Well, she finally got the chance to do a good turn and get off cheaply. Where are they, anyway?"

"Who?"

"My sister- and mother-in-law. Your family."

"I don't know. They left around noon. They said they'd be back this afternoon but they haven't shown up yet."

I checked the time. It was six in the evening. Jackie treated me just as lovingly as I did her. I looked deeply into Ana's eyes — or at least tried to. She smiled without trying to conceal her ruined teeth, which were now covered in chocolate. I mentally thanked her for not hiding them: I loved her more when she surrendered herself to me without putting up defences.

"How do you feel?" I asked.

"Sometimes I feel so guilty. But I don't want it. I've made up my mind about that. How about you?"

"So-so. I feel like I'm living in a kind of nightmare. I blame myself; I make up pointless stories to get around it and then get trapped in them. It's as if the margins of life were shrinking, or I'm making them smaller by the tales I invent."

"I don't know what you mean."

I told her what I'd said to my mother, the reprehensible way I'd acted with her, and what I'd told Aram.

"You're ashamed."

"Yeah, there's no doubt about it. I feel like I'm beginning to understand those cheap stories I've read about monsters hidden in people's attics. And we don't have an attic ... or even a doghouse. But is that all we have to fear? Sometimes I'm afraid there's a lot more to come. How about you, do you feel ashamed?"

"No, not really. But I do feel angry and guilty about having let them give me that anti-tetanus shot. I'm sure that's what caused the lesion."

I looked at her again and stroked her hair. I sighed. I was just going to hug her once moren when the door opened.

Entry 41
The First Missionary

I rose to my feet. I was sure it wasn't a nurse from our section. The cap she was wearing was different. Then I recognized it as the one worn by the nurses who worked in the nursery.

She stood there motionlessly, her grim face inspecting or studying me attentively. Then she stepped inside and I felt a slight tremor of fear. If she hadn't been dressed in the same outfit as the kind and noble nurses whose duty it is to help humanity, I would have said she was from the S.S.

She strode over and stood in front of me. We were face to face.

"Are you the father?"

"The father of whom?"

"You know very well what I'm talking about."

"If I do, then why are you asking me?"

"I suppose you're capable of denying it."

Another one who knew what I was capable of.

"Well as long as we're supposing things, let's suppose I am."

"And you're doing absolutely nothing about it?"

"About what?"

"To save him. His spinal cord may become infected and he'll die."

"Thanks for telling me. That's exactly what we're hoping."

She took another step forward. I really started believing in those cheap novels: her eyes were like daggers. I'd taken a step backward. Her teeth ground together and her fangs appeared.

"You ... you're a monster!" She turned to Ana. "And this mother, this unnatural mother ... I'll never let it happen as long as he's in my care! Give me a thousand pesos right now for his antibiotics!"

I gave them to her. She marched out the door, her heels clicking against the floor, her mission accomplished.

She hadn't spoken a word to Ana or even asked her name. Except to say ... I turned around. Ana's head was lying on the pillow; her face pale, her eyes closed. Dead? No, the eyes of the dead were always open, I thought.

Again she was crying. Again I dried her tears with my tongue.

Ana let them give her a shot of Valium. Maybe a shot of something would have done me some good too. I went to the café across the street from the hospital and had coffee. I asked the price of a glass of wine. A glass of coarse red would have to stand in for Valium.

As I drank, I reflected on the missionary's visit. She was a real S.S. type all right, but I suspected and feared that most of them were on her side, a fact that was later confirmed. For the moment, I thought of our home in Longchamps, of my parents, of their disappointment and suffering, even of asking my mother for forgiveness. How did the saying go? "The road to hell ..." I finished the wine and went back to the hospital. Ana was sleeping. I lay down on the other bed, but that night I slept badly.

Entry 42
Calculations

The same nurse came back the next morning but didn't say a word. I got up and went out on my own mission: to talk to the pediatrician.

I found him in his office, which was so full of papers that it looked more like that of an administrator than of a medical doctor. He asked me to come in (an honour), but didn't offer me a seat. His eyes danced about from one side to the other. Politically undecided, as they say. It's strange: he didn't say hello to me, nor I to him.

"Was it you who gave the order to put him on antibiotics?" I asked.

His face went pale and his eyes jumped from one side to the other.

"I didn't give any orders. Did they do it?"

"Last night the nurse asked me to buy them for him."

I think he gave me a look — though I'm not sure — as if I were a complete idiot.

"And did you?!"

"What else could I do?"

"Refuse! Medication is given to patients on doctor's orders and is paid for when the patient leaves the hospital. The nurse was acting on her own. I can't be everywhere, you know. What's more, it's time you made a decision. Today is the last day of your wife's stay here. After that, the cost would be ..."

"Excuse me, Doctor. My employers have always advised me to calculate things in my head, and I'm a little confused here. I thought today was her second day of rest. The child was born the day before yesterday."

He counted on his fingers.

"You're right. But keep in mind that this isn't some kind of charity or welfare institution."

"What with your mathematical skills and deep understanding, I couldn't possibly forget."

I left without saying another word. I wondered if people with crossed eyes could see their condition in the mirror, or how, in fact, they do see themselves. My irony was coming back, but my barbs weren't finding their mark.

Entry 43
The Solution

When I arrived back at Ana's room, my mother- and sister-in-law were already there. Ana and my sister-in-law were carrying on a fierce scientific debate in English. I stayed out of it and waited, sitting on the far bed. Out of respect for me (and quite possibly because my mother-in-law was already floating along on an alcoholic cloud and couldn't have cared less), they switched to Spanish. Ana's breasts were about to explode with milk and the pain was becoming unbearable. The staff had given her an injection in order to stop her milk production. According to my sister-in-law, it was the worst brand of lactation inhibitor they could have given her: not only would it fail to stop the flow of her milk, but it would also enlarge her clitoris or something, because it contained hormones. "They gave you that?" she said. "What a bunch of ignoramuses. The products from OUR laboratory, on the other hand, are infallible." I remembered that my sister-in-law worked as a translator for a British pharmaceutical firm, but I didn't know it was called OURS. Ah, yes, I also remembered Aram's reproaches: he wouldn't allow me to use the words "we" or "our company."

Ana defended herself.

"I don't really have any information about the product and I don't know its side effects."

"But do you think that WE, a British laboratory, would be immoral enough to …"

"Oh, no," I told her. "With YOUR product, she'd only become frigid for six months. For God's sake, let's stop all this. Come with me for a moment, Jackie, I'd like to talk with you."

I was gruff. All the same, I was amazed at the speed with which she followed me out. We went back to the café across the street. When we got there, I told her, "I'm totally broke. Lend me a few pesos and buy me a café au lait."

"Sure. It's on me."

More reasons to be amazed: Could this mean that she would loan me the money? She seemed only too willing to do so. I ordered a gin and tonic to boost her happiness and a hot dog with the works to satisfy my hunger.

I finished breakfast, lit a cigarette, and exhaled the smoke. She waved it away as it rose toward her face.

"Sorry," I said.

"It's nothing."

I took another drag on the cigarette and blew the smoke out sideways.

"Well, what shall we do?" I asked her.

"At last you'll talk about it. You're totally lost, aren't you?"

"I must admit I'm not; it's just that you've got the money."

"Oh no, no, no, no. It's not that easy. Did you see they were giving him antibiotics?"

"I didn't see it, but I felt it in my pocket."

"And what does that tell you?"

"That antibiotics will prolong his life."

"Exactly: they'll prolong his life. For what?"

"Ah, well, I thought it was part of some humanitarian mission … though rather an arrogant one, it seemed to me. Another point of view."

"Mm-hmm. And what does that woman care about your son? Didn't it ever occur to you that she might be in cahoots with the nurse that's supposed to take care of him? Maybe they don't want him to die; with the antibiotics they've got these days, they could keep him alive for who-knows-how long … and that's without their ever even finding out about the powerful new products OUR lab is developing. All the money in the world wouldn't be enough to pay for him."

"No, it didn't occur to me." I was dumbfounded by such a subtle thought.

"You see? You see? You don't think about anything; you just keep firing off ironic comments. I came up with the solution yesterday, but I couldn't tell you about it because you never listen to anyone."

I never listened to anyone? Oh well, who cared? As if I'd just stepped into a field freshly planted with land mines or the most delicate flowers, I lowered my voice.

"'The solution'? What would that be, Jackie?"

She smiled, arranged her hair, and threw out her chest. She took a sip of her drink. She was just seven years older than Ana. Lack of exercise and the calories from the alcohol had made her fat.

"Do you remember that neurological psychiatrist, Dr. Brahe, who cared for my mother?"

I had a vague memory of something, from Ana's confessions when we were going out together, about a legendary psychiatrist who had spent five years trying to cure my mother-in-law's alcoholism.

"No, not very well."

Jackie's mouth filled with saliva. "Yesterday I went with my mother to see him at his private office ... he's a real researcher, as well as being warm, charming, and humane. I told him what had happened. He understood everything immediately. I'll never forget his exquisite choice of words in order not to use expressions that might in some way be objectionable. He works in the municipal hospital and has put an incubator at our disposal. They'll take care of the baby there for free until it dies. You see? It's important to have connections."

I was about to ask her how in hell she'd suddenly spruced up her vocabulary like that — maybe from some English discourse on manners — but decided not to. I plunged onward.

"When can we get started?"

"Tomorrow if you want. You'll have to speak to Dr. Brahe first so they can get everything ready."

"And how do I take him there?"

"Oh, no. I'VE got to take him. It's got to be ME who brings him there."

Entry 44
The Wait

You didn't have to be a genius to guess what Jackie wanted. And I let her know it. As the person responsible for the child, I should have insisted on going with her. But it was easier not to. The pain and tragedy we'd been through seemed reason enough to let her do it.

That same morning we went back to the pediatrician's office. His eyes rolled about like figures in a slot machine. He kindly invited us into his office and asked us to sit down while he drew up an agreement absolving the sanatorium of all responsibility from the moment the baby left its care. Jackie read it and had him stamp it with the following day's date and told me not to sign it till the next morning. She also asked that the baby be transferred in an ambulance.

Suddenly the world was becoming more human. A single physician would now be watching over Meningito, and it would be you, Doctor. Instead of a coffin, he'd now have an incubator so he wouldn't catch cold. The baby's departure had been solved. The tale I'd invented was beginning to acquire the glimmer of truth. All that was left was for Ana to be officially discharged so she could go home. I still had to put down the rest of the down payment. The money was hidden in a book at the house and I didn't really feel much like going back to Longchamps to get it.

I dropped by the store that afternoon and told Aram the news. It was getting close to the end of the month, and he advanced me the money I needed without any problem.

I went back to the sanatorium to spend the night with Ana. I found out that my sister- and mother-in-law had offered her a room in their apartment when she got out of the hospital: a gesture of reconciliation, just in case some problem arose while the whole thing was being settled (which in fact it already almost was). I was also invited to stay. The range of human generosity is truly astounding.

Morning arrived and so did Jackie, freshly made-up and wearing a white dress with a plunging neckline that revealed half her breasts. She sported a new purse, a permanent, and a perfume that anesthetized everyone around her.

The succession of scenes that followed was as brief as those in a dream. I signed the papers and the pediatrician went with me to the nursery, where I was given the baby, who was completely covered up. Ah how light he was, nothing at all, and how defenceless against horror. Once in the elevator, Jackie virtually grabbed him out of my arms. The ambulance was waiting at the basement entrance. She got in next to the driver. Before the door closed, I asked her to let me see his face. No. Yes. It's not going to make you feel any better. Yes, it is. She drew back the cloth and I glimpsed his diminutive, wrinkled, old man's features. He was sleeping.

I watched motionlessly as the ambulance went up the ramp and disappeared into the traffic.

Entry 45
Ana Goes Home

The nurse didn't have time. I held Ana's arm as she walked slowly and with difficulty to the bathroom, her face grimacing with pain, in order to take her first bath. It was, however, a step back to normal life. As she combed her hair after bathing, she began to chew at her lips again to hide her teeth.

I don't know if she had seen her sister that morning. When I commented on how Jackie had been dressed, as if she'd been on her way to a wedding or to get picked up, Ana replied, "Pedro, for years now she's dreamt of marrying a doctor."

"Why not?" I said. "It's almost as original as dreaming of marrying a fireman, pilot, or sailor."

It was hard for Ana to walk. I asked her if it wouldn't be better for her to spend another day in the hospital.

"No, the books say the more you move, the sooner you'll be home and starting to heal up. Those two-week stays in the hospital after giving birth have gone out of style."

"All right. If you consider your sister and mother's apartment a home, I guess there's no problem. I'll probably be the one who gets sick there."

My prophecy came true.

A doctor came in to look Ana over and give her a few suggestions, and then she was discharged. We paid the bill, had lunch in the cafeteria and then, brandishing the receipt stamped "Paid in Full" to the guard at the door, we left the building at two in the afternoon.

In the taxi, Ana sat leaning to one side, almost on her hip; she was suffering more than she admitted.

My mother-in-law greeted us at the door in a very — how shall I put it? — neutral way. Judging by her face, which was even redder than usual, she'd already had several doses of her favourite medicine. Once Ana was comfortable, her mother told us in her atrocious Spanish all about her theory as to what had happened. She was clear enough, however, for me to understand. According to her, no one in "our" family had ever had a child with a birth defect. She was sure they had switched babies on us. The defect couldn't be "ours."

This was a possibility, one more doubt, that didn't help either Ana or me very much.

By five o'clock that afternoon, Jackie still hadn't come back. As a true son of the pampas, accustomed to freedom and open spaces, I already found the apartment suffocating. Ana was resting. I decided to go out for a walk. I told my mother-in-law, who advised me, "Supper, eight o'clock."

I walked through the streets of downtown — Santa Fe, Callao, Corrientes, 9 de Julio — and past the usual bookstores and cafés, wondering in which hospital Meningito had ended up. I tried to imagine what it was like for him.

Entry 46
The Happiness that Should Reign

Having overcome the temptation to return at midnight, when everyone would be sleeping, I got back to the apartment at nine in the hope that they would at least have finished dinner.

I rang the doorbell. Ana opened the door and, as soon as I went inside, threw herself into my arms and burst out crying. My immediate reaction was to get her out of there, and my first question was obvious.

"Oh no," she replied, "I'm crying from happiness. Listen, listen."

"Listen? Listen to what?"

She wiped away her tears and sniffled.

"Come on, over here." She leaned on me as we walked forward; she was limping. When we stopped, Ana pressed tightly against my side.

I found the table in the middle of the living room set for dinner and Jackie seated on the sofa, dressed the same as she had been that morning, with her legs crossed and a glass in her hand. I don't know how I managed to keep my next question free of obscenities.

"What's going on?"

Jackie got to her feet. She stepped by me, smiling, contemptuous, triumphant, looking at me out of the corner of her eye as if I were a beggar.

"What happened, did you pick up the ambulance driver?" I asked as she disappeared into the kitchen.

"Are they drunk?" I asked Ana. "Oh, sorry. I know they live drunk, but you're not, are you?"

She shook her head, her silken hair brushing against my face.

"No, no. She'll tell you what it is."

I wanted to think, without knowing about what, to prepare myself, without knowing what for. I tried to pull Ana away from me as gently as possible, but she held on.

I walked over with her to the sofa and helped her sit down. She kept one hip slightly raised. I sat down next to her.

As if she'd been observing us from behind a theatre curtain, waiting for her cue to come on stage, Jackie reappeared with a full glass. She paced back and forth in front of us before speaking.

"I'm totally disillusioned." She stopped and stared at me.

I didn't say a word. She began to pace again.

"I never imagined such a high-class private hospital could let them get away with something like that. They're totally irresponsible. How could you ever have ended up in that place? It's incredible: even I, who don't trust anyone, believed them. Well, it doesn't matter; the guilty ones will get what's coming to them."

I couldn't stand her pedantic, magisterial tone a moment longer.

"Jackie, for God's sake. What the hell are you talking about?"

She stopped suddenly and let out a shrill laugh, followed by a theatrical "Oh!" Her teeth ground together and her voice trembled.

"If it weren't for my sister ..."

"If it weren't for your sister, what?"

"I'd walk off and let you deal with the whole thing. It'd serve you right."

Ana gave my arm a squeeze, begging me not to lose my temper.

"Go ahead. I swear I won't interrupt you."

She began to pace back and forth again. I won't bother to add anything about the foam on her mouth.

"I got to the doctor's office and he saw me at once. He has a secretary and a nurse. We went into a special room that opened off to the side. He asked the nurse to remove the linen the child was wrapped in. I blushed; the baby had pooped along the way. It was awful, but the nurse cleaned it up quickly. The poor thing was crying and kicking like a bull; it surprised me. Doctor Brahe picked him up skilfully and professionally and looked him over. We both searched for the opening where the spine would protrude. There wasn't anything at all. Just a tiny red incision at the bottom of his back. Doctor Brahe looked over at me, as if to say, "What is all this you were telling me about?" He asked if anyone had diagnosed the child. I couldn't answer because that other idiot … I was afraid he'd be angry with me. He checked the baby's reflexes with different instruments. Everything was perfect. We were more and more surprised. He immediately called in several other doctors: a surgeon, a pediatrician, and I don't know who all. Six of them arrived. All of them were amazed, astounded by such a mistake. I don't know how many questions they asked me. I just smiled and looked confused. Since I hadn't been there when that neurologist spoke to you, I didn't know what to say to anybody. They asked the nurse to take the child out and have X-rays made immediately. We waited there and talked; none of them could get over how anyone could be so irresponsible as to make such a mistake. They all congratulated me on my decision to bring him in to them. "And the sanatorium?" I asked them. "Will the people who did this be punished?" They smiled sadly and gravely and said, "Don't worry, we'll see to that. Things aren't just going to stop here. This whole matter is extremely serious." Then I had a great idea: I asked them if the wound could have been made somehow while the baby was being born. They thought that this was quite possible and that it would have been entirely natural for the others to have tried to cover it up. And that seems to have been what happened: Ana told me she had seen one of the obstetrics nurses looking terrified as she set down a pair of scissors."

She paused and took a sip from her drink.

"And, since you two weren't there, I had to sign the forms authorizing them to save him."

She fell silent, closing her eyes as if from the pleasure of just completing a dangerous mission, wiped the froth from her lips and took another swallow from her drink.

I was overcome with relief, tranquility, and happiness. Then I reacted. I didn't know where to go. I leapt up so quickly that Ana almost fell on the floor. I applauded my sister-in-law and hugged her. I sang and danced around the living room. I realized Ana was still on the couch; I helped her up and lifted her in my arms as she painfully did a few dance steps with me around the room. She couldn't keep up. I kicked my feet in the air. Ana was laughing and crying, holding on to a table. I went over to Jackie, slapped her on the back, grabbed the drink from her hand, and drank it down in one gulp.

We sat down to eat and opened a bottle of champagne. The stew my mother-in-law had made had gotten burned, but I congratulated her all the same. Over supper Jackie told me the doctors would like to meet the parents. Since Ana was still so weak, perhaps I could go. She said she would accompany me, and that it would be a pleasure.

Entry 47
The Doctors

Early the next morning (I think Jackie got up an hour before I did in order to get herself dolled up), as we were eating breakfast before going to the hospital, I had a sudden thought.

"I think I'll go down to the sanatorium and kick up such a fuss that it'll all come out in the papers."

"NOOO!" Jackie shouted. "For God's sake, you'll ruin everything. You'll drag us all into it: the doctors and me. The ones who did it will get what's coming to them without any publicity; we don't want anyone to panic or lose their faith in things. It'll all be settled on another level, much higher up. You can't get involved."

I thought of asking her if she were talking about Mount Olympus, but I kept my mouth shut. I gave Ana a hug and an enormous kiss. She did the same. I noticed her breasts were becoming smaller.

"Hey," I said to Jackie, "what about mother's milk for the little guy?"

She smiled indulgently at my concern.

"Don't worry. The formulas they give them these days are even better than mother's milk. OUR laboratory makes one of the best."

Nestlé, the doctors, the Swiss laboratories, the shareholders, the lab workers, the mothers who were afraid of ruining their breasts, the fashion mavens, the last word in science, HER laboratory — she'd been the mouthpiece for all of them.

We took a taxi. As I breathed in the suffocating aroma of her perfume, Jackie recounted more details from the doctor's office the day before, practically down to a biographical sketch of everyone there. She spoke of you, Doctor, and described you as a great luminary of science who was respected by everyone — the man with the last word.

She saturated me with details. In order to entertain myself, I looked out the window: Lezama Park, Almirante Brown Avenue, and finally Argerich Hospital.

We got out. Jackie insisted on paying.

Out of the four elevators in the hospital, the only one that was working was the one reserved for the staff. Jackie was violently rebuffed by the operator.

"What an idiot. He doesn't have the faintest idea what he's doing," she commented.

We went up the stairway to the fifth floor — your office, Doctor Brahe. The door was shut. Jackie knocked; it opened slightly and a nurse's face appeared.

"Ah … you … I'm here to see Dr. Brahe."

"He's busy."

"But, don't you remember me? I was here yesterday with him and some other doctors."

"Yes, I remember."

"Well then, tell Dr. Brahe that Ms. Petersen is here to see him."

"Wait here, please."

We waited. My sister-in-law was rubbing her hands in expectation and murmuring, "Wait till you see. Just wait till you see."

Half an hour went by.

"I don't see anything yet," I said.

"He must be incredibly busy with some difficult case."

She knocked on the door again, and the nurse's face reappeared. The same dialogue was repeated, with a few variations.

"Yes, Ms. Petersen. I have informed the doctor."

"But did you tell him it was ME?"

"Yes, ma'am. Please be patient."

We waited there two hours. It was hot. Jackie's makeup began to run and her perfume had evaporated.

"I can't understand what's going on in there," she repeated. When the door finally opened and you appeared, she practically hurled herself at you. You seemed oblivious and nodded to us lightly.

"Come with me," you said.

We followed you down the corridor. I think that you motioned to other doctors along the way, because they got up from their desks to join us as we went along. My sister-in-law's head darted in every direction. She seemed to be in ecstasy. We went down a floor and entered a kind of meeting room. There was a brief silence, followed by smiles and joking banalities, as if to say, "Nothing out of the ordinary is going on here. We're in the best of all possible worlds. Everything's clear; there's basically not much left to say."

A short fat guy came over to me.

"Are you the father?"

I stepped forward, throwing out my chest.

"Yes, I'm the father!" I thundered.

The windows shook. A few of the doctors smiled doubtfully. "He's so certain of himself. In these matters, only the mother knows for sure. Anyway, let him go on." Others put their fingers to their lips or waved their hands in the air with their palms down in order to calm me down.

But by and large they were honest, friendly, and tolerant. They understood my pride. Being a father is a difficult, dubious task nowadays, full of spiritual and economic pitfalls and sometimes tainted by immorality.

The little fat guy stepped forward again and put his hand on my arm.

"Thank you, thank you for trusting in us," he said gravely. "You know that life is short and art is long. The moment is fleeting and the decision, difficult."

It sounded to me like a preamble, but I nodded respectfully. I was going to ask him a question when I was interrupted by a red-haired guy with a moustache who was carrying a large envelope under his arm.

"How admirably my colleague has put it. Our glories are obscure and unknown; our triumphs go unapplauded by the multitudes; our work is recognized in the deepest recesses of the home ... in the bedroom where a baby cries."

I felt bewitched. My sister-in-law was shooting me glances of, "You see? What did I tell you?"

A blond man who looked like he might be Polish (perhaps his name was also Pedro) came over to me, shook my hand and held it for a moment as he patted my forearm.

"My colleague has spoken eloquently. I'd just like to add one thing: my congratulations. The moments you are living through are precious indeed. To entrust us with a life so unreservedly is almost inconceivable in the course of human affairs. Perhaps some day a poet, inspired by what you have done, will sing your glory."

Something was wrong here; something was going awry despite all the pompous clearing of throats and massaging of souls, the intoning of the customer's praises, the speeches and smiles of satisfaction. There was a moment of hesitation before getting to the point, followed by a low, pensive voice that arose from the corner — your voice, Doctor, which held the room's attention.

"That which medicine cannot cure, can be cured by iron; what iron cannot cure, can be cured by fire; but that which fire cannot cure, must be considered incurable."

We looked at one another in surprise. The other doctors nudged each other in the ribs and looked in your direction. The room was filled with nervous movements; my legs trembled slightly.

With a sonorous "Hmmm," the red-haired man drew the large envelope from beneath his arm as if he were unsheathing a sabre. He called me over to a window. My sister-in-law followed. One after another, he took out five X-rays of Meningito and held them up to the light. Then he put them back in the envelope.

"Did you see?" he asked me.

"Well, yes ... I saw them, but I'm not sure I understand what ..."

"Did you see there isn't almost any opening?"

The shaking in my legs increased.

"What do you mean? Then ... there is an opening?"

"A very small one. Insignificant. Hardly anything."

"So you'll operate on him?"

"We already did. Just in time, too."

Trembling, more trembling.

"But Doctor, his head … how big will it grow?"

"We have to avoid making reckless or hasty judgements. Let's wait and see."

"But, his legs … will he be able to walk?"

"We'll see, we'll see. Nature is wise."

I was beginning to lose control.

"Yeah, the cows in the field. Why did you meddle with him, doctor?"

"I didn't want an infection to kill him!"

Red blotches floated in front of my eyes.

"Doctor, we brought him here to die."

A chorus of indignant voices.

"THAT'S HORRIBLE, INHUMAN! HE'S GOT A LIFE, TOO! YOU SHOULD BE HAPPY AND THANKFUL! DON'T SAY THAT … IT'S MONSTROUS!"

"Who says it is, for Christ's sake? What's going on here? What's happening? My God, who says it's monstrous?"

I was yelling desperately. I couldn't see anything. Blind, furious, I looked for someone to hit. As if they sensed it, they moved apart. I searched for the red-headed guy and saw him scurry toward the door.

I was going to run after him. My sister-in-law grabbed my arm.

"Are you crazy? Damn! I knew you'd ruin everything. I knew it. What a laughingstock! What a goddamn laughingstock you are!" Her mouth filled with saliva.

I struggled to free my arm from her grip.

"You … you're a …" I remembered Ana had the same mother as she did. "You, you … You'll never get married!"

I raged, and then managed to get a hold of myself a bit. I remember running up to the fifth floor but you had already left your office. It was almost noon. My sister-in-law had stuck to me like a tick, although, judging by her squeaks, maybe it was more like a rat. I turned on her and shouted that I wanted the address of your office at home. She refused to give it to me, covering me with saliva as she upbraided me: How could I act like that when I was less than a nobody, a professional nothing, etcetera. Once out in the street I threatened her with my fist and she left me alone. I went into a café across from Lezama Park and found your address in the telephone book. Your family name was rare enough that it was the only one listed. My indignation and fury, always not far from the surface and now fueled by what I saw as an injustice and deception, were infinite. Finally I calmed down a bit and managed to take a bus toward your home. An idea began to form in my mind — though still far from clear, it's true — of what I was doing.

Note: I'll never be able to forget that chorus of outraged voices. It was a foretaste of the voice of the moralizing hordes to come.

Entry 48
Interrupting Lunch

Charcas Street: an old but well-kept house still standing among the apartment blocks. There was even a front yard, complete with a flower garden and a gate with an iron grating, which was open. I followed the path through the garden, went up three marble steps, and rang the bell. Someone came running to the door and opened it: before me stood a pale little boy with glasses, wearing a school uniform. Behind him appeared someone else: a thin woman as wan as he was, with a head scarf like a turban.

"Can I help you?" she asked.

"Good afternoon, madam," I replied softly, so softly.

"Good afternoon," said the little boy.

"Is the doctor in?" I inquired softly, so softly.

"He's not receiving patients today. He'll be available tomorrow between four and eight pm," she answered.

"It's very important, madam," I replied, as softly as ever.

"Who shall I say is here?" she asked.

"No one," I answered, softly and sadly. "You don't know me, madam, but he does. Of course, I don't know if he still remembers my last name, but he knows who I am."

The woman looked me up and down, as if inspecting my clothes for lint or other identifying marks.

"Excuse me if I'm a bit dirty, madam."

Was it a small "Oh!" that I heard her exclaim?

"He hasn't come home yet. I don't know whether or not you'd be able wait for him."

"Could I wait right here, madam? Or rather, on the sidewalk in front of the house? I won't be obtrusive, I promise."

"If you have the time," and she shut the door.

Time: all the time in the world, my poor Ana. And poor me. Yes, I could stay out there till the following day. The Kalpakians would welcome me back with open arms.

I stood out on the sidewalk. I waited and waited. I forced myself to imagine deaths, wars, children crushed or with severed limbs, starving babies — to the point of even forgetting about my own child, all in a supreme effort to shed a few tears and have my eyes nice and red for you when you showed up.

And you finally did.

Someone drove you up in a Mercedes-Benz. On the other side of the windshield, on top of the controls, was a cross with a rosary hanging from it. You got out, a raincoat neatly folded over your left forearm. Waving your right hand, you followed the car with your eyes as it sped away.

By the time you noticed me, I had turned into two little red eyes that rolled along the ground. You gave a gesture of surprise, a wordless "Oh!", and a compassionate smile of infinite mercy. You seemed to comprehend me without any need of explanation. I felt at peace, soothed — as though someone finally understood.

You opened the garden gate for me; my reddened eyes wheeled along the ground ahead of you up to the door of the house, which you opened with your key. You picked me up delicately, took me inside, and deposited me to the left of the entryway, at the top of a staircase that descended and then turned and disappeared below. You said, "Wait for me here."

Then you crossed the Persian carpet. An arch with a velvet curtain, which had been drawn, divided the hall from the entrance to the dining room. The table had been set; the crystal twinkled like a star-filled sky above a fresh loaf of bread on the cutting-board and a pair of red candles. Two children rose to their feet; you stretched out a hand and stroked their hair or blessed them. Your wife, who had opened the door, finished lighting the first of the candles and presented her cheek to you. You grazed it with your lips. You handed her your raincoat and whispered something in her ear. She nodded, blew out the candle, and — after gesturing to the maid, who was just then entering the room with a steaming tureen of soup — she withdrew from the room with your coat.

You lifted your hands, touching the ends of your fingers together and putting the index against your lips as your eyes ran over the table. The force of tradition was solidly present, the children quietly seated. Nothing would be amiss if you were to slip away for a few minutes.

With two or three long strides, Doctor, you were at my side; again you lifted me up and now carried me downstairs, turning on the light as you went, lighting up the waiting room and the desk of your secretary or nurse. You opened the door to your inner office, turned on another light, and we went in. There was a small couch and glass cupboards, and the air smelled a bit stuffy. You lowered me down to the floor next to an armchair, into which I crept like a monkey and then seated myself politely. You stepped up onto a platform that reminded me of those at university; upon it was your desk, made of carved wood. You sat down behind it. You were both visible and invisible from my half-hidden vantage point so far away. You gave the rollers of your chair a push; your height, the seriousness of your expression behind your thick glasses, and your thin, drawn face, which seemed consumed with worry, gave you the look of a judge — a kindly one, of course — who honoured me with a slight bow and then addressed me in a low, deep voice.

"My office hours are Mondays, Wednesdays, and Fridays from four to eight pm."

I lowered my head as if in regret at having disrupted the order of the universe.

"But of course ..." you continued, "seeing it's the first time, and given the circumstances, I suppose that ... Well, go ahead then, I'm listening."

"Thank you, Doctor. As you say, the circumstances are terrible indeed. I came here because I want to find out what has happened to my son."

"Haven't they told you?"

"Yes, Doctor, they have told me and it's left me more worried and confused than ever. I don't know who or what to believe. My sister-in-law, Ms. Petersen, took him to your hospital so he could die in peace, and it turns out they've operated on him. Please, Doctor, I beg you to understand that my wife and I ..."

No, you didn't cut me off. I fell silent on my own. You had brought your index fingers up to your lips again and were studying me. I was afraid, without knowing why, of lying or not telling the truth. You withdrew your fingers and pointed above.

"Let us trust in Him," you said.

I looked up and saw a beautiful cross with a doleful Christ which was worthy of display in a high-end antique shop. I smiled.

"Don't you believe in God?" you asked.

Did I believe? Should I believe? Would it be better for me, or Ana, or Meningito? I smiled in the hope that my smile would be infinitely sad.

"Oh, Doctor, I confess that my conscience still hasn't solved these things. But my short, almost nonexistent experience in life has shown me that when someone sick is entrusted to God's hands, it's because the doctors either don't know what they're doing or else they can't figure out what to do next. I don't know what methods are used to interpret God's will. But no one gave my son the chance to work out anything much with Him. I hope God shows a bit more mercy now and lets my son die soon."

I remained silent, with my head bent forward. I felt better, relieved. I heard you sigh. I raised my head.

"If I hadn't have operated on him, he would have died."

"That's what I'm talking about. What could have been better for all of us?" It was I who sighed this time. There was a pause. "Now what do we do, Doctor?"

"Don't you want him?"

"What will happen to him, Doctor?"

"He might die anyway."

"Will it be soon?" I asked.

"Maybe tomorrow; maybe years from now."

"Why did you operate on him, Doctor? You yourself said, in the hospital, that that which cannot be cured by fire is incurable."

You stretched out your arms and made a gesture of powerlessness.

"I say so many things ... I try ... It didn't depend on me ..."

"But you approved the operation?"

"I wanted something else ... As a neurologist and psychiatrist, it would have been interesting for me to have observed his development. It still is, of course, but, well, what's done is done."

"Doctor, what's going to become of Meningito?"

"Is that what you call him: 'Meningito'?"

"That's what my wife and I christened him. Don't you find it appropriate?"

"Too much so," and you tapped on your lips with your joined index fingers.

I asked you again about Meningito's destiny.

"You're sure you don't want him?"

"Will he ever get better?"

"Perhaps."

"Doctor, this is driving me crazy. I don't know if you also find that process of interest, but, as a psychiatrist, you'll be able to observe me as it happens. Tell me, your colleague ... the neurologist at the Metropolitan Sanatorium ... lied, didn't he?"

"I wouldn't say so. To err is human."

"Was the lesion brought on during birth?"

"I wouldn't be able to confirm it."

"What shall I tell my wife?"

"She doesn't want him either?"

"Will he get better?"

"Don't either of you want him in any way?" Your voice, Doctor: what did it betray? Doubt? Amazement? Fear?

"I don't understand, Doctor."

"Well ... for example, he'd be able to perform some functions, though others, no."

"I swear I still don't understand what you mean, though I desperately want to. Could he end up OK ... completely all right?"

Your glasses gleamed as you looked at me.

"No. Only a miracle ..."

"How will he end up, then?"

"Well, for instance, one of his legs might develop normally, while the other might be paralyzed."

"Or he might be able to urinate but not defecate, or vice versa," I replied; "or part of his penis might be able to become erect while the other part couldn't. Isn't that right?"

You took off your glasses and rubbed your eyes before putting them back on again; the tips of your index fingers were between your lips now.

"What shall I tell my wife, Doctor?"

"I suggest you have another child immediately."

"And Meningito?"

"It's settled then? You don't want to keep him?"

"No, neither of us does. Does that seem bad to you?"

"I'm not the one to judge," you replied, lifting your hand upward and pointing to the figure on the wall.

"Doctor, I'm afraid that my wife and I are all alone in this. What would you do if you had a son like ours?"

For a moment I was afraid I was getting involved in something that didn't concern me. You smiled.

"I believe it's a personal matter: a problem of conscience, quite private. If I had one? I don't know; I've never really thought about it … I don't know what I'd do. But tell me: Don't you feel anything for him?"

"No, Doctor. But you're free to call me a monster. I can take it; I was vaccinated against it when I was a kid."

"You'd let him die without trying to save him?"

"I would help him die," I answered. I remembered how light Meningito had been when I'd held him. "Let's say I love him enough to do that."

"I take it you don't agree with what we … or rather they … have done?"

"No, Doctor, I don't."

"Would you be willing to express your opinions before a medical board, or, say, put them in writing?"

"I would," I answered, thinking how I would be the envy of my sister-in-law. "And although I've sometimes dreamt of being a writer," I added, "I've never actually written anything in my life. But in this case … How can I put it? I feel a real need to write, or at least talk to someone."

You smiled.

"It would be interesting … very interesting, as well as useful both for science and for you; you would feel relieved … Yes, go ahead: put down all the details you can; include everybody that has had anything to do with Menin—, that is, with your son: his mother, his grandparents, even the neighbours. And don't worry about the order or length of what you write: my assistants or I will select what's most important."

"I promise you I'll do it. And the child, Doctor, what will become of him?"

"Forget about him; just leave him in my hands and think about having another one."

"Do you want me to sign anything?" I asked quickly.

You smiled once more.

"No; that won't be necessary. Don't worry about it."

I thought for a moment.

"Are there places for children like him?"

"Yes, there are, but you needn't be concerned about it."

"You'll take care of placing him in one?"

I don't remember your answer, Doctor. Maybe when you took out your fountain pen and unscrewed the top and then lowered your head to look for your prescription pad, I took it for assent.

"Please don't rush into anything. No one knows what might happen: you don't even know your own future, or your wife, hers. Maybe you'll change your ... Well, we'll see."

The prescription pad was in front of you, the fountain pen at the ready. You looked at me and then at the pad. Then you let out a soft "Oh" and put the top back on the pen.

The appointment was over.

Entry 49
Where Did I Go?

You showed me to the door and wished me goodbye with a kindly smile. I remember walking all the way back to Santa Fe Street, overcome by a need for space. But I have no idea as to what I did and where I wandered until I finally got back to my mother- and sister-in-law's apartment around eight o'clock that night. I might guess, of course, that I walked down as far as Plaza San Martín, crossed in front of the Retiro station again, and went back to the open air grill along the waterfront for another plate of sausages and glass of wine. It's quite possible that I got to talking again with the cook and that I once more brought up the subject of deformed children. He probably became a bit bored as he listened to me carry on about the same thing, just like any other nut. Perhaps I realized this and changed the subject to soccer, commenting on clubs like Boca and River Plate and San Lorenzo in order to keep his interest up and not feel so alone. After that, I would have gone back downtown and roamed the usual streets again, stopping by a few cafés, as I had done infinite times before. It's not surprising that I can't remember any of this exactly, when my experiences that afternoon may in fact have been a synthesis of many such wanderings. Everything may have happened, though, in that one afternoon. If someone were to tell me that they'd seen me at a movie theatre that day, I wouldn't be able to deny it. It would probably have been an all-day cinema with cartoon shows, at least one of which would have been by Walt Disney.

The chosen one had been born in the summer; he hadn't wanted to emerge from the womb, but they'd forced him to and now they were still tugging at him. That was all there was to it. And I was in some way hesitant to perform the sad and bitter duty of telling Ana what was going on. My endless ramble that afternoon was probably to put off the moment of truth, if such a thing existed or could ever exist.

Ana opened the door for me and, for the first time in our lives, turned her head away when I went to kiss her. I wasn't too worried. The kicks and blows I'd been receiving were turning me into a sage at a dizzying speed. I was sure she'd been given an anti-Pedro injection.

I went on into the living room without saying anything. When my mother-in-law saw me she gave a short snort or bark and retreated into the kitchen. I'd have sworn that she'd gone into the living room just to perform this scene. My sister-in-law was already in her bedroom, where she stayed for the rest of the evening. I sat down on the sofa and let out a snort of my own that could be heard from the kitchen to the bedrooms. I was still a kid.

Ana stood in front of me with her hands on her hips and fixed me with an inquisitorial stare. She wiggled her hips once or twice as if to get herself going, and then froze in a grimace of pain.

"Well?" she asked.

Ana's rebellions always had a comical, affectionate charm. They never seemed serious and were easily defused.

"Well, nothing's well. What did your sister say?"

"She told me you made a humiliating scene at the hospital and acted disgustingly."

"That's the same thing she told me, so it must be true. What else?"

"And that it could all be fatal to the baby."

"Why?"

"They might get so sick of you that they'd take it out on him."

I let out a whistle.

"Your sister is as sharp as ever. Imagine the worst and you'll be right. Don't worry, Ana, according to the latest reports, Herod's given up slaughtering the innocents."

"I don't get all your subtle remarks. I just want them to take good care of him the way they should."

She was deeply upset. I sighed.

"Ana, my dearest Ana, please stop worrying. As far as his care goes, I guarantee all sorts of experts and specialists will be singing him lullabies. He'll be looked after by princesses and the fairest of maidens. Presidents, ministers, ambassadors, every general in the country, and the Pope himself will all be helping out and sending messages of encouragement. Our own Beloved President ... who I seem to remember is General Something-Or-Other, though it's been a while since I thought about the outside world ... has promised to call him up personally. Donations are on the way and a number of kind-hearted souls have promised to take as good care of him as they have of us. We'll be the living example of exemplary parents: long-suffering, resigned, poor, and humble, but honourable, thankful to God for having sent us this sublime test of faith. Meanwhile, putting our trust in the Lord and keeping our powder dry, we will wait for Meningito, the nameless one, to expire as quickly as possible ... unless we do first from all the waiting and macabre speculations. Will he walk or not? On one foot or two? Will he be able to shit or just piss or either or neither of the two? That's all I have to say, Ana."

She was shaking her head from side to side. I was afraid she might be losing her mind. She fell to my side and stared off with wide, dry eyes at something unknown. She didn't touch me and I realized it would be useless at that moment to try to console her, take her in my arms, or draw her to me. When we'd both finally calmed down enough for her to listen and for me to speak, I told her about my meeting with you, Doctor. I talked and talked and talked, answering all of her thousand and one questions until she arrived at the last one.

"And you've never wondered why all this happened?"

"No. Does anyone know? Does he know? Why do you want to know?"

"Well, the Doctor said we should have another child, and if we do ... I'd like ..." She paused. "I'm afraid, Pedro."

"Me too. Very, very afraid. In Argentine terms, we've lost control of the ball."

There wasn't much left to add. Ana rested with her arms around me. The cars and buses outside made the street and building shake.

I was thankful to my sister-in-law and her mother for staying away from us that night. For me, Jackie has forever after remained in her bedroom. I felt sorry for her; she also, in a way, had lost control of the ball. Like a temperamental kid who didn't want to lose, she'd decided to leave the game and not play any more.

Entry 50
The Endless Story

My vacation time was up. I had to go back to work the next day. My mother- and sister-in-law were still soundly sleeping off their nightly drunk when Ana woke me up with a cup of coffee. I had it in bed along with my first cigarette. Ana remained standing next to me.

"Why don't you sit down?" I asked her.

There was no reply. I looked up at her eyes, which were red. Had she been crying? I was fed up. Was my irritation stronger than my understanding?

"What's wrong with you? Have you been talking with your dear relatives again?"

"They're sleeping," she murmured hoarsely.

"Well, then?"

"I had a dream."

"That's interesting. I can't remember dreaming anything. What was it about?"

"I dreamt about him, Meningito."

"Hmm. You've never even seen his face."

"I didn't see it in the dream, either. He had his back to me."

I put the cup on the saucer and sat up in bed. She seated herself next to me and looked down at the floor the whole time she told me about it.

"We'd taken him home, or at least that's how it seemed in the dream. I was changing his diapers. Strange, I never saw him from the front, just the back. I found a wound at his waist, next to his spinal column. I told myself, 'What an oversight. This has to be taken care of before it tears open any further.' I went to look for some epoxy glue. I mixed some together and began to spread it on either side to close up the wound. Then I heard his voice say, 'No, Mama. Not like that. That's not the right way to do it.'"

Ana and I held hands as she walked me over to the subway station. She was still limping, and we went slowly. I knew I'd be late for work, but it didn't matter. My status as victim and martyr had given me certain rights.

I'm not a poet, but I know that all kinds of lies and garbage can be praised and put into poetry. Even though Buenos Aires is an urban hell, its mornings can be beautiful. I ignored the noise and exhaust fumes and concentrated on the morning's freshness as the rising sun shone through the trees along Coronel Díaz Avenue, without thinking about the unbearable heat and humidity that would soon appear.

It was the first time in days that Ana had been outside. From time to time she squeezed my hand, and when I looked over at her, that old smile of hers would appear on her lips. Her efforts to hide her teeth ruined it a bit.

Yes, the first time in days. Days can be counted, but not nightmares, which can be infinite. Just as we used to do when we were going out together, we kept an eye out for a place to be alone and finally ducked into a café on the corner of Coronel Díaz and Santa Fe. Our spoons clinked against the sides of the cups as we stirred our coffee.

"I feel like I'm being reborn," Ana told me. "I want to go back to our house and hear the chimes of the clock again."

I didn't say anything. Her coffee was getting cold. Her face darkened.

"But I have a tremendous feeling of guilt. I'm not sure I'll be able to go back to enjoying the little things in life again."

That phrase "the little things in life," which sounds so pretty and poetic, irritated me. I'd heard it all my life, generally from women and failures. At one time I'd liked it, but eventually I realized that the people in power left us the little things in life so they could rob us of the big ones.

"If you want," I told her, "they'll hand you Meningito on a platter, a bit deformed maybe, but put back together even better than with epoxy glue."

She blushed.

"No," she said, "I'd never want that."

"Well, drink your coffee, then. After all, it's one of the little things in life."

Entry 51
Parenchyme and Mesenchyme

I'd always told customers who came in for our summer sales that wool carpets didn't give off at bit of heat — "pure fantasy", "an old wives' tale", "a racist myth" — and that, on the contrary, they actually insulated a room and protected it from the heat (though in the winter, miraculously, they *did* emit warmth), but when I went back to the store and began working at my desk, surrounded by rolls of carpet three metres thick, it felt like I'd entered a miniature inferno.

I came in to work that summer morning with guilt dogging my heels, though I couldn't be sure which guilt it was. Was it on account of my Christian upbringing, my arriving late, or something not yet in the public domain?

I said hello to Enrique, sat down at my desk, took out some papers, opened my box of file cards (and, for the first time, got the idea of recording these events as a series of files), and was soon working away as if I'd never left the place — or at least pretending to. I lit a cigarette and reflected on how long I'd have to keep up the schoolboy routine.

I got up and walked to the back of the shop. Aram was sitting at his desk counting money. I said hello to him and he gave a start, stuffed the money quickly into a drawer, and shut it. He was so relieved at not being held up that he didn't notice I'd come in late — or at least that's what I supposed.

"Ah! It's you. What's new?"

"Not much. Well … We finally took the kid to a hospital where the" eminent physicians found ... that ... there was an obstruction in the lumbar sacrum of his spinal column that was blocking ... or I should say, obstructing ... the vital circulation of cephalorachial fluid between his parenchyme and mesenchyme. The good doctors operated on him and were able to restore function to his tissues. We are now expecting a second child, which will be born *in vitro*."

He locked the drawer, got up, and came over to me. The small eyes on either side of his long, hooked nose scrutinized me more keenly than ever before.

"Your mother may have been a saint, but you're a son of a bitch. You're putting me on."

I hadn't expected this. I bit my lip and lowered my head. Then I looked up at him.

"Aram, I swear to you: I learned all those terms when I studied medicine, and I used to be able to explain the difference between a parenchyme and a mesenchyme, though I couldn't even begin to now. Are you satisfied?"

He studied my face a bit longer.

"Yeah, I guess so. Get back to work."

I sat down at my desk again and lit another cigarette. A while later it was my turn to jump. Aram was standing next to me.

"Pedro."

"What's the matter? There aren't any customers. And stop swearing at me."

"OK. I won't do it again ... for now. I just want to ask you one question."

"I'm listening."

"It's better that he dies, right?"

"It's that simple, Aram."

He gave me a pat on the back and went off to inspect the other shops.

Entry 52
Magic Carpets

Human beings are strange things, unknown even to themselves. That morning I had another surprise a bit more agreeable than the first. You'll have to excuse me but, personally, I've never found Armenian

141

women very beautiful. Erminia was no exception and, as I've mentioned, she was also a bit dim. Her charm lay in her enormous eyes and in what I perceived at that moment: her warmth.

She came over to my desk and put her hand on my shoulder.

"I heard what you told Aram," she said. "I'm sorry about it."

"Thanks, Erminia," I replied, and moved slightly sideways so that her hand touched my neck.

"But what is it exactly that's wrong with your son? A tumour?"

"Yeah, a tumour."

Her hand was still on my shoulder. I picked it up and placed it on the back of my neck.

"That's it, Erminia: right there. I'm all tensed up. Squeeze."

She squeezed softly once and then again.

"A malignant one?"

"Extremely."

"It's awful these days, not like it used to be. Now they find cancers in people of all ages."

"That's right, Erminia. It's terrible."

"Poor Pedro. You have no idea how bad I feel for you."

The squeezing along the back of my neck had turned to caresses.

"And you have no idea how that comforts me," I said, pulling her toward me.

She let herself go along. I buried my head against her waist.

My heart was pounding. Suddenly, as if I were adding more problems and guilt to my life, I pulled my head away.

"Sit down here and tell me about yourself," I said, gently tapping the top of the desk.

She leaned back and propped her bum up on the desk. I pushed my chair nearer and put a hand on her thigh. I could feel her garter belt beneath the thin material of her summer dress.

"What do you want to know?" she asked.

"First, tell me why you and your husband broke up. Don Garabed told me Armenians rarely get divorced, since they prefer to marry other Armenians."

"My husband used to beat me."

"What an animal! Instead of caressing you like I do." I stroked her thighs a bit. "And what else? I mean, how do you make ends meet?"

"I don't know what you mean," she laughed.

"Without your husband, or a lover."

"Oh, I have one."

"My God. It looks like I'm too late. And?"

"And what?"

"What I mean is, how do you get along? Is he kind and affectionate like me?"

"I don't know. Sometimes he's boring."

"He's boring? That's interesting. What do you mean exactly?"

"Ouf. I don't know. It's like another job. But I think he'd make a good father."

"'Another job?' What do you mean?"

"You know. All that stuff: kissing, going to bed together. It's a job, right?"

"Don't you like to go to bed with him?"

"It's not a question of liking it or not. I just don't see much difference."

"But Erminia, when ..." I hesitated. "When you're in bed with him, don't you like it? Don't you feel anything?"

"Not much. I close my eyes."

"Yeah, but ... What do you think about?"

"Oh, I don't know. My head's still full of carpets. The plain ones and the ones with designs on them that measure 1 by 1.5 or 2 by 2.5 metres; or I think about whether I forgot something or not, like sending out a 1 by 1.5 metre instead of a 2 by 2.5. I can't get them out of my head for a second. There you are: that's what I think about."

"Magic carpets with spells on them that get inside you and fly around your head and possess you. Or maybe infect you," I said.

"Yeah, something like that."

I felt exhausted. I stopped playing with her garter belt and withdrew my hand.

"Tell me, Erminia. Do you feel like you're the infected one, or is it the job that's tainted?"

"I don't know what you mean."

"Well, am I going to finish talking to you, and then go home and think about carpets when I make love to my wife? Or Aram, Ohan and Artim, for example: Do they ever have their mind on anything besides carpets? What do you think?"

"I don't know. When I meet their wives at the Armenian Association on Sundays, they always say their husbands have nothing but carpets in their heads."

I looked at her.

"That's horrible, Erminia."

She shrugged.

Aram came in the door. Erminia hopped down from my desk and ran to the back of the shop.

Entry 53
Changes

Summer in the store: a hellish heat seemed to radiate from the shop itself, billowing out the doors, which were left open for ventilation. Sad days for the Kalpakians, who were in mourning for the lack of sales. As I sat smoking one cigarette after another, Enrique would doze off, leaning back against a roll of carpets like a watchman guarding a mailbox in some more peaceful land. I'd found out a few things about Enrique by this time — though not too many. His silence was amazing; his answers would break off in midstream, and you had to guess the rest or fit the loose pieces of information together as if they were a mosaic. He had migrated to the city from the interior of Argentina; like his father, he had dreamt of his own private El Dorado, Buenos Aires, and now dreamt vaguely of leaving it and going back to his part of the country, the subtropical Chaco, up along the Paraguayan border. When I asked him why he wanted to return, he would answer, "I don't really know, Don Pedro. Back there you've got time for everything: long afternoons, get-togethers in front of the local bar in which someone invariably comes along with a guitar — it's as though life were longer there," and he would fall silent.

Such immobility and peacefulness drove Aram out of his mind.

"Listen, Enrique, move this roll over there and that one over here. You, Pedro: check on the estimates, call up the customers, sell everything you can. Don't just lie around sleeping … there's more than enough to do!"

"Get in there and get your clothes dirty! Jump like a frog!" I would say.

Enrique would slowly start dragging rolls of carpet across the floor and I'd look over a budget or two, make a phone call, and check the time.

One day Don Garabed didn't come in. I asked Aram where he was.

"He's out of town on vacation."

"Where?"

"A place called Cheapside."

I had to laugh. The Kalpakians were a miserly lot, and Don Garabed was the model for them all. He didn't have a car and, despite his age, would walk to and from work, even on the hottest days, when the street outside was like a steambath and the asphalt melted and stuck to your feet like mud in a swamp. The word "taxi" was enough to give him a heart attack. He accused me of wanting to take away his last pleasure in life: saving money. The sale of a doormat made from carpet scraps was enough to afford him the greatest joy. I once told him that he seemed happier about the sale of a throw rug than about carpeting the presidential palace. He said that was quite possible, since the profit from doormats and throw rugs was a hundred per cent, and the income from just ten of them would pay Enrique's wages for a month. Another time I jokingly asked him if he thought he could take the millions of dollars in his Swiss bank accounts with him to the afterworld. He reacted as if I'd summoned Satan himself: he turned white, put his finger to his lips, and, looking around, made the sign of the cross before holding up his fingers like horns at the sides of his head.

Just before noon, Erminia called out to me, "Pedro! Your wife's on line one."

I picked up the phone.

"Hi. What's up?"

"Pedro, my sister doesn't want you to stay at the apartment any more."

"Why not?"

"Well, I had to tell her how you went to see Doctor Brahe and about what he said to you. She says you're going to wreck everything and end up driving us all nuts. She also says she can't stand having you spend even one more night in the house."

"How about your mother?"

"You already know how she feels."

"And you?"

"She says I can stay."

145

"And we'll screw over the phone?"

"Pedro, you know I …"

"I'm just asking how I can see you. Am I allowed visiting rights?"

"I don't know. I forgot to ask."

"PEEDDRROOOO! Customer!" Aram's shout interrupted the conversation.

"I'm coming!"

"What? You're coming anyway?" Ana asked.

"No, no, Ana, I was just answering someone here."

The customer was waiting. I could see he was checking his watch.

"How's the face of God?"

"It's still sore, but my temperature's back to normal."

"Good. Get our suitcases packed. We're going home."

Silence. I was getting impatient.

"OK?"

"Well, that's what I wanted, but I'm afraid they might be offended if …"

"Tell 'em to … Listen, just pack our stuff and wait for me. I'll pick you up at six. 'Bye."

I hung up. I took care of the customer and then went to the back of the shop.

"Aram."

"There's no money."

"Yeah, I know. It's summer, sales are slow, and all the rest. That song gets more playing time around here than the national anthem. I don't need any money."

"OK, but you need something."

"Yes, I've got to leave work an hour and a half early. I have to take my wife home."

I won't go into the ensuing discussion with Aram or how I finally got permission. Things had already been like that for a year and would go on the same way for another year longer.

Later in the afternoon Don Hagop came into the shop; I can still see him now. I was actually happy he'd showed up. There was something wise and serene, even authentic, about him. He too would sit down beside me and teach me things when he came in. One day I'll have to describe his teachings, as I've done with Don Garabed. They were quite different.

That afternoon he didn't sit down with me. He walked over and said hello, and then, without asking me how my son was, but with a slightly bitter smile, he put his hand on my shoulder and gave it a squeeze.

Before I went to pick up Ana, I bought a file box and a stack of index cards. I would use them to begin another stage in my life, that of the unsuccessful artist.

Entry 54
The Face of God

Ana was waiting for me at the door of the apartment. Her mother was with her but disappeared as soon as she saw me. Ana's bags full of clothes and gear had multiplied like rabbits; compared to all that, my file box seemed insignificant. Before I could make any comments, she told me, "They gave me money for a taxi."

I let out a whistle.

"That was generous of them! To Constitution Station or all the way out to Longchamps?"

"To Longchamps."

"I can't believe it."

"You'll never believe all the things they gave me."

"A lot less than what they've stolen from you, don't worry. And tell me: Did they give me permission to go with you or do I have to take the train?"

"Cut it out, Pedro; quit exaggerating."

I went to look for a cab.

We got to Longchamps at sunset. The house didn't seem to have waited for us; a warm, humid, heavy gust of air hit us as we opened the door. The clock had stopped. I wound it up while Ana, still limping, unpacked. I opened the windows and was thinking of going out to get some beer at Don Manuel's corner store when Ana called me. She asked me to help change the sheets. I did and then went out for the beer. Two ice-cold bottles, bread, cooked ham for Ana, and salami and fresh cheese for me. I didn't want to, but I couldn't avoid it: I had to answer Don Manuel's questions and tell him about the umbilical cord, the tumor, and the incubator. His swearing was my only consolation.

When I got back, Ana was in the bathroom. The book was on the kitchen table, lying open to the chapter "Postpartum," subtitled "For the Mother's Beauty." "Dear friends," it read, "Don't let yourself start feeling low or thinking that everything is over for you as a woman. You've got to recapture that figure you had before you were married in order to show off your new happiness. Your children love you and deserve a mother who's pretty and fresh, with the same gracefulness she had back when she was engaged. Don't forget that your new-found motherhood in no way diminishes you as a woman; on the contrary, you should feel exalted, not only as a mother, but as a lover. Do you have any of the stretch marks, cracked skin, and flabbiness that may appear during or after pregnancy? There's a new ..." I closed the book in a fury.

Eight bells chimed. I opened a bottle of beer and tried to calm down, telling myself that everything was fine, everything was perfect, that the schizoid feeling I was experiencing was mine rather than the world's. There was a glug-glug-glug as I poured from the bottle and foam rose up the sides of the glass. I lowered my nose and concentrated on the tiny bubbles as they burst. Ana appeared at the door into the kitchen in her bathrobe. She blushed as, hiding her teeth, she asked me, "Isn't it going to disgust you?"

For once in my life — one of the very few times — I wasn't irritated by her obtuseness. It broke my heart.

"Ana, please, before I get upset, tell me clearly. What do you want?"

Her face turned even redder.

"You know ... I'm not ... able ... I can't clean myself well, bathe myself. Maybe you could ... if it doesn't make you sick ... because of the smell ..."

She didn't finish the sentence. I smiled.

"Ana, are you talking about the face of God?"

She nodded.

"And since when does it repulse me?"

"It's just that, that it's ..."

She was suffering. I rose to my feet and clapped my hands.

"Nurse! My rubber gloves and mask, please."

I parodied putting them on. I rubbed my hands together. I even managed to make her smile.

"Fine then, Ms. Ana Petersen, future doctor, you'll have to recapture your maidenly figure in order to show off your happiness. What illness are you suffering from? What's happening with the face of God?"

She led me to the bedroom and gave me my instructions, some cotton, and a liquid that cleaned and disinfected, as well as an ointment to heal things up.

She lay back with her legs hanging over the foot of the bed and then separated them. If I'd had a smile on my face, it was gone now. Only human beings can do such things to God: they had destroyed his face. There was dried blood, and the flesh was red and raw. It was impossible to tell what was what. I got down on my knees, dipping the cotton in the liquids, and went over the living, wounded landscape that was so sensitive to every touch. I watched Ana's face in order to direct my hand better, to seek her approval; she had closed her eyes and was pressing her lips together. I picked up some fresh cotton and continued wiping, this time with the ointment. I was anointing her. I could feel the cooling relief it was bringing. Nothing seemed to be enough, despite her distended lips.

I was kneeling before the altar. I kissed the face before me with the hope of restoring it immediately. It didn't happen. Softly, with a slight fear of hurting her, I touched it with my cheek: Ana's hands caressed my head and pressed it against her as she searched for the right pressure, the one that would help in the face of God's resurrection. I hoped that, soothed now, the face would smile.

The clock struck again. The beer was still on the kitchen table, losing its chill.

Note: Yes, I remember I'd never loved her so much. I doubt it will ever happen again. I don't know whether my passion, or adoration, could be explained through the phenomenon of the love for lepers or people covered with sores, but suffice it to say that I loved her completely. The clock disappeared and there was no longer any beer on the table, slowly turning warm. I drank it gradually at first, then faster and faster, replacing it with wine and finally with whisky.

Dear Doctor,

Yes, speaking professionally, I'd prefer to consider this second letter an entry on a file card; perhaps it could be titled "Sorting Out", or "Summarizing", or "Selecting What's Essential" — or possibly "Doubts and Confessions".

The entries take me back once more to that dark labyrinth, though this time in the opposite direction, entering it from the present and exploring back into the past; there are now so many of them that I run the risk of becoming paralyzed along the way, or of losing myself without ever being able to find the way out. The file box has turned into Pandora's. The trembling, which I told you had diminished over the years, still returns sometimes, and seems to be intensifying as I near the end. I have the feeling that he is there, waiting for us without knowing, in the darkness in which he lives, and that I am making my way toward an encounter or reunion. Is there a way out?

(I look out the window: the snow is still there, with the pine trees through which there is no path. The world looks as if it were eternally frozen. Ana is not at home; she'll be back later. I know where my children are, though I have no idea what they're doing — or if they're happy.)

Let's continue on with the report. I'll leave out the entry in which I tried to arrange all the files that didn't have a number or title; that was chaos. I'll arrange the numbered ones, reread the others, select the most important ones, give them each a title, and transcribe a summary of the ones I consider essential.

"My Native Villages": I was born in a small city in Hungary. I vaguely remember a giant kitchen with a purring fire and a servant woman who would tell me stories and legends and then, to my surprise, hide me under her skirts when someone came in. She didn't wear any underclothes, probably because she was so poor, which, by contrast, was indirect proof that we were rich, at least according to my father. The episodes from the war years aren't relevant here. I lost that village, but Longchamps was a good substitute. There the wood stove purred on, and it was there that I went through my initiation ceremony with The Turk and continued my apprenticeship with Carmen, the fat girl. Yes, the smaller the town, the bigger the hell — but at least it was a familiar one. I knew everybody and used to say hello to them all. When our son was born, without my realizing it, Longchamps began to recede into the distance. The story about the umbilical cord tied my hands and ended up hanging me. After initially telling it to Don Manuel, I then had to repeat it to the denizens of Bocha's bar and to Don Tomás and his wife when I paid him for the ride into the city. Longchamps flung me from its breast. In exchange, I gained a wide and alien world.

Ana was never much interested in the town. I don't blame her: it wasn't hers, and she never thought of it as more than someplace she was just passing through. She was friendly enough to the neighbours, but would rarely stop to chat with them. She never felt obliged either to make up stories or tell them the truth. Whether this was due to her reserve or her pride, who knows? Maybe even she doesn't. It was probably thanks to her attitude that the legend later arose about the Polack who drowned babies in his bathtub, which certainly didn't affect her as much as it did me.

"My Parents' Behaviour": The continuing story about the umbilical cord and the tumor never convinced my parents. In the name of parenthood or grandparenthood, they drove me crazy with their endless questions and their desire to help out and be useful. Naturally, they wanted to see Meningito. At last, fed up and exhausted, I begged them to leave the three of us alone — especially Meningito. I told them where he was and admitted the truth.

After that they stopped asking me questions. We saw less and less of them, and they of us. It was as if they had chosen to step out of the story.

"The Exonerating Entry": This file is composed of a list of humanity's greatest crimes, much more important than ours, which I thought I might someday end up using in court. It runs from Sparta and Mount Taygetus through the Inquisition and right down to the present day.

"The Dream" is something that has recurred for years now, with slight variations. I'll leave summarizing or describing it until later and will include it with the entries I've already arranged at the end of the story.

"Destiny" is made up of speculations about the mark our first child left on our lives. It's undeniable that we've ended up travelling down roads that, if not for him, we probably never would have taken — and that, if there hadn't been any problems, I would probably have stayed on with Kalpakian Ltd., growing accustomed to the warmth and security of my manger and ending my days as a "man to be trusted," perhaps a sales manager in one of their outlets. Of course, upbringing and personality also affect one's destiny — especially in my case, in which I've grown irritable, intolerant, and worse over the years as I've had to deal with the burden of events. I've also no doubt that my love for Ana has led me to protect her, to voice her wishes by helping her reach out beyond the barriers of her reticence and silence. Could things have turned out otherwise? What's meant to happen eventually will, one way or the other.

"Failures": These are not to be found in just one entry, but in a number of them. They refer to my attempts to write a novel, which Ana suggested and even begged me to do. I wasn't so sure about the idea, but I did begin with enthusiasm and a desire to get it off my chest, which I subsequently lost. The novel and the report I've been preparing for you have gradually become confused with one another, as is evidenced by the number of entries that open up onto other passageways into the dark labyrinth through which I am still making my way. It's also quite probable that I don't have any talent as a writer, and that the trembling, bitterness, and tightening in my stomach that I feel when I sit down to write are proof of my inability. I'm making excuses for myself: I was hoping writing would bring me maturity, serenity, and peace.

I'll sketch in the rest. We failed to make a go of it in the beautiful country house we lived in after moving out of Longchamps and then finally left Argentina in 1977. The First World to which we immigrated had much more information about ordeals like ours than even Ana had been able to find: statistics, data on the cost of supporting a handicapped child, and specialized magazines with articles like "A Place in the Sun for the Disabled," "The Physically Challenged: A Tragic Loss of Productivity and Human Potential," which defined them as human beings, capable of having a bank account, signing their cheques, handling a credit card, buying the things they needed, paying the electricity bill — "and buying a carpet," whispered a demonic voice in my ear. They seemed to be fulfillled, normal human beings. Finally, when "The Rights of the Disabled" were declared, I was overwhelmed by the realization that "what the world needs is love," rather than my personal story. Despite what you said about "what fire cannot cure" being incurable, the handicapped who are cured but then continue to suffer from ill health constitute a different type of failure.

"Ana's Search": This file has developed from a box full of material, dating back to the summer when she first began looking for the causes. She has searched every day, for weeks, months, and years — and continues her quest even now. She says that neither she nor humanity itself can be happy as long as the causes of Meningito's deformity remain unknown. I find the material she shows me dispiriting, but there's no use in telling her not to search for any more or that no amount of information can bring back our nameless child. As soon as one cause is discovered, another appears. She looks at me across the kitchen table of our impeccable house, shakes her greying hair, and says, "You don't understand me now and you never have," and takes another sip of wine.

What kind of material does she bring me? Photocopies of scientific articles about meningocele and spina bifida, with graphs and columns of statistics. She has over four hundred of them. When she shows them to me, I leaf through them distractedly. The few articles I've read have given me an idea of what Meningito went through. Some refer to great advances in medicine that I can't begin to understand. The yardstick by which these successes are measured seems to come from another dimension or world of abnormality, a small closed circle of specialists. Moral considerations scarcely exist; they don't seem to enter into the world of medicine. The latest articles on the new horizons and hopes opening up with transplants, or the future triumphs of genetic engineering, seem to me to be postponing the basic questions until some brave new world of the future, which may or may not be authentically carpeted. Many of them are in German or other languages I don't understand. I've pointed this out to Ana, but she just shrugs her shoulders. It doesn't seem to matter to her much; she just wants to find out everything she can.

Human beings are strange. I know that the distance between Ana and me is not due to Meningito. Other than a few misunderstandings due to our different personalities, we've always agreed on most things, and still do. The distance arises from different perspectives on life and from the erosion of time as the years slowly weaken us and begin and end without our even noticing. When I left my job with the Kalpakians, for instance, after giving them the month's notice required by law, I had Enrique prepare a carpet for me — not an authentic one, but a beautiful imitation of one of those that was fashionable at the time in the most prestigious and active of harems. I gave the driver of the delivery truck our address and asked him to return the bill to me rather than Erminia after he had "transferred" the carpet from the store to our house. I considered the "transfer" a payment or settling of accounts for the way the Kalpakians had exploited me, without realizing that it was also nothing less than an effort to revitalize the love between Ana and me.

Fatherhood and motherhood are also strange — as are time, memory, and the human brain. Whenever the old trembling returns, I have no idea where I am or which window I happen to be looking out of: whether that of our first house, with the clock that we took with us when we moved, or that of the country house I obtained through a certain business deal, in which we raised our children. Then, inevitably, I realize that it is neither of the two: that is why I see the snow outside.

The wood no longer crackles in the fire, nor does the gas hiss: our stove here is electric.

And the clock is no longer with us.

Entry 55
Our First Visit to Meningito

It's ten in the morning. I'm sitting in a café near Argerich Hospital, across from the slopes of Lezama Park. A milky humidity floats through the trees. Ana has gone on to the university; I suppose that, given it's summer and there aren't any courses, she must be doing research on the causes of his disease. I must have been on my way to work and then have decided to take one of those breaks I called freedom. How poor and brief are "the little things in life." I haven't yet numbered the entry as I begin to write it in the café; I know there are still more files to come before I explain how I got here.

This entry is dedicated to my first visit to Meningito a week after his operation, and to meeting Dr. Berenger, the pediatric surgeon that operated on him. Was he world famous or famous in the world of Buenos Aires? An eminent surgeon, it must be said.

The elevators still weren't working. We walked up to your office on the fifth floor, doctor, where your nurse gave us Dr. Berenger's name and office number a floor below. We wandered through the corridors, found it, and then waited an hour. I smoked while Ana sat silently. We didn't have anything to say to one another.

The difference between actually being important and simply pretending to be important in a classy way is lost on most people. Dr.

Berenger appeared surrounded by a group of young people who must have been interns and nurses — a small court.

As far as being well-nourished, Dr. Berenger seemed to wholeheartedly fulfill one of the precepts of the Hippocratic Oath — that the ideal doctor be brimming over with health. He was as round as a barrel, yet he moved about with agility, even exuberance, as if to prove the myth that fat people were happy. I supposed that he was the same fat doctor I had seen during my meeting with the other doctors the week before, but I wasn't sure. He threw open his arms when he saw us and did a ballet step.

"Ah! A most interesting case."

"Good morning, Doctor," I said, grinding my teeth.

"Ah yes, of course, good morning. Are you the happy parents?"

"Not so happy. More like worried."

"There's nothing to be worried about. Medical science is striding forward at a dizzying pace. I'm waiting for an answer to a telex I sent to my colleague Dr. John A. Whitacker, Advisor in Pediatric Surgery at both the United and the Alderhay Children's Hospitals in Liverpool, in order to find out what's new in the field. He's a colleague with whom I carry on a constantly evolving correspondence. Yes, your son is a most interesting case. It's too bad we've lost so much time; we had to operate with the risk of meningitis hard on our heels and excessive dryness in his nuclear ... excuse me, I mean medular ... plaque. But these old hands performed a miracle."

He raised his hands and looked around. Did I really see all those open mouths and hear that "Oh!" of admiration?

"Excuse me, Doctor, but Dr. Brahe said that ..."

"Dr. Brahe," he cut in, "is a most distinguished scientist, a profoundly humane man. But he doesn't have much to do with this case. We're on the fourth floor and he's on the fifth. Statistically speaking, there's a good chance your son will improve. The numbers speak for themselves."

I tried to be cordial and keep the dialogue going.

"Doctor, I don't know much about statistics or where they're found. What interests me is our son. You're right: Dr. Brahe doesn't have anything do with all this. It was another doctor, a renowned specialist and authority in his field, who gave us the original diagnosis."

His head stretched forward like a radar screen, locking its listening device onto me.

"He said that our son would be paralyzed all his life, that he wouldn't be able to urinate or defecate and that his head would continually enlarge."

"Hmm." The listening device withdrew and he seemed to be thinking. "Opinions, criteria. Hmph. To put it in scientific terms, you're referring to hydrocephalism. Well then, I must inform you that nowadays the size of the head can easily be controlled through surgery, and that hydrocephalics are things of the past. I guarantee your son will have a reasonable intelligence and will be of use to society."

"Doctor, what is a head's normal size, or a reasonable intelligence ... and to whom or for what would he be of use?"

There was a murmur of voices around us. Doctor Berenger smiled.

"Please, no rhetorical or pseudo-philosophical questions," he said. "Mathematics is an auxiliary branch of the great tree of medical science," he added smugly. "We also have statistics, numbers, and exact averages of normal cranial circumference."

I remembered all the other problems Meningito faced and the blood began to go to my head. I was about to continue when —

"Could we see him?" Ana asked. It was the first time she had spoken. No one seemed to hear her.

I don't know whether the doctor noticed my face turning red with anger or not, but he waved his hands suddenly.

"I'm sorry. They're calling me to the emergency room." He whirled around and, with another few ballet steps, disappeared down the hallway, followed by his entourage.

For a moment I thought we'd been left alone, but a pair of large dark eyes was observing us. They belonged to a nurse in a green lab coat. She came over to us, and spoke to Ana in a cloying, unprofessional-sounding voice.

"Would you like to see your son, madam?"

Treatises could be written on encounters between women. The look Ana shot her startled and disturbed me. Was it of superiority, contempt, or rivalry? The woman seemed not to have noticed.

"My name is Mabel Benaím, surgical nurse," she said. "I took part in little Jorge's operation."

"'Little Jorge'? Who's that?" asked Ana coldly.

"Your son, madam. That's the name we gave him when we baptized him. Jorge is the name of his godfather, one of the surgeons here. We baptized him when he got the infection so he'd go to heaven if he died."

There was an embarrassed silence. I repeated Ana's request.

"Well, can we see him?"

"Come with me," said Mabel.

We followed her down a corridor past three or four doors till we came to a large room. A nurse rushed over to us.

"This area is not open to the public. What do you want?"

"They're little Jorge's parents," explained Mabel. "Doctor Berenger authorized their visit."

A smile lit up the nurse's face and then went out again.

"Oh, what a miracle. You remembered little Jorge. It's about time."

She guided us into the room. There was a row of incubators, some empty, others with babies in them. We stopped in front of one of them.

"It's this one," the nurse said. I suppose she was referring to the incubator.

It took some time to make out the baby's form inside, lost among what seemed like thousands of tubes. Ana pushed back her hair so it wouldn't fall over her eyes; her hand hid her face as she leaned against the glass and looked at him.

"Is it true you don't want him?" the nurse asked. "How is that possible? Look at him compared to the others: he's the whitest of them all. A little blond angel."

I bit my lip. Ana had finished observing the baby. She raised her head and walked quickly toward the door.

"No, no, this way, ma'am."

She had gone off in the wrong direction.

We said goodbye to Mabel Benaím, who offered to be of help in any way she could.

As we went back down the stairs in silence, I wondered where I had seen those eyes before.

When we got outside and into the open, I took a deep breath of fresh air.

"What do you think?" Ana asked.

"About what?" I was surprised by my own irritation.

"Everything."

"I don't know. I really don't. He doesn't seem to be our child any more. It looks like everybody takes care of him and he belongs to them all. As for Doctor Berenger, he's a real pig. I can't believe that with all that fat he has enough wind to keep running after the progress of medical science, let alone catch up to it. In any case, at least he didn't go on about the Indians and the cows of the field."

I fell silent, looking for a word or phrase that could penetrate through to her heart and let me know how she felt.

"You're right. What's more, his English pronunciation is awful," she said.

She gave me a kiss, said goodbye, and took the 102 bus to the university.

I stopped off at a café.

Entry 56
My Second Visit to Your Office, Doctor; or, The Miracle of Life

Ana had apparently finished her research into the possible causes. She gave me two hand-written pages so I could read you the list and you could decide which of them might be the real one.

"Tell me something," I asked her. "What do I have to do with all these libraries and this learning? Couldn't you just go yourself and talk with him? He's a professional, and you're on your way to becoming one; you'd understand each other better. The whole thing seems pointless."

"No it's not. I don't want to go because the two of you will be able to talk it over more easily if it's just between men. He'd never tell me the truth."

"That's pure science fiction!" I said angrily and didn't bring it up again.

So I went to see you. I don't remember if it was a Monday or Wednesday, though I do know it wasn't a Friday. Your front door was open and the dining room had disappeared behind a curtain. A cotton pathway had been laid from the door into the house, covering a corner of the Persian carpet and ending at the stairs. The protection for the carpet showed how much traffic there was and how successful your practice had become — or at least indicated bourgeois care and conservation.

A secretary or nurse and three or four patients were in the waiting room. I greeted her with a mellifluous "good afternoon" and asked her to take my name. She handed me a card.

"It's a thousand pesos," she said.

"I'm not a patient."

"Oh, I'm sorry. Are you a medical representative?"

"Yes, exactly."

I was carrying the Kalpakian Ltd. portfolio, which didn't appear particularly full and I'm sure didn't correspond to the professional look of a medical sales agent. She eyed it doubtfully.

"Some new medication, is it? What laboratory are you with?"

"Kalpakian Limited."

"Is that a new laboratory? Do you have a card?"

Yes, I had one featuring a flying carpet with a Turk smoking a hookah, which didn't seem the appropriate image for a laboratory; it should have been one of test tubes with the serious, intelligent face of some scientist or researcher bending over them, or perhaps waving a bubbling tube in the air with a smile as if to say, "Eureka! I've found it! Humanity's been saved!"

"No," I told her, "I don't have a card. The company is just starting up."

The look of distrust on her face grew more pronounced: it must be some dilapidated laboratory with neither the feel nor a feeling for the market. At that moment the door opened and a patient came out.

"Please let the doctor know I'm here," I told her quickly, trying to hurry her on.

She stood up unwillingly.

"'Kalipikin,' you said?"

"No, no, 'Kal—' but listen, to make things easier, just tell him it's Meningito's father."

Her startled face as she headed to your office showed me she knew where things were heading but couldn't find a way out. A minute later she was back.

"You may go in," she said, with a touch of irritation.

And enter I did. You were behind your desk, up there on the other side. We greeted each other and then, after your "What's new?" "How are you doing?" "How's it going?," and so on, like a gaucho from the pampas, you finally got around to the subject.

"I'm afraid I don't have any news for you at all. We shouldn't rush things."

"Doctor Brae …"

"It's 'Brahe,' with the 'h' pronounced gutturally."

"Excuse me: 'Brahe.' I don't want to bother you, Doctor, but it's not for me … it's on account of my wife. She's worried, and I'm here because I want to help her follow a piece of advice you gave us."

"Which one? There were so many."

"There certainly were," I thought. "Half a loaf is better than none."

"You suggested we forget about everything and have another child," I told him.

"Ah, yes. What seems to be the problem, then?" he answered. "Go on; I'm listening."

"It has to do with what caused Meningito's malformation. My wife's a medical student who's going to become a doctor, like you. She's made up a list of possible causes and would like to know which one you think it might be … so we can avoid it happening again, I guess."

You smiled and shook your head from side to side.

"Will it take long?" you asked. "There are quite a few patients waiting."

"If you'd like, I can come back later this evening. That way …"

"No, no, that won't be necessary. Let's hear then," and you put your index fingers to your lips.

I took out the list from my pocket. Since you hadn't asked me to sit down, I did so on my own. I put the portfolio on the floor and opened up Ana's list. I didn't clear my throat, just sniffed back some nonexistent mucus in my nose.

"By way of introduction, I'd like to say that there's a theory floating around the family that they switched babies on us. These things happen, especially considering that this country is a swindler's paradise. But, laying that possibility aside, here's the rest of the list: the anti-tetanus vaccine; the penicillin; her previous abortions; the painting of the Pindapoy oranges; the testing of atomic weapons; those Chilean lobsters that were contaminated with cesium 137; carbon 14; strontium 90; vaginal sprays with rose or strawberry fragrances; the lettuce and tomatoes …"

"Excuse me," you interrupted, separating your fingers. "What was that about vaginal sprays? I don't ..."

"Oh, just one of those intimate kinds of products that women perfume themselves with, you know, instead of washing. Personally, I prefer ..."

"I don't understand."

"They come in a little gas-powered tube. The woman puts it down there and psshht, that's it. I was curious about how things would be after using it, you know: the varieties of lovemaking, I guess. She only used it that one time. But when she found out that synthetic products like that contained chemicals that could ..."

I realized you were no longer listening. You weren't there anymore: not that far away, perhaps, but not there. You nodded your head two or three times and even seemed to wrinkle your nose a bit. Then your eyes came back to me.

"Go on," you said.

"... the lettuce and tomatoes from that Japanese guy's farm next to the chlorinated match factory; the secret formula for Coca-Cola; the electric, radioactive smile of a survivor of the atom bomb dropped on Hiroshima ..."

"Is that what she wrote?"

"No, Doctor, it isn't. She didn't say, 'sprays with rose or strawberry fragrances,' either: it was 'with hexachlorophene and propellants.' But the way she's said things is either infinitely boring or distressing, depending on your point of view. Unless we change planets, the whole list seems useless."

You sighed.

"It is," you agreed. "It's an endless road."

You stood up. I put the papers back in the briefcase and got to my feet.

"Tell your wife that all those reasons are good ones, but that none of them are necessarily valid. Life continues to be a miracle," you added philosophically.

"And health even more of one, don't you agree? Even despite doctors. Though I'm not referring to you, of course," I put in quickly.

You accompanied me to the door of your office. Before saying goodbye, you told me, "Don't forget that I'm waiting for your notes on all this."

"I won't. Thanks for everything."

I never went back to your office. I preferred to visit you at the hospital.

Entry 57
New Sales Techniques

I was becoming unsociable at work. It seemed as though Don Garabed had run through all his teachings and was now repeating himself. His fretting about how many doormats he'd sold each day, which I'd always found funny, now began to seem more typical of a narrow mind that was going round in circles. His questions about Meningito's health seemed more inspired by nosiness than humanity. They were getting on my nerves, and no matter how many times I told him I didn't want to talk about it, he'd insist on returning to the same subject. Perhaps due to Meningito himself, however, Aram's attitude toward me had softened. We not only went out for coffee together now, but for lunch, too. As we talked during our meals, I realized that he was actually a rather solitary soul who was dragging around a number of dead dreams through life. He didn't ask me anything about Meningito. When I hit him up for another loan in order to get Ana's teeth fixed, he gave it to me without a word. He probably thought it was to cover more costs for Meningito's treatment. Erminia didn't ask me anything else either. When she noticed I was sad or lost in thought, she would quietly caress the back of my neck. Yes, I was becoming out of sorts, impatient, overly irritable, even aggressive at times.

But I kept on selling—that was what mattered. I had gradually built up a certain clientele, and it was about that time that I developed a new sales technique. I admit it was based on Don Garabed's teachings about the vanity, vacuousness, and pride of human nature. I'm not sure whether my technique could ever be formalized or taught as part of a course on the progress and development of mankind, or whether it was ultimately only applicable to me at the Kalpakians' carpet store in Buenos Aires. I no longer chatted along with the customers, entertaining them with the stories and legends I invented, nor did I listen intently and nod as they went through their "buying experience," in which they proved to themselves that the purchase of luxury goods set them apart from other, less fortunate mortals. I would still smile a bit, though, my face a slow, subtle mask. Customers think they know what they're buying. Softly, courteously, I would introduce a note of challenge — "You think so?" "I don't believe you." "You don't seem quite sure about that." "Yes, but could you prove it?" or "Buy it. Show me who you really are!" — all the time creating a circle of ambiguities, a margin of indecision, a fear bordering on panic leading to an empty space that the customer would hurriedly fill by buying the item in question.

It was a difficult, dangerous technique, but it worked marvelously, its basic elements being resentment and the "Horror of the Void." As I say, it had to be applied with tact and affability, so as to keep from gnashing my teeth.

The only thing that comforted me a bit or that I was able to tolerate was my occasional talks with Don Hagop. His gently ironic teachings, reflections, and doubts seemed like nostalgic yearnings for some personal Paradise Lost, much farther away than my own, and, combined with my bitterness, I found they fit like a glove. I'll transcribe them; I've got to fill up the time and space with something before arriving at the defining or fatal moment.

A Brief Summary of the Teachings of Don Hagop

Don Hagop had fathered Aram and was Don Garabed's older brother. He must have been about seventy-five years old. He was the tallest of all the Kalpakians. He had grey eyes — or perhaps they had simply faded over the years; his face was angular and his skin was lighter than that of other Armenians. I don't know what colour his thick white hair had once been, but I'm sure that he'd been quite handsome in his youth. He was the true black sheep of the family; he had broken with Armenian tradition and married a Hungarian woman, which was a crime similar to that of a Jew marrying a Gentile.

He didn't come into the shop very often — no more than once or twice a week. He would stop by in the evening so Aram could give him a lift home when the store closed. Like Don Garabed, he didn't have a car and couldn't bear to spend money on taxis, but that was where the resemblance ended and the differences began. After much reflection, he had come to view avarice as an existential problem.

He always had a book or two with him. Quite uselessly, he would say, he attempted to find in them what he had not found in life. When he would be seated near me and sigh, it sounded as though the years were crushing or demolishing him. From time to time a flash of mischievousness would light up his normally gloomy gaze. Unlike the other Kalpakians, he never got worked up about things; he always spoke in a measured voice and never asked how sales were going. He was not an inquisitor, and his questions could just as well refer to himself as to anyone else. He never gave advice; he said it didn't accomplish anything, and that he couldn't remember ever following it in his own life, despite having received a lot of it.

According to Don Hagop, the Kalpakians had overflowed the banks of human existence. The money they made had long since ceased to have any meaning for them. How many steaks can a man eat in a single dinner? If he's normal, just one, along with a little salad. As for the business, buying low and selling high was neither an art nor a virtue. The Kalpakians took pride in very little. That fact that they could deceitfully vaunt the quality of carpets in eight languages didn't mean they could actually speak them at all. But the worst was that the Kalpakians (and at times he'd include all Armenians), had forgotten the only art that was really worthwhile: the art of living. For him, the Kalpakians' greed was genetic. He never actually put it that way; he just used to say that they "had it in their blood." He explained to me that never in his life had he owned or even considered owning a car — not only now that he was old, but even in his youth. The notion that something could constantly depreciate and deteriorate was intolerable to him. Everything about a car wore out, from tires to transmissions, and, for Don Hagop, even the idea of windshield wipers moving from side to side in the rain, imperceptibly eroding away, was horrible. It was a curse. But didn't his son and nephews have cars? "Yes, of course they do, but they suffer from having them; they don't enjoy them. Understand? They're not like the Jews, whom you know I don't like. Being a Jew is terrible. It's like carrying a cross. Did you ever notice that, when someone finds out we're cheating him, he insults us by calling us 'fucking Jews' and things like that? Somebody who insults the Jews evidently doesn't know much about Armenians and Greeks. But I'm losing my train of thought — it must be my age. What I mean to tell you is that, even though Jews may be stingy, they aren't that way with each other. They know how to live and I envy them for it."

Don Garabed and Don Hagop had been born in Istanbul and had

studied together. In order to escape the extermination of the Armenians by the Turks, they had fled the country and looked all over the world for a new one. (Both Don Garabed and Don Hagop maintained that the Armenians hadn't gotten nearly as much mileage out of their holocaust as the Jews had from theirs: the Armenians had never received compensation and, although one or two novels had been written about it, along with a few history books that no one ever read, it had never made it to Hollywood.) The two brothers had bought carpets in Tehran, Baghdad, and Isfahan, and then had sold them in Budapest, London, and Vienna. That was why they spoke so many languages, though their vocabulary was limited to what was needed for buying and selling. Both of them described their travels, though the substance of their stories differed greatly. Don Garabed told me how much it cost to rent a camel or buy a dish of *kebbe* in a restaurant in Tehran in 1935. Don Hagop, on the other hand, transported by the memories that returned to him as he recounted his stories, would pause in the clicking of his worry beads as they ran between his fingers, lean his head back with his eyes half-closed, and hum some Middle Eastern melody, swaying along to the rhythm. Then he would invoke the women of his past, with their almond eyes, delicate waists, and hips like ... (here the worry beads would clink together as he traced a curve with his hands). He would tell of caravans of camels, of desert winds, of empty landscapes beneath Arab moons, of oases, of tiny villages lost in the seas and dunes of sand, villages where girls could still be found weaving carpets for their dowry on homemade looms, sometimes making a mistake as they worked, a sign of the carpet's authenticity. Every so often, following her heart and breaking with traditions grown monotonous from years of imitation, one of them would throw herself into some fantasy inspired by dreams and the desire for love, and would end up weaving a carpet of great value. The rest of the carpets were all a big lie: the ones supposedly from Bukhara were actually made in sweatshops in Pakistan, where a hundred women would be given a handful of rice per day for keeping their two hundred hands busy as a voice on a megaphone called out, "First thread, first knot: red." Those carpets were perfect, without the slightest flaw or fantasy in their wool. They were like the men of today, robots that always performed the same task. Falsifying colours was another "modern" secret, performed by an Armenian in London who was half wizard himself, in a laboratory worthy of the most advanced science. Changing green to red and brown to yellow was nothing more than chemistry at work. The patina of antiquity and "natural" shine, much like silk, given off by a pure wool carpet, which we all praised so highly when we'd sell one, were easily counterfeited by burning it with different kinds of acid.

Don Hagop believed that the last true carpets had disappeared in the fifteenth century, when they were still associated with authentic Asiatic luxury, with its rituals of prayer and purification, and maintained that all carpets since then had simply kept endlessly repeating the same designs.

As closing time drew nearer, the old man would fall asleep with his worry beads between his fingers and a faint smile on his lips. I used to go over to him and hum his melody; he would sway back and forth or, if he woke up suddenly, threaten me with his worry beads. And I would tell him, "Quick, Don Hagop, the camel caravan is at the door. When do we leave? I feel like getting out of here."

Entry 58
Visiting Meningito

Despite what the newspapers said when our story finally became public about our never having so much as glanced inside the hospital doors, the fact is we paid Meningito many tortured visits. Perhaps it would be best to summarize a few of them and group them together as a single entry. Usually, after going to Argerich Hospital either alone or with Ana, I would sit in the café across from Lezama Park and jot down the latest events, which were not very dramatic during the first three months. I never got to know the hospital staff by name, though they knew me, distrusted me, even hated me. The self-righteous nurse who had demanded I pay for penicillin months before had multiplied like a plague, until there seemed to be hundreds like her, exclaiming, whispering, clearing their throats, or making sarcastic remarks. I was also forever bumping into Mabel Benaím. She was the only person who didn't seem hostile, and her large dark eyes were filled with kindness. Sometimes she would stand at my side in silence, as though on the verge of saying something left unsaid. She asked for my telephone number at work, in case something happened, and she gave me her number at her parents' house, where she could be reached in the evening.

It was during one of these visits that Doctor Berenger informed me that Meningito was making wonderful progress, updating me on his urination and defecation, about which he was sure much more could be done. In any case, even if Meningito eventually proved incapable of urinating, he could easily be fixed up either with the Foley medical probe or the Credé manoeuvre, a fantastic solution that would stand him the rest of his life. Walking? Much more could be done there too. The best thing for the moment would be to buy him a special pair of pants that would straighten out his dislocated hip. What dislocation? How had it happened? Didn't I know? Dislocation was quite normal in these cases. I refused to buy the pants, saying we couldn't afford it. And we couldn't. Ana's teeth were costing a fortune: they all had to be crowned with porcelain caps, unless we chose the other option, which was to have them pulled. And even if I had had the money, I still would have refused.

At any rate, the world is filled with good people and generous souls, and I sensed that no one would ever abandon Meningito or let him die. He had become incredibly useful to those around him, and would end up being much more so not only for his own society, but even, without exaggeration, for that of the United States. Love was all around him, like a viscous swamp, sticky and dangerous. And I was splashing about in it, without realizing how perilous it was.

Another Visit

Through the café window I can see the yellowing leaves on some of the trees in Lezama Park. Once again, Ana has left me here on her way to medical school; once again we've just visited Meningito.

When we said goodbye, she told me, "This is the last time I come."

I don't blame her. The battering we took this time was cruel, a veritable assault. It was quite probably a plot hatched by Dr. Berenger.

Mabel Benaím had taken us over to Meningito's bedside. She informed us happily that little Jorge had taken a great step forward and had been able to leave the incubator. And there we were, bent over his crib: he was sleeping soundly under the covers. The tubes were gone. Then Doctor Berenger appeared with his clipboard.

"Hi. Hello there. Good to see the happy parents. Careful, eh, not to rob me of my favourite patient. But, well, everything has to come to an end, doesn't it? Get his little crib ready: he'll be going home in no time. A few more adjustments and he'll work like a clock."

Ana turned pale and gripped the edge of the crib.

"A clock or a diesel motor?" I asked him. "Which do you think is more human?"

"Aha. How witty you are … a most likeable fellow. Well then, where were we? Ah, yes. We have to take little Jorge over to radiology now in order to see about that hip. Why don't you carry him there, madam, and use the time to become more familiar with him and give him your love."

Ana was now not only pale, but trembling. She couldn't decide. Mabel Benaím bent over the crib and uncovered the baby's legs, which were sheathed in orthopedic pants. She picked him up and Meningito began to cry and then continued to whimper softly. I couldn't see his face very well.

Ana's arms trembled when she received him. I don't think she realized that her nose was twitching: Meningito smelled of piss.

"Don't be afraid; he won't bite," said Dr. Berenger. He was the only one who laughed.

Ana and I followed Mabel Benaím to the door and out into the corridor. We'd only gone a few steps before faces began appearing in doorways and people approached us as they saw us coming. An entourage of nurses, good Samaritans, orderlies, nurse's aides, and doctors formed around us, all making comments.

"Look how cute he is." "How sweet." "How adorable." "How blond his hair is." "How white his skin is." "He looks like a little German." "And to think they don't even want him." "Oh, if he were only mine." "They'll change their minds." "He looks like his mother." "More like his father." "Of course, both of them are fair, too." "He's such a cuddly little thing." "So strong, so plump … so …"

Life and its associations are strange. Ana was wearing very high heels, which she sometimes used to put on when we would make love standing in front of the mirror at home. I remembered this when I saw her legs begin to shake so hard I thought she would fall, but this time they were trembling from pain.

I couldn't stand it any longer.

"Yes, and how strong he is! Just look at the way he walks and runs around!" I shouted jubilantly, gasping for air, in a hoarse voice.

The eyes around us filled with hatred, but there was finally silence, like a balm. Ana …

"Watch out, he's falling!!"

I don't know if he would have fallen or not, but Mabel Benaím was already there. She held Meningito up while I steadied Ana.

The entourage became a funeral procession. A sepulchral silence fell over the group as feet shuffled forward. By the time we arrived at the X-ray department, only Ana, Mabel, and I remained. Mabel took the baby in her arms and disappeared inside.

Ana and I left. She waited for me in the café while I ran upstairs to look for you.

Luckily, you were just leaving your office when I arrived. I told you breathlessly what Dr. Berenger had said about us taking the baby home. I was about to remind you of the promise you'd made us when you suddenly spread your arms, flapping them in the air like a bird (I'm not suggesting that you looked like a crow; you were dressed in white at the time), and begged me to calm down.

"Listen to me," you said. "All of that would be far too fast. There's still so, so, so much left to do."

I went back to the café and found Ana, her eyes red. I told her what you'd said.

I stayed there after she'd gone, smoking and trying to scribble down these notes.

Entry 59
Meningito's Head

Most of the trees in Lezama Park were now bare. It was winter. The café had become a cozy place, but the gusts of cold wind that whistled in around the edges of the door reminded me what the world was like outside. A printed sheet that Mabel Benaím had given me lay next to my

169

coffee cup. I reread it once more. It began with: (Code 825 01), and went on: Pediatric Scalp Vein set; (Cutter P.S.V. Set), (1 Team = III).

The story that had been predicted in the original diagnosis by the neurologist at the sanatorium (a true prophet) was now coming true, step by step: Meningito's legs were paralyzed and his head was growing disproportionately.

No, I didn't write this entry that day. I couldn't do it. I smoked and thought — or thought I was thinking. It was the height of the season at the store, and I had to fight against the feeling that I should be at work as I let a succession of images parade through my head. There was no better place to be alone and concentrate than that café across from Lezama Park. I saw caravans of camels and remembered an Arab story or saying that Don Hagop had told me or that I had read somewhere: Life consists of being born, growing up, suffering, and dying.

I thought about the last times I'd come home from work. Dinner was ready when I arrived. As we ate, I would tell Ana about the news at work and, without her ever asking, I'd describe my visit to the hospital if I'd gone there that day. The meal would end and, without a word, she would get up and go into her study. And I would sit there smoking a cigarette, listening to the clock as it marked the passing of time.

Making love had become a physiological necessity, an accident, a coincidence. Our sweet perversions had grown limited and had almost disappeared.

I never saw my parents anymore, nor my old friends, either. And there weren't any new ones.

Yes, the café was the best place in the world to think and make decisions. I don't believe I decided anything that day, or else I followed decisions I'd made in the past. The printed sheet from Mabel Benaím was still there in front of me.

She was a strange woman. She was of Arab ancestry, with large dark eyes and somewhat high cheekbones, like Ana, but her skin was a dark peach colour; she had well-defined lips and, when she wasn't wearing her green hat, her face was framed by jet-black hair. Her breasts pressed tightly against her green operating nurse's uniform. She was short, even in her operating room shoes. She was also soft and quiet. She must have been about my age, but we treated each other with a certain formality. Without feeling embarrassed or uncomfortable, she would stand by my side longer and longer, always on the point of saying something, though she never did. I was tempted more than once to ask her to have coffee with me, but I never did. I was always afraid of what our subject of conversation would be. Maybe I was wrong. I almost never actually saw Meningito or Dr. Berenger anymore. Her reports were enough. Meningito's head had begun to grow rapidly about a month and a half before. Dr. Berenger, whom I considered a monster but Mabel thought was "basically a good person inside," had done everything possible to control the growth of the child's head, measuring it and extracting the cephalorachitic liquid with a syringe. I can't remember whether he gave him feeding bottles with teats made of glycerine or Vaseline, or if he injected other substances into him that absorbed the excess fluid. It didn't matter much.

Nothing worked. The child's head grew and grew and threatened to explode. It was time for an emergency solution. In order to convince me, Mabel took me to visit Meningito. When I saw him, I stretched out my hands.

Except for the recurring dream I mentioned to you, Doctor, in which I see him clearly, I don't remember Meningito's face. Or I remember various faces: the little wrinkled one when Jackie took him away, or the squinched-up one when he was crying, or the one I saw that day, in which his enormously dilated eyes, as if full of fear, were about to pop out and roll across the floor.

I had put out my hands to catch them.

The fantasies of a frustrated writer. His eyes, Mabel explained as she tried to calm me down, were just part of the syndrome: the "sunset effect", which was normal in hydrocephalics and cases like Meningito's. It was due to the pressure of the liquid against the cranial ...

"Oh, no, that's enough, Mabel. I can see that everything's as normal as normal can be, but in some other dimension, some other world. Let's get out of here, for God's sake."

She went on explaining in the hallway outside. The quantity of liquid and the imbalance in pressure were more intense than usual in such cases. They'd have to ...

"Ah!" I exclaimed. "Then thing's aren't quite so normal."

Mabel stopped talking. Her body swayed from side to side.

"But ... but ... how can you be so ...? He's your son. Don't you feel anything for him?"

Her dark eyes were moist, or at least they seemed to be. Or I wanted to believe they were, even though it was just their normal gleam.

"I could say I'm over-sensitive. I could say I can't sleep sometimes. I could even say I don't know what I feel: rage, anger, guilt, desperation, fury, or impotence. But none of that matters here. The thing that's in that room and that should have been resting in the cemetery months ago isn't my son anymore. It's the son of Dr. Berenger and the hospital." And I added brutally, "If you want it, it's yours."

Mabel looked startled. She thought for a moment.

"And your wife?"

"She told me she'd never come here again."

There was a long silence.

To put it in precise, scientific terms, Meningito had to have an emergency operation. The doctors had to install a valve that would drain off the cerebral fluid into a vein or artery, so his head wouldn't explode. It would function automatically, but in case there were some problem or obstruction, which Meningito himself would indicate by crying with pain and holding his head, all they'd have to do was press a small button on the outside of his head and everything would be all right. The valves they had at the hospital were made of plastic and had been removed from children that had died; other ones were made of stainless steel, but they eventually rusted. He had to have a new one.

The printed sheet I now had next to my coffee cup contained the technical details for the valve.

On the opposite side was the address of a surgical supply store where it was sold. As if abusing the privilege that came from having a sick child, knowing that I would get to work extremely late, I went to the store. The salesman who waited on me had the attitude that he knew more than the doctors themselves, which was probably true. I gave him the paper.

"Pshhh. They must be dreaming. They certainly don't know what they're talking about. Nobody carries that here."

"But … it exists, doesn't it?"

"Sure, in the United States. It's either a special order or it gets smuggled in."

"How long does that take?"

"Ouf. With all the hassles at customs, it could take up to three months. It's cheaper and faster to get an airline pilot to bring it in."

"Thanks," I said, and left.

I'd never actually thought of buying the valve, but a strange, morbid destiny seemed to have locked my fate into Meningito's. I simply, or not so simply, wanted to know more.

At the last minute, when the surgical store was closing, I called Mabel Benaím at home to tell her the valve was unobtainable. Our conversation was brief.

"I hope they can't get one," I said. "Or that something happens to him before they can. Thanks, and goodbye."

Note: It's true I can't remember Meningito's face. The face that appears to me in my dreams now is very different. Even so, I can't understand why his weightlessness when I held him in my arms that one time in my life, as light as a feather, a lightness that needed protection, has never left my mind. I can still feel it.

Entry 60
International Solidarity

But I had forgotten about all the noble souls and Good Samaritans. I'd forgotten about what I myself had predicted to Ana. It was a hurricane of love and kindness that devastated my soul. I never thought the world could be so good and I so bad.

By the time the valve was finally installed, the newspapers and magazines were running headlines such as "What Being Human Is All About," "How to Save a Life!" "Mission Accomplished, John," and "News That Makes Life Worth Living." The articles that followed used phrases such as "a human being, just like everyone else", "a crusade to save a life" and "a major link-up."

There were also philosophical or mystical touches: "A woman on a street corner in Buenos Aires broke into tears when she heard of the child's needs. In this era of materialism, of overlooking things, of living for the moment, and of rank commercialism, it was an act of giving that purified us from our sins. For one brief moment we all held our breaths; Catholics, Jews, and Protestants took advantage of the occasion to look within themselves and meditate on how best to bring a bit of improvement to a harsh and unrelenting world."

It seems it was Mabel Benaím (as I later learned) who first notified the hospital auxiliary committee that the valve was not available. Meningito's head was about to explode. A ham radio operator who worked with the committee sent out a desperate message over the airwaves. His transmitter wasn't very powerful, but another amateur radio enthusiast in Brazil picked up the message and rebroadcast it, as did one in Mexico, until finally a certain John Clement in New York, "just an average citizen", also heard the message and swung into action.

Hours later the valve was on its way to Kennedy Airport under police escort. A pilot with the Argentine national airline brought it back personally on the next flight to Buenos Aires, where another police escort, sirens wailing, took it directly to Argerich Hospital. "This was the way a life was saved."

The anguished parents could not be found for an interview.

Quite understandably, many of the details of the event — such as a new drug being involved or the valve being shipped in a refrigerated compartment — changed in the telling. The main thing, though, was that a life was saved. There were photos of the pilot, of the police motorcycles roaring through the city, and of the ham radio operators involved, among them the smiling, wholesome, optimistic, and satisfied face of John Clement.

Entry 61
"A Spectacular Operation"

The newspapers spoke of an operating team of some twenty medical professionals, when in fact there were only five — an error that probably stemmed from their adding in everyone on the floor, including the cleaners. They recounted how a four-hour operation had transformed a hydrocephalic into a normal human being, depending on your opinion or point of view. The story about the sisters and Mother Superior of the Divine Face Convent getting involved was standard fare, as was the one about the president of the time congratulating the surgical team on having placed Argentine science at the forefront of modern technology. I don't know if there was a message from the Pope or not. The newspapers reported that the father was present all during the operation, anxiously awaiting the results, but was too overwhelmed with emotion to speak.

That the operation was a success and the patient was in good health were, of course, foregone conclusions that were as inevitable as death.

I, the father, was totally out of touch with what was going on inside the operating room as I leaned against the wall or paced up and down with my hands in my pockets and a cigarette hanging out of my mouth. I watched the television camera and the lights on Dr. Berenger's freshly powdered face. He was accompanied by Mabel Benaím and other nurses and doctors, all with their cheeks and noses touched-up.

I jumped. You, Dr. Brahe, appeared at my side. We said hello. Whether out of jealousy or envy, or because you knew the truth, your eyes took in the scene and your head shook from side to side several times. You turned to leave and I followed you.

"Doctor, Doctor, just a moment, please. What happens now?"

You stopped and raised your arms.

"Calm down, calm down. You've got to take it easy. There is still much to be done. Let's have faith in this little valve, because it's … Let's trust in it for now."

Entry 62
Mabel Benaím

The trees in Lezama Park were budding once more, just as they were in Longchamps and along 9 de Julio and other avenues, as well as in other parks and forests. Then suddenly it was summer again, the season of lament for the Kalpakians.

Meningito would soon be having his first birthday, if he hadn't already. My visits to the hospital were becoming less frequent. Unless I ran into Mabel while I was there, I would leave without checking on anything or speaking to anyone.

Things were bound to turn out one way or the other. I kept on waiting, without knowing for what. Something had to happen.

And then one Friday that summer, just before noon, when sales were slow and the store was quiet and Don Garabed was on vacation in Cheapside while I sat listlessly at my desk, Erminia called out, "Pedro, telephone." I picked up the receiver.

"Hello?"

"Hello, Pedro. It's Mabel Benaím."

"Oh, hello."

There was a long silence.

"What's new?" I finally asked.

"They're discharging little Jorge. On Monday. This time it's for good."

Another long silence. My mouth was dry.

"What should I do?" I managed to ask.

"Come in on Monday and pick him up."

"I'm not going to do that. I'll talk to Dr. Brahe. Things are all settled with him."

"What do you plan on doing?" she asked.

"Put him somewhere: in Cotolengo, for instance."

She sighed. There was a brief silence.

"Could I talk to you?" she asked.

"That's what we're doing."

"No, not like this. I mean personally."

"All right. You can come by during lunch hour or after we close at seven."

"No, that's not possible for me. Why don't you come to my house this weekend? That way you could see little Jorge. His mother could come too."

"What do you mean, 'see little Jorge'?"

"He'll be there. I've been taking him home now on weekends for a month or so."

I sighed.

"Yes, I can come. But I don't think my wife will want to. I know what she'll say."

"That's fine. Just you then."

"All right. I'll come alone."

I jotted down her address: a street in the suburb of Temperley. Sunday afternoon.

I hung up.

Human beings are strange — if not in general, then at least in my case. Ana did not want to go. I knew, though, and was even sure in those days that I had enough power over her to force her to go. My excuse for not doing so was that I wanted to spare her any more suffering.

Entry 63
Sunday Afternoon at Mabel's

I suppose there's no need to point out that the summer heat turns the city of Buenos Aires — or in this case, the greater metropolitan area — into an inferno. It was Sunday afternoon and, dressed in a tie and jacket, I was on my way to visit Mabel. I got off the train and set out down the scorching streets of Temperley in search of her house.

I walked past grand old homes surrounded by venerable trees and shrubbery, with cooling shadows in the corners of their patios. Nobody was around. It was siesta time. Every once in a while I would stop beneath the shade of some tree and catch my breath.

At last I found it. It was a large, ramshackle house that looked half-abandoned. There didn't seem to be a doorbell, so I knocked on the door. The sound resonated, leaving a chain of echoes.

I hardly recognized her. Of course: it was Sunday. High heels, firm legs, a light summer dress, low-cut to ease the heat. Where had I seen those dark eyes before?

She smiled in embarrassment.

"Hi. Come on in. Little Jorge's out back on the patio."

I went in, stepping by her. She was nervous; her breasts rose and fell. We walked through the house and out the back door to a patio with tables and chairs. The only person there was Meningito, lying propped up on a chair in the shade of an umbrella. I avoided looking at him, but I could see he was dozing off.

"The sun's good for him," she said. "He needs the vitamin D. Have a seat."

The remark about vitamin D irritated me. I'd had enough of science. I sat down in a chair on the other side of the patio, behind Meningito.

"You're not afraid of him, are you?" she asked. There was a slight challenge in her voice.

"Yes, absolutely, and I always will be," I grunted.

"But look at him, how nice and white he is, with those blue eyes. How can you keep from loving him?"

"For God's sake, Mabel, quit harping on it. He's full of deformity and death."

The heat must have been getting to me. I found that I too was nervous and confused.

Mabel hesitated. My reply must have seemed curt, even violent.

"You wanted to speak to me: so, talk," I said.

"No one will bother us back here," she continued evasively. "My parents are asleep upstairs, and my brothers are at the soccer game. Wait a second."

She picked Meningito up off the chair and took him over to a crib with a mosquito net under a tree. Then she came back.

"Would you like something to drink?"

I looked at the table. There wasn't a thing on it.

"All right. Just a glass of cold water, thanks."

She went back into the house. Her legs reminded me of Ana's, though they were more muscular. Her hips were wider; they swung from side to side as she walked. She didn't hold them a little to the back the way Ana did. They made her whole body sway.

Mabel was an operating room nurse — a step above the rest of the nurses, whom the doctors thought of as foot soldiers. But ...

She reappeared with a glass of water, pulled a chair toward the umbrella, and invited me to sit in the shade with her. I moved my chair over. The shadow of a branch fell over her face. Those eyes ...

"Come over a bit closer. I don't want my parents to hear."

I moved my chair until our knees were practically touching. She crossed her legs. I could smell the heat from her body.

"I'm all ears," I said.

She thought for a moment.

"Are you truly, positively sure you don't want to keep little Jorge?" she asked in a low voice.

I sighed.

"I don't know how many times I've told you: no, we don't want him." My voice was also low.

Mabel thought for a while.

"Do you know there are lots of famous men who are living today with metal valves in their hearts?"

"Tell me who they are, Mabel. Give me their names. Can they walk around, run from danger, make love? Yeah, I'm sure there must be one, a model and example for others, but I wouldn't know who it is. I don't read the *Reader's Digest.* I'd be willing to bet, though, that it's a doctor."

Mabel was watching me. She wasn't sure she'd understood.

"Well, I can't remember either now, but ... well ... If you don't want him, then I'd like to adopt him."

To say I froze would be an exaggeration. But to say I felt a certain ambiguous comfort in my heart would be very close to the truth.

"But Mabel, you're not married. Do you have a boyfriend?"

"Yes, but he's threatened to leave me if I adopt little Jorge."

She grasped the arm of my chair with both hands and leaned toward me. Her breasts were close to me now.

"How do you feel about that?" I asked.

"I don't care."

"But Mabel, what's driving you to do this?"

"I don't know. He's so white, so tender. I've grown to love him as if he were my very own."

Her eyes searched for mine and then looked into them. I held her gaze.

"Mabel ... Mabel, for me ... it ... it wasn't that hard. What I mean is that ..."

The shadow of the tree branch across her eyes suddenly made me remember where I had seen them. In the shadows of a shaded room, many years before: the dark eyes of The Turk. Now, in those same eyes, I found what I had missed so deeply back then: a gleam, an interest, and a warmth that could enfold you.

I was shaken, upset. I leaned forward and lowered my voice, "Mabel ... Mabel ... you aren't ...?" I whispered.

"Aren't what?" she breathed.

It was driving me crazy.

"Nothing, nothing. Sorry. Your skin ... Why does skin have to be so white for you? Your dark skin has a warmth to it that ... Oh, no ... I don't feel too well ... I didn't think that ..." I stopped.

Mabel opened her lips. In surprise? Bewilderment?

I really was feeling ill. There was a burning sensation. Or at least that's what I wanted to believe. If she had heard ...

"According to my lawyer, both you and your wife would have to sign a document ..."

No, she hadn't heard. I reached forward blindly to take her hand in mine. It wasn't there. She rose to her feet. Embarrassed — Would that be the word? — I did the same.

We stood there in silence. Or perhaps she said, "What do you think?"

At first it sounded like the "ek, ek, ek" that locusts make in the summer as they begin to wind up, and then a cry broke out from Meningito. Mabel ran over to him.

My face was burning with shame, fury, and impotence. I was going out of my mind. I raced through the house and out the door. I heard her high heels clicking against the sidewalk as she ran after me. I turned and opened my arms. She stopped short about ten feet away from me, panting for breath.

"You ... you haven't given me an answer."

I felt horrendously ridiculous with my arms outstretched.

"Shit!" I yelled.

And I went off without another word.

That night it didn't bother me that Ana shut herself in her room to study. I drank a couple of Golden Lions, a beer from Santa Fe, as I sat listening to the slow chiming of the clock. I went over the visit in my mind. Regrets. My hand trembled slightly whenever I raised the glass to my lips. It occurred to me that death had been on the prowl that afternoon and had made off with one of its own. Or maybe it had only been the infinite helplessness or need or whatever you might call it that I had felt — a need that was probably impossible to satisfy. I wasn't really sure. Now I know, though: nothing is enough. The beer cushioned my fear.

Entry 64
The Institutional Machine

Nevertheless, I went back to the hospital on Monday. Once Ana makes up her mind about something, she rarely changes it; that's why she got through medical school. However, given that we had to decide things one way or the other — and probably that I was pushing her on — she agreed to go with me.

We didn't even notice whether the elevators were working or not. We found Dr. Berenger in a room full of cribs, one of which held Meningito. Mabel Benaím was also there, more silent than usual. A feeling of revulsion comes over me when I think back on the discussion we had next to Meningito's crib. It was violent. And although I may have seemed high-handed, repeating, "He's all yours, all yours! Understand?" Berenger was saying more or less the same thing, adding that we couldn't ask the government to keep on paying for his upkeep, that Meningito was now perfectly fine, and that we were refusing to recognize the quality of his work. "And yet he never moves a muscle!" I howled. I think I even threw in words like "fat", "filthy pig", and "son of a bitch". It wouldn't have been out of character for me. That was probably the reason — along with the tedious bureaucratic process involved in writing up a discharge form — that a policeman finally appeared in the crowd of onlookers. Dr. Berenger stepped outside and spoke to him, pointing at us.

We had to get Meningito out of there. Dr. Berenger's cries of "Take him away! Take him away!" resounded down the corridor. We found ourselves standing in the hallway with the policeman at our side. Ana was pale as could be; I was red with rage; and Mabel had Meningito in her arms. I turned on her.

"I thought you wanted him."

She lowered her beautiful eyes which, at that moment, seemed hateful and full of lies.

"We ... we never settled on anything. I don't know, I thought that ..."

"You thought what? What?" I said. I waited.

Her silence and inability to respond were as passive as Ana's and were quickly nullifying her remaining charm.

It's incredible. I had sunk so deep into the darkness of rights and laws — real or imagined — that until that moment I had even forgotten about you, Doctor Brahe.

When I did remember you, I began forcing my way through the crowd, with Ana, Mabel, and Meningito in my wake and the police officer bringing up the rear. At last we stood at the entrance to your office.

It was the first time I had ever found your door open. Your office was large; after the dark halls of the hospital, the sunlight that flooded in through the windows made your desk seem to float above the clouds. And there you were behind it, our guardian angel.

Yes, it was like entering Paradise. Probably (just probably), the door was open that day because you weren't on duty and weren't expecting anyone.

It didn't surprise me that you gave a start when you raised your head and saw us. Neither did your "Oh!" We exchanged feeble "good mornings." You invited us to pull up chairs around your desk.

"What brings you here today?" you asked. And we responded by explaining, or rather I explained what had happened. You listened with your index fingers held against your lips. I ended by reminding you of your promise. The "ehems" and "hmms" were deafening.

"So they're letting him go?" you asked, in the same way that one might ask (excuse my saying it), "So it's raining?"

You reflected for a moment.

"Lay him down over here," you told Mabel, pointing to a cot in the corner.

Mabel crossed the room, put the baby on the cot, and positioned herself at its side as if next to an operating table.

You also got to your feet. You took out a small hammer from the top pocket of your medical coat and went over to him. First you watched him for a while. I suppose that's the way you do things. Then, using the handle, you began to fiddle around (I think that would be the word for it), jabbing it against his legs.

Ana didn't look. Mabel watched, though. At one moment, I thought Meningito might roll off the cot, but my fear was unfounded. I remembered the scene of the doctors examining Pinocchio. You took the role of the talking cricket.

You finished your examination. You put the hammer back in your pocket and sat down. You looked at us. I'd never seen you so mortally serious. You murmured something like, "No, obviously … Hmm, the valve …"

Your eyes fixed on us.

"Don't you want him?" you asked, with a sweet humanity that struck me as false and reproachful. For a moment I hated you. Then I thought that it was probably nothing but a routine question.

Ana took my hand: I felt her cold sweat.

"No," I said.

There was a long silence. Ana's hand was trembling. Mabel was looking down at the floor.

"Well, then," you said in a professional tone. "Well, then, there's a lot to do. Let's keep our hopes up. The case interests me. Next week I'm due to receive a machine for performing myelographies from the United States. I think we could use it to detect exactly which muscles are active. It'll be important to have a precise diagnosis. Leave him with us."

I managed to speak.

"Thank you, Doctor."

We stood up. I remembered something.

"Doctor, there's a policeman outside."

You accompanied us to the door.

"Officer, the child is not yet ready to leave the hospital. He will stay here with me. Please let them know at the discharge desk."

The policeman nodded.

We said goodbye.

The policeman walked back to the discharge office with us. The paperwork was quickly taken care of by the aging, heavy-set woman who worked there. She listened to the policeman's report, eyeing us with contempt (or was it my imagination?); then she opened a folder, glanced at the papers in it, jotted something down, closed it again, and put it aside.

Was the case closed? The momentary relief that came over me quickly faded. There was another, younger woman, in her late twenties, dressed in a white medical coat, standing next to her. She came around the side of the desk and walked over to us.

"So you're little Jorge's parents, then?" she asked, as if just making a discovery or seeing a legend materialize.

Worn out from the struggles and emotions of the day, I stammered out a "yes." She introduced herself. I can't remember her name, though I do recall her occupation: she was a psychologist and was on the psychiatric "team" at the hospital. She politely invited us to come and talk things over with her, offering us her help which, even if not of immediate use, would nevertheless allow us to deal with the problem more calmly.

It was the first time I'd heard the word "team" in a hospital: it sounded quite modern and advanced at the time. It was also my first encounter with an engineer of souls. Tired but curious, I hesitated. I heard Ana's voice.

"No, we're not interested."

They call it intuition: more enemies? Had the time come to behave properly? I told Ana to wait for me in the café and accepted the woman's invitation.

Ana went off with a loud sigh that sounded weaker than she intended. I followed the psychologist into an office. I suppose the whole "team" was there, consisting of two other psychologists, both women. Looking back on it now, I suspect they were only medical assistants, although at that moment it didn't matter.

They asked me to sit down; each of them was holding a ballpoint pen and a notebook.

One of them laid out the problem: my resistance (and possibly Ana's, though I don't remember exactly) and refusal to assume my role as father, which was something quite rare and infrequent. I asked her what fatherhood she was referring to, and if cases like Meningito's were that common. Another one of them — I think it was the woman who'd dragged me down there — leafed through a file and told me that, according to the doctors' reports, our son had progressed and cooperated with them magnificently, and that they couldn't understand why we couldn't follow his example and do the same. They weren't accusing us of anything, she said, just sounding us out, because according to Freud, a parental rejection at that age could mean ...

I interrupted her to ask which doctors had made the reports and told her there were plenty of others who had said just the opposite. I had vaguely heard about sessions with psychologists and psychiatrists replacing confession in church, but when they began digging around in my life with Ana, no matter how technical and emotionless their language, I growled that they were touching on a topic I didn't want to discuss. There was the inevitable offer of free treatment so Ana and I could better understand and accept the obligations of parenthood and adjust or adapt to the problems it entailed. I was about to tell them I had to be on my way when the one who'd been sitting a bit apart and hadn't opened her mouth till then — perhaps thinking she had at last discovered the key to the problem: my unconscious motivation for rejecting my son — asked me if I had been born with a hare-lip. I raised the bristles of my moustache with my index finger and thumb and assured her I hadn't, though I was afflicted with other, worse deformities. I added that I believed I had had quite enough for one day, thanked them unconvincingly, and left.

When I got to the café, Ana had already finished a second cup of coffee. She was in a hurry. I didn't ask her why, nor did she inquire about my session with the psychologists. She gave me a kiss and disappeared.

I didn't feel like writing or noting down what had happened. I stayed there a while longer, watching an old retired fellow who was reading the paper, a woman who seemed to have been crying, a drunk who kept asking for more wine, which they wouldn't give him, and a guy who looked like a travelling salesman, perhaps peddling books or safes. He'd placed his briefcase on the seat across from him and was jiggling his legs as he had a quick lunch and a glass of wine.

That day it occurred to me that practically all the cafés in Buenos Aires were alike and that, except for the ones downtown where the people were a bit more dynamic, the customers in the others were essentially idlers and loafers.

There was no use waiting: Mabel never showed up, not even as Meningito's guardian angel.

Entry 65
A Place for Meningito

Despite what it may seem, my life with my friends and Ana was not an endless string of cafés where a man could withdraw and take refuge from the world, either to be alone or wait for someone else to arrive.

I've never mentioned that I had once been an acolyte — the starting point for a race to the papacy, just as being a paperboy is for the presidency in the USA — as well as a deeply devout believer.

If I came across a church as I strolled along in search of my customers' houses, I would usually stop and go in.

I'm not a theologian, nor do I wish to be one. As I sat there quietly in the darkened silence, I don't know whether I was searching for a lost faith that would enable me to confront my destiny or if I was praying that God, in whom I no longer believed, would welcome our son to his heart, especially since, when all was said and done, He'd been the one who'd condemned him. Perhaps because I had lost my faith, or because my request defied His design, like a heresy, He never listened to my prayers.

In the darkness and silence, I limited myself to asking where I had lost my faith and whether or not I would ever get it back. I never received an answer and yet, when I got up to go, I would somehow feel rested from all my internal torment, with my energy recharged so I could continue on my way without knowing where I was headed.

The same day we were to take Meningito home, or maybe a few days later (not that it really matters), hounded by fear and haunted by punishment, I again entered a church, in hopes that the devil couldn't get in there to drag me off to Hell.

I was afraid that you would fail us, doctor, or, as it finally turned out, that you wouldn't be able to hold on to his life any longer. The punishment I dreaded was that we would have to take him home.

A priest or sacristan was arranging things on the altar, stopping to genuflect every time he passed in front of Jesus on the cross; he reminded me of another priest I had talked to in the hospital, the one who had baptized Meningito with the much more human name of Jorge, though Meningito was, in fact, human only in name.

Our conversation had been long, doctrinaire, and—despite touching at times on the deeper issues in life — ultimately pointless. The priest didn't succeed in convincing me of anything, nor I him. It wasn't a confession — my sin was already too well known for that — nor was it an appeal for pardon or absolution. Perhaps he would have absolved me *in pecto*, the same way he gave me a small religious image and the name of a place for Meningito: Cotolengo.

Not that I hadn't heard of Cotolengo before. It was located near Longchamps and I had heard legends and stories about it as far back as secondary school. It supposedly held the most varied creatures the Good Lord had ever made: the Wolfman in his cage; the Fishman or Human Crocodile in an underground passage that had water running through it; and the Spiderboy, with four hands and four feet.

I spoke to Ana about my fears and about the possibility of sending Meningito to Cotolengo. Strangely, without ever saying anything about it or my even being aware of it, she had come to trust you implicitly.

That may have been the reason why, without checking to see if there were official visiting hours — as I suppose there were, since Hell itself must have a schedule — I decided to go out to Cotolengo late one Saturday afternoon.

The bus dropped me off at the gate around five-thirty. The sky was overcast, and it threatened to rain. Low, dark clouds were being swept along by the wind, heralding nightfall. It was hot. The chill I felt, the cold in my hands and face, was my own.

Above the main gate was a sign: "Little Cotolengo." I don't remember if it said "Argentine" or not. They said Cotolengo was as ancient as the New World. I opened the gate and walked up the asphalt drive.

Trees, lots of trees with whispering leaves; aside from them, silence. Peace? If it hadn't been for the cold I felt, I would have said "yes," it was Paradise. The church immediately to the left of the entrance seemed to confirm it. I stopped and looked inside. It was a modern building whose architecture and decoration spoke of simplicity, modesty, and seriousness of purpose — or perhaps simply of the lack of money for luxury, ornamentation, and elegant decadence. It was the exact opposite of the old churches I had known, filled with darkness and gloom, with hidden corners where one could imagine the devil crouching, ready to spring. This was a building that, with its stylized designs on large stained-glass windows, seemed to be floating with light. For a moment, I felt peace and tranquillity — and possibly reconciliation.

My doubts came back, as did the cold in my hands. I stayed a few minutes and then left and went back up the road.

There seemed to be less light left outside now than there was in the church. The feeling of cold was becoming more intense.

I continued forward, farther into the grounds. It was getting dark. The houses and buildings among the trees and bushes were fading into the dusk. Far off, beneath the clouds along the horizon, the sun was setting. I stopped. Yes, it would be better to turn back and return at an earlier hour the next day, or perhaps the following Saturday, or never. I heard something.

It was a tapping sound, along with a muffled noise that sounded like a grunting "mmm," but wary, incapable of expressing itself, something like a moan. The church bell began to ring. It was time for the evening rosary.

It — or they — appeared around a bend in the road. At first it was a swaying smudge against the darkness. The tapping sound and the grunting or moaning became louder. The smudge continued on toward me and began to dissolve into segments: the tapping was being made by crutches on the asphalt as paraplegics in wheelchairs were pushed along by cripples, their feet dragging along the pavement; there were heads that were too big and others that were too small, the blind leading the blind; two or three wriggled along in a St. Vitus' dance, jumping out of formation and then back in again. The muffled grunting was now passing by in front of me, with two meditative priests walking alongside the procession, missals in hand, the wind ruffling their robes. The mass advanced by spasmodic jumps, puffing along with toneless grunts. The silence, the absence of human voices, was terrifying.

They went by blindly, without noticing me. Or else I, for them, was just one more thing among many, a stupid tourist in search of something new.

I looked on as they neared the church, whose stained-glass windows were now illuminated, and watched as they entered. I considered following them in so I could observe them more closely, be with them, see if ...

I started back for the gate, and then stopped for a moment in front of the church. Yes, maybe among them Meningito would feel he were part of a family. But there was no point looking for my own place. I would never, ever find it.

I looked up at the sky: not a single star was visible. That was normal: it was overcast. Or perhaps it wasn't that dark after all.

The first drops of rain made me lower my head. Getting drenched as I waited for the bus was a purification.

Entry 66
Bereavement Leave

Aram didn't yell at me any more. He probably thought I'd made it through the worst and was now able to get along comfortably on my salary. He left me alone all during the supreme boredom of the summer months and would walk by my desk without saying a word, even when I was writing up these entries at the shop.

But, with his temper, he finally couldn't let it go by any longer.

"Haven't you finished filling out the bills yet?"

He was referring to the sales slips they falsified in order to balance their illicit income from smuggling Persian rugs and loansharking. There was so much cash around that they had to stuff it into safety deposit boxes in bank vaults; converting it into gold would stop its earning power. They had to launder it some way.

"Yes, Aram. I've already complied with the God of the Armenians' greatest commandment. They're with the accountant."

"What are you writing, then? How come you're sitting here scribbling down this bunk instead of looking after the customers?"

"What customers, Aram? I'm writing a pornographic story, or maybe just an obscene one, so I can become a millionaire and won't have to work anymore."

"Since you're writing it on our time, we'll have to get a percentage."

He fell silent. I felt his eyes on me. He sighed.

"You'll never amount to anything. A hopeless case. You waste your time on junk like this instead of learning English, for example." He left the store to have coffee or inspect the other branches.

It was another Friday, about eleven o'clock in the morning.

"Pedro! Telephone!"

I picked up the receiver. There was a moan.

"Hello? Hello?"

"It's Mabel ... Little Jorge died last night ... at four in the morning. A brain hemorrhage. Dr. Berenger fought to save him, but couldn't. I hope you're happy now."

Trembling. Again the trembling. No, I was neither happy nor sad. But I did feel a certain obscure relief.

"I'll be right over," I said and hung up.

I looked for Aram. He was in the café on the corner. I told him what had happened.

"It's better that way, Pedro," he said quietly.

"It is better, Aram: much better." We were both silent for a moment. "Yes," I said, "I feel a sense of relief, but it's a little strange. It's not as simple as a toothache." I stopped and then added, "Two things: money and how long can I have off because of his death."

"Let's see," he said. "Today's Friday. Take until Wednesday of next week."

I walked back to the store with him to sign the receipt. He gave me two thousand pesos, which I thanked him for. Before I left, he asked me, "Anything still hanging over you?"

"No, Aram, no. It's summer; sales are down."

He looked at me. I suppose the bitter smile on his face was a reflection of my own.

In the taxi, for the first time, I no longer needed to pretend: I sighed to relieve the pain that was spreading up from my chest, rising into my the throat and clouding my eyes.

Entry 67
The Valve

One of the elevators was working, but the line of people waiting for it was interminable. Typical Argentine laziness, a German would say. I was young in those days and ran up the stairs to your floor in one burst. Your door was closed; you must have been seeing patients inside. I knocked and your nurse came out. You appeared at the door a minute later.

Doctor, I don't know how to say this to you, but you seemed even happier than I did. You didn't actually perform any dance steps, but you could have.

"What did I tell you about that little valve," you repeated. "That little valve. That little valve."

I didn't know whether your happiness was due to your diagnosis being confirmed, or the weight and responsibility being lifted from your shoulders, or the sad happy ending to the story.

When your joy faded, we were suddenly cut off from one another — wouldn't that be the way to describe it? In the end, without that small dose of humanity — which I was often afraid was only apparent — our relationship wasn't even that of a patient and his doctor. Meningito's death severed the tie. There wasn't much left to say. Probably nothing.

A few questions and bits of advice about the future, best wishes for success and happiness. Ah yes, the notes: you asked about them. I told you I'd made them out as file cards and, thanking you for everything, promised you that as soon as I finished them, I'd bring them in.

We said goodbye.

The ups and downs I was to have for the rest of my life: at that moment, with solace in my lightened soul, I went down to the children's ward and looked for Mabel.

She was in the staff room with a group of nurses. I opened the door and stood at the threshold. When they saw me, their mouths closed and there was a wave of silence. Mabel got up, came into the hallway, and stood next to me. I shut the door.

I asked her to have coffee with me. She didn't have time. We talked in the corridor.

"I … I'm sorry about what I said on the telephone," she told me.

"That's all right, Mabel, that's all right. It's not worth feeling bad about. It's all over. What are they doing now?"

"Right now they're performing an autopsy on him and taking the valve out."

"Even when he's dead they won't leave him alone."

"They have to do it for the next case … so that in the future …"

"No, don't start in on that with me. I want to have kids. For God's sake, no more about the future and medicine's giant strides ahead."

I was going to ask her why she had changed her mind about Meningito. She spoke first.

"What are you going to do with little Jorge?"

"What do you mean, 'do with' him?"

"Well, are you going to take him away to bury him? I'd like to …"

I sighed.

"Mabel, I'm not a religious person. All my life I've asked myself if the Bible was actually of any practical use. In this case, I think it is: that line about the dead burying the dead."

"What do you mean?"

"What I'm saying is: Isn't there a municipal service for these things?"

She looked at me horrified.

"You're going to … you're going to …?"

"What do you want me to do? I didn't want him when he was alive, so I don't know why I should once he's dead."

The speed of your reply astonished me.

"You're right. Could I ask you for something?"

"Sure. Go ahead."

"Little Jorge has been a kind of son for all of us. Would you let us have a funeral for him and bury him?"

"If you want. I don't really know how those things work, but after all the macabre things I've been through, I'd be glad to have you free me from the last of them."

"No, you're the one to thank. I'm going to find out where we could hold the wake so that you can come."

"To be frank, it's not the kind of party I like. Thanks anyway."

There wasn't much left to say. We were about to say goodbye to each other when I remembered something.

"By the way, Mabel: What happened to the valve?"

I'd never seen dark skin turn so pale. And the fear. Or was it something else? She looked to each side, and then at me.

"Maybe you're not as much of a … as the others say."

She came closer, lowered her voice, and, still looking over her shoulder, whispered, "I don't know if it's going to be of any comfort or help to you or not, but I think the valve they put into little Jorge wasn't the right one."

"What do you mean it wasn't …?"

She whirled around and disappeared through the door.

Note: I don't know what in these files has made me realize that in fact I have not refused to give them to you, as I believe I did the last time we saw each other. I had promised them to you, but whether out of spite, as I mentioned in the very first entry, or laziness, or the desire not to open old wounds, I simply never kept my word. But now I am fulfillling my promise, and in a more orderly fashion than I would have been able to back in those days.

Entry 68
Nap Time

"It's all over," I told Mabel — how naive could I be? Now, four or five years after saying that, as I write up this file in our country house, with Ana outside hanging out the laundry or playing with our children, I realize that in fact it was all just beginning.

I've always tried not to judge people, without being able to avoid it; to be frank, without succeeding; to tell the truth, without saying it — and to confess when I need to. Isn't writing these files a form of confession? A useless one, to be sure, because if God exists, He's the only one I'll have to settle with. The go-betweens are corrupt. And no, I'm not looking for acceptance.

After this preface, I think I can afford myself the luxury of saying that, either out of convenience or to humour Mabel or out of ignorance, I had consigned Meningito to carrion. I do not search for forgiveness.

When I left the hospital, I didn't head for a café; I didn't need any more of those pathetic moments of free time that I'd stolen from the Kalpakians in the past. I was free until Wednesday. I went home.

I stopped by Don Manuel's corner store and bought a couple of Golden Lions. He was surprised to see me so early and asked if I were on vacation. I told him I had in fact been able to get a few days off. I was destroying myself with these stories without realizing it. In any case, I'd been doing so now for quite a while, and what's one more spot to a tiger? I also bought two hundred grams of Parma ham: a luxury, but I had to celebrate. I stopped by the bakery and picked up some fresh baguettes of French bread.

Ana wasn't home yet. I celebrated the event alone, listening to the chimes of the clock. Helped along by the Golden Lions, all I could think of was taking a good long nap, sleeping off a year of fatigue, and forgetting.

I lay down. As soon as I closed my eyes, I fell asleep.

The Sleep of the Just?

I heard the chime of bells, either from our clock or the church in Cotolengo. Then the muffled tapping, the moaning, and the inarticulate voices came down the road again or else appeared out of the depths of the horizon. I don't remember too well: the world seemed deserted, but the group drew ever closer in a ragged march, like in a circus or carnival, but with a firmer pace.

Suddenly the silhouettes take form. Yes, there he is among them. I recognize him: he's fleshless, a tiny skeleton. There's a hole in his head where they'd run the tube or valve, patched over with two crossed bandages that are lifted on the wind as it whistles through the hole as he moves. He smiles, but without lips his smile is eternal. Despite his finally being with his family, I pity his loneliness. Who's going to take care of him? I calm down, before the group passes in front of me and disappears. I think I see a nurse holding his hand.

Entry 69
Meningito's Brothers and Sisters

They touched me delicately. It was summer, and I was sweating. I felt a hand on my forehead.

"Pedro, Pedro, are you all right? You're drenched with sweat," Ana observed in a soft voice.

"No, no, it's nothing. Just some good news. I feel like sleeping through till tomorrow morning. Celebrate. You can sleep too."

"I don't know what you mean."

"I don't feel like talking. Leave me alone."

But do-gooders never rest. They couldn't get our address, but they did find that of my parents. At ten that night there was a knock at our door. It was my sister and Mabel Benaím.

That was how Ana found out about Meningito's death.

As if torn from eternal sleep, I fumbled around, got dressed, and attended to our guests.

Mabel told us we had to go back to the hospital to sign a form authorizing Meningito's removal from the morgue so that the wake could be held that night and he could be buried the next day.

"I'm not going," I said. "I think he's fine where he is, far away, safe from human hands. At least no one there will keep on making him sick, or making us sick either."

"Monster!"

My rage finally woke me up. I looked around for whoever had dared say those words. In back of my silent sister, a very pale Ana, and Mabel, whose eyes were lowered, stood a woman I'd never seen before, who must have come in after the others. Half of her face was grotesquely red and swollen with what I supposed was a cancer.

"Speaking of monsters," I said, pointing at her and grinding my teeth, "Get out of here!"

She hesitated, as if she couldn't believe that the rights she'd acquired with her deformed face had suddenly vanished.

"Get the hell out!" I howled.

Mabel had to push her out the door.

Ana and my sister were used to my reactions. They weren't overly upset by the episode, but Mabel asked permission before coming back in.

No one tried to calm my rage, knowing it was impossible and that any attempt to do so would only make it worse. But monsters can also have strange ideas, and I naively wanted to finish everything up. Twenty minutes later I was on my way back to Buenos Aires in somebody's car, seated next to a driver who I think was an older person, perhaps a volunteer of some kind, with Mabel and the woman with the cancerous face riding along in the back seat.

I didn't say a word during the whole trip. Though I am not a religious man, I have always believed in following tradition, in respecting one's ancestors, and in burying the dead with dignity, and I found myself wondering exactly why I was so opposed to taking part in this particular funeral.

It must have been at least eleven-thirty by the time we got to the hospital. We went in at the back. Back doors are places where they take out the garbage from restaurants and the dead from hospitals. I never found out what the purpose of the poorly lit room we entered was supposed to be, other than the one it served for us. It had one tiny window, a long wooden bench, and quite a crowd of people.

As soon as we entered, the cancerous woman seemed to spring back to life and told everyone assembled what I'd said that night. Meningito's brothers and sisters, the crippled and the maimed, including a paralytic on crutches and others with I don't know what all kinds of deformities and anomalies, gave a roar of solidarity and rushed forward at me. A voice was raised above the din.

"Wait a minute, friends. Let's hear what he has to say in his own defence."

The noise died down. The one who had spoken must have been the twin sister of the woman with cancer. She had the same disease, but on the other side of her face. Her sunken eye was barely visible in the red mass of tissue.

"We're willing to give you a chance to repent for what you said. Come and take a look at little Jorge."

"Thanks for the offer, but isn't he in the icebox?"

I realized my voice was trembling.

"We're having a wake for him in the hospital chapel."

"Without my permission?"

There was a murmur and then silence.

"We don't mind if you see him," said a generous voice in the crowd.

195

"So that I can thank the doctors for all they've done?"

"Are you afraid of him?"

"Yes, exactly. I'm afraid he'll bite me."

I was beginning to feel weak. I looked around for the only sane person I could appeal to. She was standing to one side. I went over to her.

"Mabel, for God's sake," I begged her. "What is all this? I came here to sign to have his body released, not to be torn to pieces by a pack of self-righteous wolves."

Mabel was also upset.

"Yes, yes, I know. There's the morgue superintendent."

Maybe he'd already been there for some time. He stood watching us, smiling, as thin as a noodle, with a folder in his hand and a cigarette hanging from the corner of his mouth. He seemed to be amused. I went over to speak to him.

"Tell me, please: Where do I need to sign?"

His smile broadened.

"Quite a carnival, eh? Step over to the wicket there." He pointed to a darkened corner.

He ducked down through a small door into a long, low room that ran along the side of the building and turned on the light. There was a rustling about and then he emerged behind the grate of a wicket. Things had to be done right. He opened the folder, looked through it attentively, and then passed me a slip of paper under the grate. I signed. Another one. I signed again.

Commentaries from the spectators: "Look! He knows how to sign his name. The guy's a genius!"

He thanked me and then checked through his papers once more before handing me the death certificate.

"It's a bad business, my friend," he said, "a bad business. If he'd been a mestizo, the crowd here would have chucked him out themselves."

He withdrew from the wicket. I also stepped back in bewilderment, nauseated, and searched desperately for the door. One of the women with a cancerous face — I can't remember whether it was the one with the red mass on the right-hand side or the left one — blocked my way and shouted, "I'm giving you one last chance!"

I don't know how, but I finally got outdoors again. The café across from Lezama Park was still open. No, I didn't go in. It had already served its purpose, as had all the other bars and cafés where I had sat in search of my lost peace of mind.

Entry 70
Events in the Public Domain

Saturday

Although they'd kindly given me a lift to the hospital, no one, not even Mabel, offered to drive me back home. I, the monster who had spurned their forgiveness, was good for nothing more than a signature that would allow them to continue playing their dark and sanctimonious game.

I got back to the house at two in the morning. Ana was still awake. The look on my face kept her from asking any questions. In any event, what would I have told her?

I got into bed. She did too. Although she never held herself back from me, she rarely initiated our lovemaking. That night she did. At first I didn't react, but death was on the prowl and she longed for life; she searched and searched for me and we made the saddest love we'd ever made in our lives.

I slept badly. The next morning I drank my *mate* in the kitchen, listening to the chimes of the clock, while she worked in her room.

Ana emerged from her study clutching a slip of paper. "It'll be born in the spring," she said, without showing it to me.

I shuddered. She put the paper away in her room and came back into the kitchen.

"Who'll do the shopping today?" she asked.

"I will, if you want, but not till this afternoon. I don't want to see anyone."

She went out to do it.

I was alone. As if this were the moment of truth, I felt a deep contempt for myself. I wondered what in hell had happened to my defiant spirit the night before, how I could have let Meningito's brothers and sisters treat me like that, why the police hadn't been there.

The insults and threats of the night before turned out to be nothing but a run-up to what was to come.

I didn't hear it on the news. My sister dropped by in the evening and told us that, at two in the afternoon, Radio Colonia, my father's favourite station that he always listened to, had carried a story about two heartless parents who had abandoned their child. Whether out of journalistic incompetence or false respect, they hadn't pronounced my name correctly. But the other details, such as the town, Ana's name, and the fact that she was a medical student, had all been precise enough to erase the shadow of a doubt. My sister stayed for a while but neither of us said much more. I think we both wanted to, but the difference in our ages separated us. The hug she gave me when she left was enough.

My parents came over that night for more silence and painful confessions.

They agreed that it was better that Meningito had died. Just the same, though, like all true missionaries — anonymous, silent, and humble — they had secretly been visiting Meningito behind my back. They were the ones who had paid for the special pants for his dislocated hip. Perhaps their love, like that of so many others, had helped prolong his agony. I felt I'd been betrayed. Should I thank them or forgive them? They justified their clandestine activities by pointing to my aggressive, intolerant character and my anti-social behaviour. The news report on the radio had been my punishment. I was so exhausted with my now almost incurable fatigue that I was glad to see them leave.

That night I shared a bottle of wine with Ana, which helped us get to sleep.

Sunday

Over the years we'd developed a taste for communing with the Sunday papers at home rather than with something more holy at church. The weather was hot, but cloudy. I set off to get the newspapers and a few other things we needed. Nothing remarkable occurred on my way into the village until I got to the newspaper kiosk at the train station. The owner, besides being a news vendor, was also the local bookmaker — a short-term businessman, you might say. They called him Fat Tito, because he liked to eat so much.

I said hello to him; he snorted.

"You got a cold, Tito?" I asked him for *La Nación* and *La Prensa*.

"Humph. I'm doing better than some. And in case you're interested, I suggest you get a copy of *Crónica*. Oh yeah, and *El Mundo*, too."

If there was ever anyone without much of a sense of irony, it was Fat Tito. He was nervous and flustered.

"What's bugging you? Did the betters break your bank?"

"I pay my debts. Not like some."

At last I got it. It took a while, but I finally understood.

"Tell me, Fats ... or should I say Doctor Eggplant? You've known me for fifteen years but can't even ask me a straight question. Why don't you fuck off, you bastard!"

A revolver appeared at the kiosk window. Fat Tito was shaking and the gun was too.

"I don't know why I don't just pull the trigger. I don't know why I don't just pull the trigger," he repeated.

Strange. I wasn't afraid. I'd even say I was ready for the bullet. Or perhaps I trusted in fifteen years of supposed friendship.

"Because you're a wimp," I said. "I don't know why you bother having a gun, since you pay out more to the cops more than you do to your customers. And sorry about calling you a bastard: let's leave it at just fucking off."

I turned and walked away. After a few steps I looked back. The revolver had disappeared.

"Give me a copy of *Crónica* and the other paper you mentioned," I said.

I didn't thank him. And if I didn't pay him, it wasn't because I didn't want to, but because I forgot. Nothing remarkable had occurred on the way into town, but things did start happening on my way back. Or maybe I was just aware of them now. A lot of people I knew refused to say hello, and as I passed by I heard comments such as "People like that should be castrated", or "Hang him up by his balls."

I didn't mention anything to Ana. I'd long since realized that neither the village nor the opinions of its inhabitants interested her. She was searching for higher, more serious, more authoritative judgments.

On Tuesday, a mass-market magazine carried a fairly long article about Meningito, along with a photo of him in his coffin. Of course it was full of errors, and of course it described the doctors' heroic, even titanic struggle to save him.

Was there more? Yes. One day I overheard Jackie's commentary: "I knew he'd ruin everything." Aram was clearer: "How could you have been such an idiot? It's obvious you're not Armenian, or even Jewish.

You're incorrigible. But don't worry, the Vatican has already said that no miracle lasts longer than three days." There were also phone calls at work: some kind, some insulting, and others threatening. The first day back on the job, Mabel Benaím called up. She didn't say much, but cried a lot and repeated "I'm sorry," several times. We said goodbye for good.

Yes, there was more, but it's not worth mentioning: it would be too much. On the other hand, as Aram said, no miracle lasts longer than three days. Apart from the newspaper archives, I'm probably the only one who still has the clippings. I suppose I'll soon be able to burn them, along with all the other articles I've saved.

We moved out of the village a long time ago now, leaving behind the legend and its variations. I don't know if the Polack in the legend is named Pedro.

Entry 71
Every Cloud Has a Silver Lining; or, Señora Taboada's Stockings and Garter Belt

Life went on. Our next child was due in the spring. We had to be ready and prepared for any eventuality. No, there are no insurance policies against deformed children.

Amidst all the wonderful diversity of the student body when I was in high school, from its dreamers of paradise and conquerors of better worlds to the hosts of students who aspired to become philosophers, poets, scientists, and politicians of left or right, Horacio always stood out as the typical fascist. He was short, with a long, thin face, and black hair slicked over like Hitler, whom he used to imitate by putting a comb under his nose and raising his hand in salute. Even though I, of course, was on the left — another of my springtime itches — he and I got along well. Unconscious of ideology, we shared a passion for discussion and the warmth of friendship. I had often visited his home, where I'd met his father, a rich and famous lawyer.

Two weeks after Meningito's death, as I stood leaning against the doorway of the store looking out at the street, I saw him go by. I called out to him, and we greeted each other warmly. I was happy to see him. We went to the corner to have coffee. He had just passed the bar, as I remember. He told me, without referring to the particular noose I'd just been hanged with, that — by sheer coincidence — my name had come up just the week before when his father had been looking for someone to do a bit of work for him. "Come on over to the house this weekend," he concluded.

I did. I won't dwell on the description of the house, or on the cigar I smoked with his father as I coughed, or on the imported whisky that burned my throat and stomach as I went from middle-class to apprentice millionaire and sybarite. No, he never named my noose, but its existence underscored the confidence with which he offered me a job for one or two weeks in Patagonia, all expenses paid, with a million-peso advance and ten million more when it was over. The whole deal didn't entail much, just a quick transaction involving two or three houses — one of countless such arrangements that have long been part of Argentine history. I asked them for a week to think it over. They gave me two and a month to get prepared.

Patagonia brought back memories of the Hungarian woman I'd met at the restaurant downtown, conjuring up images of freedom and independence, of infinite space, of Don Garabed's teachings (I wasn't a priest, after all), and of Pepe, the businessman and promoter. It stimulated the admiration and envy of every Argentine: to be liberated from your job, to be free and independent. It was El Dorado. Nonetheless, I hesitated.

In the end, the decision was made for me. Once again I was sent out to Palermo Chico to one of those houses whose price, with all the inflation Argentina has gone through since then, must by now be astronomical. Once again it was a mansion, with a salon, a valet, and a bedroom that Madam Taboada-Teherán wanted to have done in white with a soft carpet fourteen millimetres thick. Once again, I thought, someone wanted to rejuvenate their love life.

The valet took me up to the second floor. Madame Taboada-Teherán received me in a negligee. She was short, a bit thin, with dark skin and eyes; in spite of her double last name, which may or may not have been from some aristocratic line, she would have given her eye teeth to have the eyes above them be blue.

She acknowledged my greeting with an "Oh" that seemed reserved for visitors from other planets. She showed me the bedroom with a beautiful parquet floor and mirrors on all four walls. I put my briefcase on a chair and began to take out my measuring instruments. She called out and a maid appeared with her clothes. The bedroom was large; she paced nervously from one end to the other, stopping in front of me in her bra and panties, with the maid trotting along behind. The servant girl's presence squelched any provocative or immoral interpretation of the scene. The maid gave her her slip, which the lady of the house donned with a flourish like a writhing snake. She took a few steps forward. Ah, yes, now I understood: she walked from one mirror to the other in search of herself. Next came the garter belt and stockings. She pulled up her slip and fitted the garter belt. It didn't look too bad on her, actually: this was a striptease in reverse, in order to conceal rather than reveal — all quite moral, of course. She sat down on the side of the bed. No, she wasn't my type, but with all those overlays gliding across her dark skin ... I am a man, after all, and something made my heart beat faster as she slid the stockings over her legs as if getting ready for a cancan and then, raising her skirt once more, attached them to her garter belt. The maid brought over her dress, adding a decorous touch to the scene.

I finished up measuring while she was putting on the dress. "No, I'm not a man," I reasoned, "I'm a white slave, like the black slaves and eunuchs of old who used to watch their mistress get dressed without batting an eyelid and without the right to feel."

"I'm done," announced the lady of the house, continuing to gaze at herself and adjust the dress in one of the mirrors. She turned to me.

"When will you have the estimate ready?" she asked. "I need it as soon as possible. Send it to my husband's office."

"The carpet slave will serve his mistress," I replied, in a snakelike hiss. She gave a start and looked at me intently.

"Do you know what, madam? Once before, another woman, of more modest means, who only wanted a six millimetre carpet, worked me off by hand. I think it was more authentic than what you've done today."

I took a bus to the Retiro train station. The clock on the English Tower showed ten-thirty in the morning. With the upkeep things get in Argentina, it probably still does today. At the time it served its purpose.

The cook at the outdoor restaurant next to the port had just begun putting the flank steaks on the grill.

"Hello there," I called out to him. "Do you remember the sweetbreads?"

He turned around.

"Hey, it's you. You know what? I don't get many spiffy customers like you. Beef or pork sausage? I'm just getting the grill going."

"Pork. The long ones, like before. They seem to have agreed with me up till now. I'm still alive."

After lots of *chimichurri* sauce, a glass of wine, and a conversation about where the country was going, I got up to say goodbye.

"So long, man," I said. "I'm off to Patagonia to line my pockets with money. And if you don't have any sweetbreads when I get back, I'll never drop by again."

"Don't worry. If you've got the cash, we'll open a restaurant that specializes in them, just for you. See you later. I hope the deal works out, and remember to stay out of jail."

"No problem. The lawyers will be watching over me like hawks. So long."

"See you later," he called as I walked away. "And by the way, don't sell your mother the way everyone else does in this country. There's hardly any of them left."

I came back to the shop renewed, refreshed, and with a lighter heart.

"I didn't make the sale," I yelled triumphantly. "But I'm giving notice. Aram, I'm off."

"Where to?"

"Patagonia. I quit."

"Don't jerk me around." Aram attempted an uncomfortable smile.

"I'm not."

The Kalpakians, with Aram as their spokesman, offered me four times my salary if I'd stay and manage a new branch they'd just opened.

"Aram, Aram: listen. How much is a man worth? I mean really, how much is he worth? How could you be such a ...? Sorry. You asked me never to insult you again. What I need, though, is room to move."

The Kalpakians gave me a farewell dinner, at which they presented me with a Parker 51 pen. Their warmth made me consider confessing to them about the carpet I'd taken back to the house. But I'd learned a little, too. I decided not to mention it, because it was one thing to cheat and rob the customers, but stealing from them was a crime.

They left the door open for me whenever I wanted to return.

Entry 72
Patagonia

There's no point in trying to explain exactly what the spurious business deal in Patagonia consisted of. Maybe the lawyers and clerks involved in it understood it all clearly, no matter how shady it seemed, but even today the whole affair is still a mystery to me. I know it had to do with an estate that was left without heirs and involved a beautiful *estancia* nestled in a valley at the foot of the snow-capped Andes, somewhere between Bariloche and El Bolsón, with cattle and ancient trees that it was against the law to cut down. It may also have had something to do with a certain territory that belonged to the province, because the governor himself got involved. I had to pass for someone I wasn't, sign various names that weren't mine, and leave someone with power of attorney.

Due to the vast distances involved and to the nature of time itself, which decelerates as the land spreads out, so that fewer and fewer people seem to hurry, the whole business took more than a couple of weeks — more than an month, even. For a while I was a tourist, travelling beyond those lands to ideal places in my mind, imaginary paradises where I never managed to find my place in the sun, let alone El Dorado.

When the deal was finalized, I bought three more houses to rent out and the country house where I'm writing this now. The power of money gave me time. I looked up a few friends, and we began to have dinner together on Friday nights.

And life went on.

Entry 73
Ana's Confession

We were now living in the country house, five or six months later. Ana was pregnant for the second time and was again losing her teeth. It was Saturday night. We were having dessert after a barbecue I'd cooked up for us, when I once again noticed how much her breasts had grown and suddenly, by a rare mental association, I remembered.

"Ana," I said, "tell me: The day you got out of the hospital and we went to see Brahe with Meningito, how come you didn't introduce yourself, or didn't have me introduce you? You didn't know him then."

She didn't lower her eyes, but as she looked back at me they flashed a challenge.

"I'd already been to see him."

"What? Without telling me?"

"Well, let's just say it was a professional consultation."

"Not a human one?"

"Whatever you say. I know all your sarcastic barbs and ironic ploys by now." She fell silent.

"Please, tell me about it."

She did.

"I went to see him at the hospital. I'd already read up enough on Meningito's condition for them not to be able to deceive me. But I was filled with doubts and wanted to discover a definite solution, to be absolutely sure, to really know the truth. It was six months after his birth, before they put in the valve. Brahe was very attentive. He looked surprised when I told him it was too late to put in the valve, and that it should have been the first thing they'd done. He sent for the latest X-rays of Meningito's head. Let me tell you, Pedro: by that time there wasn't any brain left at all; the pressure from the cephalic liquid had destroyed it all."

"Unlike the brains of geniuses like Dr. Berenger."

"That's right. He was already a vegetable, a member of the living dead. Dr. Berenger was playing the sorcerer's apprentice. Or maybe he just wanted to experiment a bit to discover something new or make a point. I don't know."

"Why didn't you tell me all this? It would have made it easier for me when I spoke to him."

"You seemed so sure."

"Sure of what? Ana, I've never been sure of anything, and I don't think I ever will be."

She didn't seem to believe me.

"I don't know; I don't know," she answered. "Maybe I didn't want you to think I was weak."

She looked at me. I hesitated for a moment before telling her, "No, Ana, there's something else. It's true that I'm not sure ... but you ... I'm afraid ... I'm afraid that you aren't either."

She stood up abruptly. She hesitated and then turned around, went into the bedroom, and shut the door. I heard noises, blows, and then absolute silence. I know now that there are many ways to suffer.

I wasn't sure then, and I'm still not now, as to whether I should have gone in to speak to her.

Still wondering whether or not that was the only time Ana had visited Brahe behind my back, I poured myself another glass of wine.

Final Entry

Perhaps, Doctor, I would have wound up this account or report — I really don't know what to call it now — long ago, if, strangely enough, life hadn't continued blindly on, without the characters in it ever finding happiness.

There are still a lot of entries scattered about on my desk or lying unclassified in the file box. Most of them are incomplete or begin with sentences that I've never finished; I don't know where many of them were leading.

Perhaps some are still important. One of them reads:

"Some good soul, writing anonymously, maybe to give me the chance to reform, sent me the number of Meningito's mausoleum and niche in the Chacarita cemetery. Ana didn't want to go; but, one Sunday, I did. Sure enough, there it was. The flowers next to his niche had dried up. I don't know why I went: perhaps to make sure he was really there and not where I had dreamt he was the day he died."

Here's another:

"The clock moved along with us out to the country house. It's in the living room. It goes on telling the hours and its chimes have probably invaded my dreams, making the first one I ever had of him return again and again. The dream is almost banal in its tenderness. I no longer see Meningito among his brothers and sisters but, thank God, the nurse hasn't abandoned him. He appears in different landscapes, holding the nurse's hand, and at times comes over and talks to me. I ask him how his life is going out there and how he likes his niche in the Chacarita. He says that sometimes he gets bored and has to get out to stretch his legs. I offer to accompany him, and he thanks me but says that it's all right, it's not really necessary. Relieved, I see him walk away, or sometimes he disappears, as if by magic, on one of the chimes that brought him."

And life goes on.

It seems as though the file cards have become my diary. I read this one and transcribe the following:

"Money was disappearing faster and faster due to the increasing rate of inflation. The rents we received were no longer enough, so I sold one of our houses in order to open a small carpet store in a shopping mall in Buenos Aires. I was free and independent. But, say what you may, in reality I had simply tethered myself to my own manger. Like all merchants, I was a slave to myself, indifferent not only to the world, but also to my own desires and wishes, which I was never able to define or fulfill. When friends dropped by, I would spend far too much time talking with them in a nearby café, and I also discovered that my talent as a salesman, the patience I needed in order to keep plumping up the stuffing of my clients' vanity, was now completely exhausted. My childhood dreams of the pampas and the infinite sky returned, as well as my longing for a beautiful, clean, orderly, real-life El Dorado, with multicoloured flowers and neatly kept green lawns — the same world of easy-to-wash nylon carpets that the customers at Kalpakian's used to fantasize about. Horacio's father unselfishly helped me through an honest and profitable bankruptcy. We sold the houses and all the furniture, except for the clock, which we left with a friend until I could come back for it and find a way to take it out of the country. Then, just as my parents said they had done when they emigrated from Hungary, telling us children that we were going off on an extra-long vacation, Ana and I and the children set out for the North, El Dorado, where she, thanks to the fabulous advances of medical science, was sure to find the answer.

"And — minus the clock — life went on, albeit in another place.

"Ana, my ever-quiet Ana: our departure ended her career. The two children she had finished off the rest of her teeth. Her smile is not the same, nor will it ever be. Perhaps it's nothing but the passage of time.

"Here, without their recognizing her degree and without any desire to study and take their equivalency exams, she found a job with I can't remember which research council in order to continue her own investigations. I don't know exactly where it is. All I've got is her phone number.

"Life goes on, both here and back there. My gaze is often lost in the snowy landscape I see from the window. I look back on the past and am seized by a melancholy, sometimes painful nostalgia. I miss my conversations with Don Garabed, though I miss the few I had with Don Hagop even more, along with his gentle bitterness, those fifteenth-century carpets that no longer exist, the caravans of camels, and perhaps even the Three Wise Men. And yes, I also miss Aram's shouting, Erminia's tender foolishness, Viamonte Street, and those Friday suppers, especially now that I don't have a manger in which to rot away. And although there are some beautiful churches here, heated in winter and air-conditioned in summer so the Lord may be worshipped in comfort, I never visit them: they're always filled with tourists. Sometimes I find myself wondering time and again about ridiculous things, such as whether Erminia still uses a garter belt or whether she's opted for the pantyhose preferred by the dynamic, modern women of today. And is her head still full of magic carpets?

"Three years ago my father died and I went back to Argentina. I had a list of things to do, an itinerary to fulfill. That's how life goes: my father was already buried by the time I got there. I saw my sister again, who was now married with two children, my nephews. It was as if I were rediscovering her; I realized that I had something in common with her and that she was part of me. She told me that when they put the lid on my father's coffin, my mother smiled more tenderly than she'd ever done before, and said, "He was a good man." She also told me that just before dying, in the tradition of heroes and great men, my father spoke his last words, which perhaps he'd been preparing during his entire existence, waiting for the opportunity to say them: 'Life is strange. It's odd how you can spend the whole time hoping that one day you'll see the smokestacks of your own factory rise up on the horizon, knowing all the while they never will.'

"In our parents' house, which was the original homestead of the area, other people live now. I didn't dare, or want to, knock on the door of the home that had once been Ana's and mine. Neither did I go see Pepe, whom I heard had been in and out of the Villa Devoto Penitentiary. Bocha's bar and Fat Tito's newspaper kiosk had both disappeared, their owners ruined by the racehorses. Don Tomás the Italian, Don Garabed, and Don Hagop were all dead. Sometimes I think that life is nothing but a Shakespearean tragedy in which, in the end, everyone dies. Aram and the others, though they'd aged, were still in good health. Erminia had stopped working years before, so I wasn't able to ask her if she still used a garter belt and if her head was full of carpets. The silent Enrique had disappeared. Meningito's niche in the Chacarita cemetery now belonged to a different owner, someone named Pérez or Álvarez — it doesn't matter which. I tried to bring back the clock for Ana, but my friend's wife had fallen in love with it and used to tell all her visitors it was a genuine antique; she refused to acknowledge the deal we'd made and wouldn't give it back to me. My friend felt badly about it and apologized repeatedly without doing a thing. I forgave him and told him that by now I was familiar with the gamut of human shabbiness. But what I couldn't understand, I also told him, was how he could live with a woman like that, without being afraid that one day she would refuse to acknowledge him too. The Friday soirées were still going on. Some participants had left the ranks and others had joined. All the same, I came away with the feeling that the tradition of those suppers was slowly falling apart — or else that either I or the times had changed.

"The grill next to the Retiro train station had vanished, along with its owner.

"I didn't visit Argerich Hospital to see either you or Mabel. I still hadn't fulfilled my promise.

"Life goes on and fifteen years have passed. Our children have grown up and my fascination with well-kept lawns, flowers, order, and cleanliness is over. The beautiful kitchen in our beautiful house doesn't do anything for me. It doesn't have a fire that crackles or purrs, or even a gas flame that hisses: everything's electric. There's plenty of light and the noise from the appliances scares off all the ghosts and legends. There's not a single corner in which to house your imagination. The stews I make are awful, completely lacking the taste of pumpkin and the scent of the pampas. At night, when the witches make their rounds outside, a drink or two — or even three — helps me get to sleep and make it through to another day. Ana joins me. Apart from the daily things of life, or the future of our kids, we hardly talk to one another. I finally decided what to do: in order not to keep grinding myself down any longer, as well as to try to distract Ana from her obsession, I've succeeded in convincing her not to bring me any more information. She seems permanently locked up within herself and often disappears into her study. I've long since given up interest in going through her purse;

I wouldn't find anything anymore that would interest me or reveal anything new, except maybe a flask of whisky.

"From here on in, life will go on. All that's left is for me to thank you, Doctor. When Ana and I do talk, she maintains and assures me that you are a great scientist and a deeply humane individual, and that it is quite possible that you yourself killed Meningito, either out of pity or a desire to help him; all you had to do was move the valve a little. I myself put forward other reasons: professional jealousies or rivalries — things like that. But life comes in a single package, so how can we pigeonhole our feelings? Sometimes, in order to comfort myself and not feel so alone, I find myself wishing I could believe Ana's version of things. The alibi she found in the valve has brought me closer to a certain truth. Regardless of whether — out of humanity or not — you did or didn't kill him, I have discovered that, falteringly, uncertainly, often in direct contradiction to yourself, you have supported us and have not failed us, and for that I wish you many, many thanks, Doctor Brahe.

"The child we christened Meningito and whom we would have liked to have named something else, walks across snow-covered fields but says he doesn't feel cold. The immaculate whiteness of the snow makes me realize that sometimes I dream of him in colour. Spring will be here soon. The dream will return, along with the swallows, the buds on the trees, and the flowers, and in my dream, which I've grown accustomed to and sometimes even invoke, the heat of the sun will tinge the snow with green, and across the field will come the one who holds the nurse's hand and we will talk about what a warm and beautiful day it is. I'll beg his forgiveness and will confess to him that, in telling his story, I'm not sure I haven't told a love story in which there were a few seconds — perhaps a minute or two — of fulfillment. I'll also tell him — if he doesn't disappear or vanish on a chime, as if being called back to the place where he belongs — that of all the things that have happened to me in life, with my corroded breastplate of culture, without a single El Dorado to fantasize about or go to, all that's left is the hope of being able to give some testimony of my fortitude for love, a shining white carpet beneath a winter sun that barely warms the world and soon will set.

"I've never told Ana about my dream. We've never delved into the problem — if there's really anything to delve into. Perhaps it's simpler than that: there are deaths, like crosses, that we carry with us the rest of our lives."

About the Author

Pablo Urbanyi was born in Hungary in 1939. After World War II his parents immigrated to Argentina, where he was raised and educated. His first book of short stories, *Noche de revolucionarios* (Night of the Revolutionaries), was published in Buenos Aires in 1972. His second book, *Un revólver para Mack* (A Revolver for Mack), a parodic detective novel, was published in 1975. In the same year he began to work as a journalist for the cultural supplement of *La Opinión*, the principal liberal newspaper in Buenos Aires. When the paper was shut down after the military coup of 1976, he immigrated to Canada with his family, eventually becoming a Canadian citizen.

After settling in Ottawa, he continued his literary career, establishing himself as one of the foremost satirical writers of fiction in contemporary Argentine literature, particularly for his ability to touch on basic societal and existential problems in a comical way. *En ninguna parte*, a satirical novel set in a Canadian university, was published in Buenos Aires in 1981. It was translated into English and French, and published in Canada as *The Nowhere Idea* (Williams-Wallace, 1981) and *L'idée fixe* (VLB, 1988). Over the next few years he published three books of short stories: *De todo un poco, de nada mucho* (A Little About

Everything, A Lot About Nothing) in Argentina; *A hagyaték* (The Legacy) in Hungary; and *Nacer de nuevo* (Born Again) in Canada. In 1993 he was a finalist in the Argentine Planeta Award for his novel *Silver*, the story of a gorilla raised as a human being by anthropologists from California. *Silver* was published in Buenos Aires in 1994; it was also translated into French and published in Montreal in 1999. A French version of *Un revólver para Mack* was published by VLB in Montreal in 1993. *Puesta de sol* (Sunset) was originally published by Girol Books of Ottawa in 1997. His latest work is the science fiction novel *2058, en la Corte de Eutopía* (2058: In the Court of Eutopia), published in Buenos Aires in 1999. Urbanyi has received several awards for his work, as well as grants from the Canada Council for the Arts and the Department of Foreign Affairs and International Trade. He has given conferences and lectures in Hungary, the United States, Spain, Argentina, Germany and Canada, and is a member of PEN International.

About the Translator

Hugh Hazelton is a poet and translator who specializes in the work of Latin American writers living in Canada. He co-edited, with Gary Geddes, and was principal translator of *Compañeros: An Anthology of Writings About Latin America* (Cormorant, 1990). His other translations include *The Better to See You* (Cormorant, 1993), *Jade and Iron: Latin American Tales from Two Cultures* (Groundwood, 1996), *Túnel de proa verde/Tunnel of the Green Prow*, (Broken Jaw, 1998) and *Cuerpo amado/Beloved Body* (Broken Jaw, 2002) from Spanish and *Headstrong All the Way Round* (Graff, 2000) from French. He teaches Spanish translation and Latin American civilization at Concordia University in Montreal.

A Selection of Our Titles in Print

www.brokenjaw.com hosts our current catalogue, submissions guidelines, manuscript award competitions, booktrade sales representation and distribution information. Broken Jaw Press eBooks of selected titles are available from http://www.PublishingOnline.com. Directly from us, all individual orders must be prepaid. All Canadian orders must add 7% GST/HST (Canada Customs and Revenue Agency Number: 12489 7943 RT0001).

BROKEN JAW PRESS, Box 596 Stn A, Fredericton NB E3B 5A6, Canada